WHAT WE LEAVE BEHIND

Siôn Scott-Wilson

Deixis Press

First published in 2023 by Deixis Press
www.deixis.press
ISBN 978-1-7397081-4-6 (HB)
ISBN 978-1-7397081-5-3 (PB)

Cover image: "Carlo Ferrari: The Italian Boy"
from *The History of the London Burkers* (Wellcome Collection)

Typeset using Crimson Text

Cover design by Deividas Jablonskis

WHAT WE LEAVE BEHIND

Siôn Scott-Wilson

Deixis Press

For my boys, Cameron and Rory

CHAPTER I

'Heave to, the boat.'

'What's that?' bellows Facey, pulling hard. 'What d'ye say there?'

'You heard me, Mr Facey. For I know it is you, just as I know you have a dozen half-ankers of spirits aboard. Stow oars and come about.'

'Put your back into it, Sammy, heave away,' hisses Facey, bending to his oars. 'I cannot hear you, sir, the wind is too strong,' he roars back at the Revenue officer.

The Tide Surveyor, perched on the rail of the Revenue cutter, places a speaking trumpet to his lips. 'You will submit yourself to an inspection by His Majesty's Revenue. This instant, if you please.'

'We are fishermen, sir,' calls Facey, 'working our nets and so happened to bring up a few casks from the sinkers and warp.'

'I know you, Mr Facey, sufficient well to be sure that you have never hauled out an honest mackerel in your life.'

'I should not know the difference 'twixt an honest mackerel nor dishonest one, Mr Armstrong.'

'You have been given a lawful order, Mr Facey, and now shall have a shot across you by way of final warning.'

'I cannot spare the time to heave to, sir. There is a fresh catch of honest mackerel, which must be carried to Portsmouth market without delay. For as all know, fish keeps like knowledge, which is to say, for but the shortest time.'

'Fire,' comes the peremptory answer. A small carronade to the rear of the cutter belches flame, sending a piece of wadding flying over our heads.

'Keep rowing,' hisses Facey.

'Their next effort will blow us to kingdom come,' I object.

'They will do no such thing. Not for a few paltry gallons.'

With Ben Barrett indisposed, his arm broke in a tavern brawl two nights previous, and requiring a confederate to manage the second pair of oars on this tiny craft, my old friend Facey prevailed upon me to accompany him on this doomed enterprise. I should have known better.

These days, I am no desperado, but, for the most part, a mild schoolteacher alongside my wife, Rosamund, at the John Pounds School. Three nights a week I put in my shift at our own little tavern, the Bedford In Chase on Wickham Street, which we purchased with a splendid bounty some two years previous. It is, as yet, only a humble establishment, a single tap-room serving ale and rum to sailors where we employ a keeper, one Sidney Griffith, for the day-to-day regulation of the place. Though the cove knows his trade, I have my doubts as to his honesty since the takings have always seemed strangely modest. This, in combination with unwise speculation in a cargo of Prussian spruce, has left the three on us precious short of ready money.

And so, here I sit, in a fish-stinking, clinker-built boat full of contraband spirit, buffeted by the choppy waters of Portsmouth harbour, peering down the barrel of a Revenue cutter's carronade. If I am not already blown to flinders by a six-pound ball, Rosamund will scrag me for a certainty.

'Kindly haul on the right-side oar alone if you please, Sammy Boy,' orders Facey.

I have only a view of Facey's broad back and cannot read his expression since we are seated arsey-versy, which is to say, in the opposing direction to the front of the craft. It is but one of the many things I cannot like about boats and is the reason Facey has not used the terms "port" and "larboard", knowing full well that I should only make a hash of it.

We pull together on our right-side oars, which has the effect of turning our small boat sharply round the back end of the cutter.

'All hands to come about,' bellows the Tide Surveyor. There is the sound of running and men swarm up ropes on board the cutter.

'Haul away, Sammy, give it both oars now with a will. Armstrong must tack his cumbersome vessel 'gainst the wind and, barring catastrophe, we shall be snug in the East and West with a hot toddy apiece afore this Duty-sniffer has managed to find his arse with both hands.'

Sure enough, the cutter is barely half turned when we are at the harbour steps. Facey throws out a rope which is caught by a young lad and swiftly tied off. Willing hands reach for our casks, which are loaded onto a cart, concealed with a tarpaulin and spirited away before I have even managed to catch my breath. 'Be sure and reserve a cask for our Bedford In Chase,' bellows Facey to the departing crew.

Facey grins and pounds me on the back. 'A fine morning's work that, Sammy. What say we revive ourselves with a glass of something warming?'

'I should like that, though I might tell you that I am not made for ocean-going, nor am I willing to risk my neck a second time on such a desperate venture.'

Facey chuckles. 'A piece of tomfoolery, is all. Armstrong must blow off a little powder to make a good show and that was scarcely the raging sea but the harbour, which is not near so perilous as a autumn puddle on the Fareham Road.'

'That's as may be, but a man might drown as well in three foot as thirty fathom. Besides I am soaked to the skin and every stitch is sodden.'

'You would never deprive His Majesty's seamen of a few perquisites for the sake of your own comforts, Sammy. They have little enough as it is, being paid more by the rope's end than coin. Moresoever, I have no doubt that our Sailor Billy, being a naval man, would most likely look the other way and not trouble hisself on account of a few coppers in lost duty.'

Out on the harbour a watery sun is burning off the low-lying morning mist; the cutter has abandoned its slow turn and is making slowly for one of the larger vessels, no doubt to undertake an inspection of its cargo. Facey gazes out with his one good eye, the other lost to an old injury, these days concealed beneath a black leather patch. There's a satisfied expression on his dial. 'A man must have his grog, Sammy, without his family go hungry in consequence. 'Tis a public service we do here in keeping the price of rum to an affordable degree. And never forget your own cut of the profits.'

'No need. What I endured this morning was out of friendship alone.'

Facey smirks. 'Endured, is it? A pleasant morning's oar across the millpond; you ought to pay me for the lark, Sammy. But, since you will take no recompense, I shall stand the full expense of young snotty's dinner tonight.'

'That is very handsome in you, Facey.'

Facey nods towards the horizon. 'Like the devil, here is our young snotty approaching even as we speak of him.'

It is Pure John he refers to, an orphan lad from London. Having no remaining kin, my wife Rosamund and me cared for him and brought him away to Portsmouth with us. Rosamund should have liked to bring him up as our own, but by nine years of age a boy's character is often set, and Pure John, being a wilful, venturesome spirit, showed a strong inclination to go to sea. In accordance with his wishes, and through Facey's old naval acquaintances, he was found a berth on the brig, *HMS Pandora*. Unable to recall his own family name, Pure John took mine and I am proud to say that he appears on the *Pandora's* muster book as John Samuel, Ship's Boy.

I peer out across the harbour seeking Pure John's vessel. As always, dense crowds of masts jostle and sway at their moorings like clusters of winter trees, but I see naught of approaching sails.

'Was you to squint your eyes just so, you might observe the merest scrap of canvas on the borderline 'twixt sky and sea,' advises Facey.

'I have it,' I say, taking his advice. 'And that is our John's ship?'

'Brig. And I believe so, if his missive is to be credited.'

He means Pure John's note, arrived by the Ushant cutter, in a very poor hand I regret to say, which confirmed for us the *Pandora's* expected arrival into Portsmouth this very day. The boy has been granted shore-leave and, to that end, under Rosamund's very particular direction, Facey has appointed for a good dinner at the Keppel's Nob to mark his return. Furthermore, it is no small thing that Facey has agreed to bear the entire cost. I should never describe him as the easiest of men, but he has always had an affection for Pure John and, like Rosamund and me, has been looking forward to the event for some days now.

'How can you be certain?'

Facey shrugs. 'I do not wish to come it the pedant with you, Sammy, but for a Portsmouth man, your knowledge of nautical matters is truly pitiful. As anyone, even a cove with but one glim can see, yon is a two-master, thus a brig. And so, of a certainty, 'tis the *Pandora*.'

I give him a look.

He grins and claps me on the shoulder. 'Now, now, Sammy, it is not so very often I am able to lord it over you by the workings of my noggin that I should not take some small pleasure in the occasion.'

'I am chilled to the bone, Facey; I believe I might welcome a toddy.'

'Certainly. The younker shall doubtless have a parcel of duties to detain him and we should not expect to welcome him until evening.'

'That is as well since we have been at sixes and sevens at home with Rosamund determined to ensure that all is just so for the lad's return.'

Instead of acknowledging, Facey's eyes narrow as he gazes in the direction of an old, somewhat tatty curricle on the harbour path. A couple of disreputable-looking individuals stand alongside it, one with a steadying hand on the horse's reins. They peer out to sea with the avidity of a couple of ratters. 'I do not like the looks of them coves overmuch,' he announces.

'Leave them be, they are none of our concern.'

'They are strangers here, neither seamen nor dock-hands, and have the appearance of city bruisers; I am well accustomed to the type. A pair of fish out of water, to be sure.'

'Most likely they are on a jaunt, having come down to take the sea air. What offence do they give?'

'If you must know, Sammy, I am uneasy at the abrupt appearance of outsiders at the very moment a valuable consignment has been brought in.'

'I do not see much harm in them and should like my toddy afore I am quite froze, one with an abundance of rum, since it appears that spirit is now become so affordable.'

The chill is still upon me as we take our ease in the East and West, despite a roaring fire and my beaker of rum and hot water. 'It is said that almost six thousand have succumbed to this Blue Death in a matter of weeks,' I say.

Facey grunts, immersed in a small stack of Penny Illustrated Papers, a newish periodical, which he much enjoys.

For myself I have three of the London papers to examine: *The Times*, *The Morning Post* and *The Standard*, which are provided gratis to patrons of this Broad Street Inn.

Two years previous we were forced to flee the metropolis, having given offence to parties of considerable influence and power. Though we may not easily return, it is some small consolation to keep abreast of events in our old city, despite the papers being a week or so old by the time we have them.

'I speak of the Asiatic Cholera, which holds all London in terror.'

'There is always something to be feared in the metropolis.'

'This is worse by far than some mere bug-hunter or cutpurse. There is no known cure and once caught it is invariably fatal. Here,' I say, reading a paragraph out loud since Facey is somewhat ponderous with his letters: 'Symptoms of this deadly disease include stomach cramps, looseness of the bowel, vomiting and severe pain in the limbs. Sufferers appear sharp and contracted, the eye sinks, the look is expressive of terror and wildness. The skin is often deadly cold and often damp, taking on a markedly bluish aspect. The tongue always moist, often white and loaded, but flabby and chilled like a piece of dead flesh.'

'Then we are fortunate to be here in Portsmouth, Sammy, with almost a hundred miles betwixt ourselves and that foul contagion. It is perhaps the one solitary blessing we may lay at Pimlott and Chuffington's door.'

I take a pull at my toddy, which is still good and hot; Facey refills my beaker from the steaming jug. 'Yet even here it seems we may be in some peril,' I continue to read from the *Morning Post*. 'Coastal residents are warned of the danger to which they expose themselves by engaging in illicit intercourse with persons coming from the Continent and should be mindful of the imminent risk which they incur by holding any communication with smugglers, and others who may evade the quarantine regulations.' I give him a meaningful look.

Facey snorts, 'They are obliged to say such things to discourage the trade in contraband. Besides, our dealings are with honest British seamen, certainly not your parlour-voos, silver-plate Frenchies with whom we have been at loggerheads for a hundred years or more. We leave such things to the Jerseymen, who speak a form of gibberish and so are able to make themselves understood by the crapaud.'

'Still and all, 'tis a frightful thing.'

'Never fret, Sammy.' Facey shakes out his Penny Illustrated, indicating the intricately engraved image adorning the front page. 'Here is a monkey-looking creature for your attention, labelled a Kin...Kin...Kinkajou, which his secondary name, in the language of the Romans, is *Potos flavus*.'

'I had not heard of it.'

'Nor seen it neither, I should say, until this moment. And yet here is an image of the very beast drawn from life, transposed with great exactitude onto the page of a periodical for our convenient edification as we sit and sup on toddies. A marvel, no less.'

'It is an excellent likeness, I am sure.'

''Cording to the natural philosophers the animal may turn his feet entirely backwards. A useful trick, I imagine, should you wish to evade the law without appearing to skedaddle.'

'He seems a meek, law-abiding enough creature.'

''Tis the law of the jungle I speak of, which is to say, his natural habitat.'

I chuckle and take another sip at my toddy. Facey is not ordinarily one for quips or jocularity but I see now it has been his intention to goad me into better spirits. With a half-pint of rum, lemon and water inside me, he has achieved his end.

'Here now is a cove in a most prodigious great hat aiming a fowling piece, or some such, at a antelope called a Springer...'

I am spared further commentary on the rendering, since Facey's attention has been caught by the entry of a hunched, circumspect individual in a pea jacket and woollen cap. 'You will forgive me, Sammy, I must attend to business.' With that Facey collects his beaker and hurries over to a corner table where the pair conduct an urgent, whispered conversation.

I continue to immerse myself in the dismal reports of this new pestilence though I cannot help but notice the brief clink of a heavy-sounding purse being passed by Facey's accomplice.

CHAPTER II

There is no lack of vittles with a great succulent beef pie before us, vegetables and any number of floury potatoes with a fine gravy. Nor is there a shortage of good ale and porter, even a bottle of fine claret to be shared, and yet the party, here in our snug private room at the Keppel's Nob, is somewhat downcast this evening, the mood soured and dampened by the absence of its principal guest.

'You was quite clear on time and place in them letters of yourn, Mrs Samuel?'

'Certainly, Mr Facey. John writes me of little else; he would not miss his own feast for worlds.'

'Then I cannot fathom it. The *Pandora* is firmly anchored and there is no damage evident to the rigging from a blow or tempest or suchlike.'

'Signifying what?' asks Rosamund.

'Meaning that the brig does not appear to have been savaged by wind and weather over and above the usual wear and tear. So, saving your presence, Mrs Samuel, it is not likely that any of the company has been washed overboard or dashed to the deck from the yardarms. Furthermore, had there been injury or loss of life that news should be all about the town.'

Rosamund sips at her tiny glass of claret. I can see she has no appetite for the viands. 'Well, that is something at the least.'

'Indeed, the brig is not in the slightest mauled and shall doubtless remain in Portsmouth this fortnight for a modest refit: shifting of ballast, replacement of spars and rigging and so forth.'

'Would that account for John's absence then? All this shifting and shunting about the ship?'

'I do not believe so. He is not rated seaman, nor likely to be for a good while yet, being only ship's boy and so more of a impediment should he remain aboard.' Facey reaches across the table for the large dish. 'Here, let me help you to a slice of this pie, which is still good and hot. You have only nibbled at a half a tater, Mrs Samuel, and shall waste away should you continue to deprive yourself.'

'You are kind, Mr Facey, and I will take a very small piece for your sake.'

'There will be a simple explication. Most likely, I believe, would be a postponement of shore leave in consequence of some minor infraction such as young lads are prone to: a spot of skylarking; inattention to duties or any number of transgressions frowned upon by the navy.' Facey transfers a wedge of the beef pie onto Rosamund's plate. ''Tis not a institution much given to mollycoddling, but a bluff, unforgiving service and a fine one for that, since it will be the making of him.'

'I shall take your word, Mr Facey, and admit that you have set my mind a touch easier.'

'In course, you might recall that the lad has a mouth on him like a runaway horse and was ever inclined to be saucy. I should not be at all surprised if it is that, which has got him into a little of hot water.'

'True enough,' I say. 'I expect he has been set some dismal task in the bilboes by way of atonement.'

'Bilges,' corrects Facey. 'Bilboes is restraints, shackles you might wear should you have done aught especially wicked.'

Rosamund shudders.

Facey sighs. 'I see this excellent pie is to be wasted entirely if we cannot quickly find another subject for discussion. So, to that end, I will make a solemn undertaking to you both. In the morning early, I shall take out the skiff and meet with Jack Sullivan who was able seaman alongside of me back on the old Billy Ruffian and is now boatswain of the *Pandora*. He is a no-nonsense cove and will tell me straight what is become of our wayward lad and when we might expect to see him.'

'You may not go tonight?'

'I cannot. 'Twould be a fool's errand to approach His Majesty's vessels at night. The guard-boats are out and I should be instantly taken up and placed in Sammy's bilboes.'

'Then tomorrow, and I thank you for it, Mr Facey, you are very good.'

'And now, a glass of wine with you both.' Facey raises his glass, we join him in a toast. 'To our young snotty.'

I can tell that Rosamund is somewhat calmed by Facey's efforts, certainly a promise to speak with his old crewmate has put her in frame of mind whereby she might enjoy a few mouthfuls.

My oldest friend and my wife have not always seen eye-to-eye, for he is quick-tempered and even quicker to throw the mauleys, whilst she is a woman of considerable spirit. However, to my great satisfaction, since we three removed ourselves to Portsmouth, they appear to have reached an accommodation. These days, when he is not putting in his shift at our tavern, Facey will often sit by our fire in the evenings in company with Rosamund and me, supping his porter and telling stretchers while she gently joshes him. He is a man of some contradiction, to be sure, rather like a great, savage mastiff, docile only in the presence of a select few.

'It is most perplexing,' announces Facey, shaking off the rain as he steps across our threshold. He unships his oilskin coat and I get him seated before our fire. 'I am informed that the lad was given leave to depart the vessel yesterday, at around seven bells, which is to say mid-afternoon. His departure in the jolly boat, alongside those others on shore leave, was observed by many a envious eye 'mongst the remaining crew.'

'You have heard this from your boatswain?' Rosamund bustles over with a bottle of porter and a leather mug.

'Thankee,' acknowledges Facey, filling his mug. It is early, indeed not long past dawn but, unlike Rosamund, Facey and me have never acquired a taste for tea. I will often begin the day with small beer but for Facey it must be porter and we keep a supply on hand to accommodate his needs. 'Certainly, it is from the very horse's mouth. Oaring out at first light, I made my acquaintanceship with Jack Sullivan known to the watch and was fetched aboard with much consideration.' Facey takes a long draught from his mug. 'Jack was summoned, and after a few well-I-nevers, how-d'ye-dos, fond reminiscences and suchlike I was able to come directly to the business at hand.'

Rosamund nods, standing at the fire, her face expressionless, yet, since her ways have become so well known to me, I am able to read her unease by other means. She tugs at her fogle, relentlessly pulling at it through her bunched left hand. By this I can tell that there is a turmoil of emotion within. 'There can be no error?'

'I do not believe so. The *Pandora* is a vessel of no great magnitude and Jack is a stickler; it is his business to know the ins and outs of his brig down to the last nail. He is quite certain the lad is no longer aboard.'

'Then where, Mr Facey?'

Facey sighs. 'Since he was observed departing in company of some of the other hands; it may be that he has been led astray in spite of his better nature. I hesitate to declare it, but there are certain places in this town where sailing men are wont to visit following a spell at sea. Low places, Mrs Samuel.'

'You need not consider my finer feelings, Mr Facey. You well know that I am no wilting violet.'

'Dens of vice then I should call them, where all the sinful pleasures may be had for the price of a few coppers.'

'No. I cannot credit it. Pure John is too sweet-natured a boy, so named for his pure heart.'

'He has been almost a year at sea.'

'All the more reason why he would come to us without delay. Though we are not kin, this is his true home, insomuch as he ever had one. I do not believe that he would choose to stay away.' Rosamund tugs at her fogle so fiercely as to tear the fabric. 'It is my belief that he has come to mischief. Might there be a shipmate with some manner of grudge against him?'

Facey slowly shakes his head. 'The *Pandora* is a easy-going, cheerful vessel. 'Cording to Jack, John Samuel is well-liked by all on board and made much of by the older hands. Indeed, Jack himself has considerable affection for the lad. He is known to be a willing, cheerful sort, though in course, at times, inclined to impudence.' Facey downs his porter with a single, mighty draught before rising. 'I have only ducked in momentarily to give you this news, though I know it to be worrisome. Now, Sammy, do you accompany me and we shall brave the elements; you may be certain, Mrs Samuel, that between us we shall roust out every squalid hole and seaman's haunt in Portsmouth 'til your lad is found, most likely with a sore head and an empty purse.' He retrieves his still-dripping oilskin coat from the hook. I do likewise, clamping my hat firmly to my head, ready to face the wind and rain.

'I shall fetch my shawl and accompany you.'

'Better you do not, Mrs Samuel.'

Rosamund's jaw sets. No doubt Facey wishes to spare my wife's sensibilities since these are likely places of considerable viciousness and depravity but he forgets that she is a woman of considerable resolution and our sentiments will butter no parsnips with her once her mind is firm. Another tack is required.

'What if John returns in the meantime?' I say.

Rosamund pauses. 'That is a consideration.'

'Well then, one of us must hold the fort.'

'Very well, I shall remain. But you will be sure to comb every inch of the town since I have heard that seafaring men may sometimes be discovered in the middens or gutters, insensible with the drink, robbed and left for dead, which on such a day would indeed be mortal. Now go, with all speed, there is not a moment to lose.'

With that Rosamund bustles me out the door directly into a foul Easterly blow filled with icy rain. I am compelled to put a hand to my hat against the force of the wind. As the door shuts behind us, Facey turns up his collars, retreating his head into the protection of his oilskin like a tortoise. 'My best guess, Sammy, would be perhaps amongst the fire-ships of Blossom Alley.'

'It is as likely a place as any to make a beginning, though I almost hope we do not find him there. It is a desperate, wretched location.'

'We shall start with the worst and hope for the best.'

We set off, taking care insofar as possible to keep our boots from the gutter, running as it is this morning like the Fleet Ditch, carrying along all manner of filth and rotting detritus in its tumbling waters. Ordinarily, on a narrow pavement such as this, folk will surrender the right of way to Facey's menacing bulk, yet curiously, this oncoming cove seems determined to do no such thing. Indeed, he seems fixed on a collision. At the final moment he stops abruptly and snatches at my sleeve. 'Begging your pardings, sirs, but would you be, by chance, Messrs Facey and Samuel? I have your two phizzogs in the mind's eye, having clocked you hereabouts on occasion, only my actual peeper is not entirely to be relied upon, it being skewwhiff as a busted gimbal.'

The inquirer is a shabby, whey-faced villain with an atrocious squint and a bristling, scabrous head, which is bare to the rain. I wrench my sleeve from his grasp being fearful of lice.

'Who is it wishes to know and for why?' booms Facey.

'I was informed that the dwelling from which you have lately emerged is home to a Mr Samuel Samuel.' He flaps a grubby, bony-fingered hand in the direction of my tiny fisherman's cottage. 'If you gentlemen are them as I believe you to be then I have a message for you.'

'We are on pressing business and should you be some species of cadger with no more than a hard-luck tale this hindrance will go the worse for you.' Facey looms over the cove, who extends placating hands, his glocky glim flicking wildly back and forth like a lantern in a gale.

'I am no sponger but a seaman who has did his duty for king and country, sir.'

Facey is often easy with sailors down on their luck but on this occasion remains stern and forbidding. 'We are the men you seek. Here is Mr Samuel Samuel; should you have a message, spill it and waste no more of our time.'

The cove leers, showing no more than three remaining teeth and them all snaggled and brown. 'It concerns a certain John Samuel, lately with the *Pandora*. Kin to you, I should imagine, Mr Samuel?'

'He is,' I affirm. I do not like the looks of this one, nor his shifty ways. If John has fallen in with his kind then I truly fear for him. My heart is in my mouth. 'What news of the lad?'

'He is well enough for the moment, sir, though concerned shipmates have charged me to inform you of his circumstances with all speed.'

'And? What are these circumstances?'

'Well, sir, I shall tell you, pausing only to remind you of the many hardships endured by a seaman cast up on the land without the means to earn his bread.'

'Earn his grog more like,' sneers Facey.

'A man must eat, sir, whether he choose to wash down his wittles with Adam's Ale or a pint of good rum.'

'Here is a sixpence for you. I care not how you spend it. What news of him?'

'A sixpence sir? It has been a hard morning's trudge and the weather, as you see, is not kind.'

'Sixpence is more than generous,' insists Facey.

'Well, I say,' casting about in the pockets of my old coat, 'there may be another copper or two about me; certainly Rosamund would pay any amount for news of the boy.'

The cove cocks his head. His good eye narrows, slyly assessing me, while the glocky one strays, fixing on something else entirely, most likely the old Square Tower at the foot of the High Street. 'Any amount of tin is it, Mr Samuel?'

'No,' rumbles Facey, ''tis either the sixpence or a clump of such magnitude that them three remaining teeth of yourn shall instantly pack up sticks and take residence elsewhere.'

'Then I'll make do with the sixpence, though it be grudged and hard-earned.'

'Well then, what of the lad?'

'I am charged to tell you that your John Samuel has departed Portsmouth in company with a group of youngsters from the self-same wessel. Having no great liking for the hardships of shipboard life, John Samuel and his confederates betook themselves to London by last night's stage in conformity to a plan long in the making. They are determined never to return and are set to make their living in the city by means of pickpocketing and other petty crimes. In short, sirs, he has skedaddled.'

'How do you come by this information?' asks Facey.

'The lad does not lack friends on his wessel and, as I have mentioned, them persons have charged me to convey this news to you with all speed.'

'Why should them parties not come to us themselves?'

The cove considers the question, gazing down at his boots for a moment, which are cracked and have seen not a lick of polish in an eternity. 'Not all have been granted shore leave, sir.'

'True enough,' confirms Facey.

'And the youngsters,' I say, 'is their destination known?'

The cove raises his head, surer of himself now. 'Indeed so, them concerned parties was most insistent I inform you of this. In accordance with their scheme the youngsters are to hole up at a house in New Road, in the parish of St. Marylebone. Number Seventeen, I am told. You are urged to make your way to that destination with all speed since nothing good can come of a delay, for once your milk is spilled, it is spoiled, as they say.'

'I do not take your meaning.'

The cove leers at me, glocky eye rolled alarmingly inwards and taps his nose. 'The instant your lad cuts his first purse he is every bit as liable for a scragging as the wickedest willain in the Devil's Acre. Make haste, gents, I beg you, afore your lad embarks on a calamitous path what cannot be undone.' The cove lays a sodden hand on my sleeve. 'I see you to be a man of compassion, sir. I have discharged my duty to you and your kin, surely you agree that be worth more than a paltry sixpence.'

'Alas, I have only two coppers about me, which you may have.' I drop the pennies into his outstretched paw. He swiftly pockets them without a word of thanks and lurches away in the direction of Spice Island.

'Well, this is cold comfort, to be sure.'

'At least the lad lives if that wretch is to be believed.'

'You were hard on him, Facey, it may be that he has done us a great service.'

'I mislike him and his cranky orb. Either display a proper glim or do without,' responds Facey, tapping his own leather eye-patch. 'That glocky article is neither one thing nor another.'

'He seemed a low sort, but you are usually kindlier to the old salts.'

'That one is no seaman, Sammy. Nor never has been, I warrant.'

'On account of his wandering orb?'

'By no means. A faulty glim will never disqualify a man from the sea. The great Nelson is testament to that. No, your seaman's complexion is invariably hearty, ruddy or brownish, often like to a walnut, whereas that phizzog has seldom felt the touch of God's blessed sun; a cistern slug has a more wholesome shade. Neither have those soft mitts ever hauled on hemp.'

'So we may not credit his tale?'

'That I reckon our man to be a wharf-side loafer and scrounger don't mean the information is counterfeit. I cannot see the advantage in it. No, I believe there is truth enough in the tale. Boys will do such things without thought of consequences. You may recall that I myself ran away to sea.'

'And so it appears our lad has run away to land.'

Facey nods, plants a firm hand on my shoulder and speaks quietly in my ear. 'Now, Sammy. I did not wish to mention it earlier since there was no call to. But I must tell you that the *Pandora* sails in a fortnight. Though Jack Sullivan has a fondness for the lad, should John Samuel not appear at the expiry of his period of leave, there is naught for it but he will be recorded in the muster book as "run". Regardless of his conduct in London, if we cannot fetch him back in good time he will surely be taken up by the navy and hanged for a deserter.'

'Then I must prepare to depart for London directly.'

'Hold your horses, Sammy, I expect Mrs Samuel will have something to say on the matter.'

'I shall certainly accompany you,' is what Mrs Samuel has to say on the matter. She has already begun to prepare a basket for our journey with a stone jug of cider, the remains of last night's meat pie, bread, cheese and a few apples.

'There is the new Asiatic Cholera plague to consider. I would not have you put your life in peril.'

'And what of you, Sammy? How is your life any less precious to me? No, if we are to go, then we shall go together. Besides, I believe that gentle persuasion may result in a better outcome than, say, the brute force of your crowbar. You will forgive me for saying so, but it is where my capacity indubitably trumps your own.'

'Then with the two on us absent for an indefinite period, our young charges shall be deprived of schooling entirely.'

'Pish, Sammy. I shall call upon old Mrs Muir, my particular friend. Though it has been some years since she has been governess, I have no doubt that she will manage our little school admirably in the interim. She is inclined to firmness, I believe, but that may be no bad thing. The tap-room shall run well enough under the hand of Mr Griffith along of Mr Facey.'

I grimace, choosing, for the moment, not to air my suspicions of this Griffith.

'And how should the pair of you intend to pay your way?' asks Facey gently.

'We have some savings set aside, though meagre enough, to be sure.'

'And yet, here I stand, pockets weighed down with good, honest silver.'

'Less honest than I might perhaps wish,' says Rosamund tartly with a sharp look in my direction.

'That is to split hairs. Silver don't moralise much, nor do them as take it in exchange for good vittles and clean beds.'

'Then I am obliged to you, Mr Facey. Since they weigh so heavy on you, we shall accept some few of your shillings, though I should like it strictly understood that it is to be a loan and shall be repaid in due course, every penny of it.'

'You misunderstand me, Mrs Samuel. There is no need of a loan, nor will you find yourself short of tin in the metropolis.'

'How so?'

'I am coming along with you, a course.'

CHAPTER III

The three of us have secured seats inside the one o'clock Mail Coach; a less fortunate cove perches up top, exposed to the winds and rain outside. Though it is early afternoon, the interior is somewhat gloomy since the leather shades are pulled down against the inclement weather. We share our benches with a pair of gents and, since there are five of us rather than the usual four, we are somewhat cribb'd and hugger-mugger. Mercifully, our companions seem decent, affable sorts: the elder, Dr Trimble, is a florid, portly physician of about fifty years; the younger, Gates, is a reserved young midshipman off the Hawke. Me, Rosamund and the doctor have managed to squeeze onto a bench together. Gates is settled opposite, alongside Facey who, with his prodigious bulk, occupies the lion's share of the seat. The odour of damp wool and stale linen permeates the air; we are fortunate that Rosamund is accustomed to employ a toilet water about her clothing and skin, which imparts the mitigating sweetness of roses.

Gates remains silent as we clatter though Horndean. I watch his head begin to sink as he is rocked by the motion of the carriage on its springs. It is soon apparent that our physician is more than happy to assume his share of the conversation: 'Well now, I should say that we embark on a hazardous venture,' he announces. 'You will no doubt be aware of this current pestilence, which has struck terror into the hearts of all in the capital and yet here we are, conveyed towards it at a velocity of no less than eight miles per hour?'

'Certainly we are aware of it, sir,' I reply.

'It is the reason for my journey, don't ye know.'

'How so, sir?'

'I have been requested to attend a meeting of the Royal College.'

'Forgive me, I do not know of it.'

''Tis the foremost association of physicians in the known world. I myself am a Fellow of that august body and have been sent for most urgently to speak upon this current blight.'

'I take it then, sir, you have some particular knowledge of the Blue Death?' adds Rosamund.

'Indeed I do, Mrs Samuel. I had some experience of it back in '24 when first it reared its dreadful head across the countries of the Mediterranean. The Grand Tour, to be specific, wherein I conducted an investigation into the antiquities of the Corinthian city of Syracuse on the Island of Sicily, described by the great Cicero as "the most beautiful of them all".'

''Pon my word, sir, you must be one of those sometimes described as a polymath.'

Dr Trimble chuckles and attempts a modest bow from his seated position. 'I would never say it, but should others choose to dub me so, then who am I to disagree?'

'Well, sir, we have pressing business in the metropolis and would certainly be obliged were you to share your evident wisdom in the matter of this contagion and, more specifically, what steps we might take to keep ourselves safe.'

'I should be delighted, Mrs Samuel. Barring obstruction and, heaven forbid, highway catastrophe, we must expect a further seven hours of jouncing in close company and so conversation may banish the tedium most commendably.'

'You are very good, sir. In return, might we offer to share a bite, for we have a surfeit?

Rosamund fishes in her basket, producing the remains of our last night's pie, which she places on her lap before carefully unwrapping it. The young middie, who has been napping, head against the coach wall, comes wide awake, alerted by the savoury aroma which has filled the air.

I pass my folding pocket knife to Rosamund, which she uses to cut five even slices. She has even thought to pack a few small pieces of clean linen, which she uses to hand out the portions.

At one time, in the days before we were wed, Rosamund would never allow anyone to observe her eating on account of a small chip in her front tooth, believing it to be unsightly. It has never been in the slightest bit discomfiting in my eyes but is rather one of the many small imperfections, which a man and woman might find to love about one another. Nevertheless, even now she will only take small and discreet bites at her own portion, chewing carefully and with uncommon grace.

Trimble has made short work of his slice and in consequence of a stray crumb lodged in his windpipe, is prey to a violent fit of coughing. 'You must drink something, sir,' orders Rosamund, producing a small leather beaker from the basket. She fills it with cider from the stone jug.

Trimble drinks it off with great satisfaction, smacking moist, puffy lips. 'Though I am the physician, it is you have provided me the perfect remedy, dear lady.'

The beaker is refilled and passed around until all have had their share and the jug is quite empty.

'Now, should you wish it, you shall all have an apple and a morsel of cheese.'

Rosamund's little picnick has been a great success, even the silent middie is all smiles and obliging nods. Trimble hunts a last crumb of yellow cheese from his leg and pops it into his mouth while Rosamund packs away the basket and stows it beneath the bench.

'Now, I shall sing for my supper as it were,' announces our physician. 'You wish to hear further of the Asiatic Cholera?'

'We do, sir. Since learning is never wasted and, in this instance, may be the saving of us all.'

'True enough. Its origin, as the name suggests, is the Indian subcontinent, most likely Kolkata. Thereafter there were reported outbreaks across the Orient. Alas, it has now made its way to our shores, the poison no doubt brought home by our own Jack Tars, no disrespect to Mr Gates.'

Gates, blushing a little to find himself the recipient of our attention, nods sagely. 'Likely, sir, very likely,' he mutters.

'The symptoms are marked, commencing with a sickness of the stomach, nervous agitation, followed by profuse vomiting and, saving your presence, Mrs Samuel, purging. The pulse is invariably thready and irregular. In many instances the skin will take on a deepish blue or purple tint, hence the sobriquet: Blue Death.'

'Is there aught to be done by a medical gentleman such as yourself?'

'Alas, no. In most cases, death is an inevitable consequence. There is no cure, Mrs Samuel, no salting nor immunity. Avoidance is the thing.'

'And how might that be achieved, sir?'

'Disease is known to be transmitted by miasmata, which is to say foul airs. In London, during the hours of darkness, these rank and foetid airs may rise up from the river and marshes, mingle with the night mists and be borne upon breezes into parts of the city. Once ingested by inhalation or introduced through the skin, the poison may be further passed by a noxious breath from person to person.'

'I shall certainly endeavour to avoid a foul breath as I am generally wont to do. My husband employs a liquorice root, sir.'

'Good, very good, though in this instance vinegar is superior.' Trimble nods at me approvingly. 'And be particularly cautious of a night fog or a mist since that damp air may convey pestilence. Furthermore, the prevailing moisture which settles upon all and sundry in such conditions is to be considered deadly. In short, the water of London generally is best avoided. In the capital, small beer is the thing for thirst.'

'And porter, sir? I have a great liking for London porter,' queries Facey.

'Porter is adequate though too strong for most.'

'I shall stick to porter then, sir, which I have often found to be the remedy for much of what ails us.'

'Just so,' agrees Trimble without much enthusiasm.

Rosamund, no doubt mindful that we are in receipt of the kind of wisdom that would ordinarily be charged at a guinea or two an hour, endeavours to return Trimble to his deliberations. 'Vinegar, you say is a specific? And how is it to be took, sir?'

Trimble chuckles. 'It need not be ingested, dear lady, but rather employed to rinse the mouth once or twice daily. Indeed, vinegar is a prime defence against miasmata of all kinds. Should you find yourself assailed by noxious odours or enveloped in the London mists, a rag or kerchief soaked in vinegar will provide admirable protection.'

Trimble lifts the leather shade and peers out, quickly retreating his head against the unceasing rain. A fat drop trickles slowly down his nose. 'I fear the weather remains unkind and I cannot envy our fellow passenger.'

'I wonder if we might make room for him inside.'

'Great heavens, no. You are too soft-hearted, my dear, the coachman would never permit it. The gentleman has paid the lesser fare and having done so must remain up top and take the consequences. Most likely a head cold, I shouldn't wonder. Though he is well muffled. Which brings to mind another piece of advice for your consideration. Miasmata have a tendency to rise and will infiltrate the elevated parts of a residence; avoid high places and upper floors and be sure to keep your doors and windows well shut at night.'

'And is this to be the substance of your address to your fellow men of learning?'

Gates, having lost interest, yawns mightily before tucking himself more comfortably between Facey's bulky shoulder and the carriage wall.

Trimble taps his protruding lower lip. 'In good part, Mrs Samuel. Though much of what I have discussed is already well-known to men of science. I shall also concern myself with methods for combating this menace. Bearding the lion in his den, as it were.'

'Yet you have said there is no cure.'

'No cure but an eradication perhaps. We must fight fire with fire. I shall be urging the liberal application of flame as a preventative measure. Decayed articles, rags, cordage, papers and hangings where found must all be consigned to the flames. Filth and its concomitant stench, driven out. Where conflagration will not suit then copious effusions of water must be applied with the addition of lye or chloride of lime.'

'We are fortunate to share a carriage with a gentleman of such parts, is that not so, Sammy?'

'Indeed, sir. We are school teachers and my wife is not without some learning, but your understanding of these matters is greatly to be admired.'

'You are very good to say so.' Trimble inclines his head, the effect somewhat ruined by the violent rocking of the carriage followed by the cessation of forward motion. 'Heaven forfend a pothole,' he mutters.

Facey flips up his blind, peering out. 'Never fret, sir, 'tis only the Anchor at Liphook.'

Trimble is all smiles now. 'So soon? Upon my word, the miles do indeed take flight on the wings of a little edifying conversation. I believe there may be sufficient time while the horses are changed to take a chop, a few boiled taters and a pot of ale.'

'I shall brave the rain and step out for a little air,' announces Rosamund.

The deluge has finally ceased and it is full night by the time we arrive at the Bolt-in-Tun, Fleet Street, some six hours later. Doctor Trimble, having gorged himself into a stupor, dozed away the remainder of the journey, as did our middie, who, being a young naval fellow, has refined the ability to cat-nap whenever and wherever the opportunity presents.

Perhaps on account of having endured something of an ordeal together, Trimble condescends to shake hands with us all, despite his gentlemanly status. A liveried carriage awaits him. 'Remember your vinegar, dear lady, and you shall thrive,' he advises, afore embarking his conveyance. His effects are collected by the postilion and he is swiftly whisked away to his accommodations and no doubt, a late supper.

The middie, blushing furiously, steps forward and treats Rosamund to a brief bow. 'Madam, I am most grateful for the vittles. I have ate nothing nearly so good as that meat pie in three months and shall tell you frankly, I have done naught but dream of it since Liphook. I wish you joy of your venture in the city.'

Rosamund returns the courtesy with a small bob. I can see by a small, private smile that she is fighting not to chuckle.

The middie collects his small sea chest, hoists it onto his frail shoulders and is quickly swallowed up by the dark streets.

Finally, the poor cove from the roof descends slowly and stiffly, so bundled in coats and scarves that we can only discern the very tip of his nose. He is still damp from the earlier soaking, as we can discern wafts of steam rising from his garments. He gives us the briefest of nods, perhaps envious of our comparative comfort.

Facey and me have brung a single housekeeper between us, which is to say a small roll of canvas holding toilet articles. Other than for Rosamund's basket and her modest reticule, we are without baggage but since it is already after ten in the evening by the St Bride's clock, we decide to go no further and put up here at the Bolt-in-Tun. Any concern that accommodations might be scarce is swiftly put to rest by the appearance of the inn keep who is only too keen to oblige us. 'What luck, what fortune,' he declares, rubbing his hands. 'There is fine rooms going abegging tonight and you may have your pick of them.' His enthusiasm noticeably wanes once inside the hallway, where he is able to more closely inspect our threadbare, travelworn appearance in the lamplight. 'Should you wish it, there is cleanish room on the upper floor where you may top and tail it with two or three other gents what came earlier.'

'I mislike other parties in my bed,' announces Facey.

'On account of your size, I daresay. I cannot help that lest you wish to pay the extra.'

'Your bedding is clean and free of vermin, I hope?' asks Rosamund.

'Laundered only this last week, Mum.'

'You will allow us view your private rooms and if satisfied, will have two on 'em' announces Facey.

The taverner smiles, though without sincerity. 'You will make no objection to first giving me sight of coin. In London, rooms are not gratis and must be paid for. Same as all else.'

Facey's eyes narrow as he looms over the man. 'You believe because we lately stepped off the Portsmouth post that we are bumpkins without means, sir?' He reaches into his jacket and produces the heavy purse from which he takes a silver crown. 'Your rooms are empty and like to remain so on account of the pestilence.'

'Now, now, sir. I had no intention of giving offence, only that times is hard just lately, which, as you say, is in consequence of the sickness.'

'Well then, here is my proposal, which you may take or leave: this here crown, no snide coin but the king's new silver, shall account for two days of bed and scran for the three of us. It is a fair price, the best you will have this night, what's more, you would do well to consider that I am not so much the yokel that I cannot tell when the dinners you send for are made of scrag nor that I lay in a bed that crawls with lice.'

''Tis ordinarily a shilling for a private room and another for the vittles. I am to be gypped of three shilling here.'

Facey shrugs. 'Better you see it as five shillings to the good.'

The taverner nods slowly, 'Indeed, it is a sensible philosophy; I shall take the crown,' – he appraises Facey – 'and will add that you are no bumpkin, sir, but drive a more swingeing bargain than any of them Ikeys of Spittle Fields.'

'Done then,' grins Facey, slapping his silver piece onto the counter.

CHAPTER IV

Despite its moniker, the New Road is a deal more venerable than many, having been constructed almost a hundred years past as a thoroughfare for the drovers to bring cattle to town. It does, however, retain its impressive width and is bordered by a number of fashionable residences. Every so often there is a once grand edifice, now decaying and in need of repair or even derelict entirely. Number Seventeen is such a one. It is a good size, ascending to three floors, but the red brick facia is crumbling and pitted, the windows dusty and neglected with many a cracked pane.

We step up to the peeling front door where the brass knocker is green from verdigris but still serviceable. Facey gives it a pounding and, almost immediately, we hear bolts being drawn from inside.

The door is flung wide to reveal a diminutive, smirking fellow with a great bush of hair in a greasy, plum-coloured weskit, breeches, stockings and pumps. 'Welcome, welcome. I see you are astounded at my alacrity. Rest assured, there is no flummery, nor no hint of the supernatural about it, merely that I had already spied you in the street from the upper window.'

'We are here in search of a John Samuel, ship's boy, lately off the *Pandora* at Portsmouth,' rumbles Facey.

'Don't I know it, sirs. And haven't I been peering through them windows on watch for your party these past two days 'til my peepers have quite dried up, shrivelled like a pair of currants and all but rolled out of my skull?'

'You have kept a lookout for us?'

'Indeed so, sir.'

'We are expected then?'

'You are, sir.' The odd little fellow takes a dainty step back and appraises us with great satisfaction. 'Given your bulkish appearance you must be Mr Facey. The cove what resembles a parson who mislaid a sixpence and found a penny, would be Mr Samuel, and this dainty creetur is a Miss Howlett, I believe.'

'Mrs Samuel,' corrects Rosamund.

'Indeed? I was not told of it. Allow me to offer my felicitations. I am Weggums.' He executes a brief but formal bow.

'We are not at a levee, you dolt,' objects Facey. 'We are come for the lad. Is he within or no?'

Weggums claps his hands in delight and emits a shriek of high-pitched laughter such as one might hear echoing from the walls of Bedlam, 'Certainly he is within.'

'Then you must fetch him.'

'Alas, I could not. A little more patience and you will set eyes on him anon.'

Patience has never been a strong suit with Facey and so I decide to interject before violence erupts. 'We have come a long way, sir, our only wish to retrieve the lad. I assure you we harbour no interest in the doings of this house, should that be your concern.'

Facey wags a warning finger in the little man's face. 'You will cease with these incessant riddles and fetch him this instant or I warrant it will go the worse for you,' he growls.

'Oh dear me, no, Mr Facey. You would never wish to chastise me, there is no advantage to it. Especially not if you wish to see your young friend safe and sound. It is not in my power to fetch the lad, but should you follow me I shall surely bring you to him.'

Weggums twirls and, light as a dancing master, ascends the bare wooden staircase. 'Quickly now. It would never do to keep your hosts waiting.'

Rosamund throws me a perplexed frown. I shrug; we none of us have any inkling of what awaits, but it seems we are committed. We quickly follow.

'Take care now, the middle stair of our upper floor is busted and should you try your weight on it you will fall clean through and never stop 'til Van Diemen's land.'

We arrive at the third-floor landing, where Weggums awaits, smiling broadly. 'Splendid. All present and accounted for I see, without mischance or catastrophe to life and limb on account of these here treacherous stairs what are creaking and groaning for want of repair. A mournful racket you will agree, like lost so many souls damned to the pit of hell.' He casts a thumb behind him in the direction of the landing door. 'Only, certain parties don't approve of the expenditure of tin for the purpose.' He turns and scratches gently at the door.

It takes some moments for it to be opened by an elderly individual, a man I recognise. He nods gravely and ushers us all inside.

Although no doubt once an upper bedroom of sorts, the room has been laid out as a comfortable place of business, entirely at odds with the dilapidation of the rest of the house. There is an armchair by a brightly burning fire, thick-piled rugs cover polished floorboards, while the walls are decorated with beautifully rendered engravings. Dominating the centre of the room are two polished wood desks covered in piles of paperwork and assorted trinkets. Occupying them are two men I had hoped never to set eyes on again.

Without a word, the elderly clerk, whose name is Crockett or Croxley if memory serves, returns silently to his place at the high desk by the window and begins casting his accounts.

Weggums claps his hands, before dancing a little jig. 'No, your glims do not deceive you,' he announces gleefully, 'It is indeed Mr Pimlott and Mr Chuffington.'

'Enough, Weggums,' snaps Chuffington. We stand in awful silence while he removes his specs and carefully polishes them with a pristine fogle. Finally, he peers up and addresses us. 'Good day to you all,' he says.

Facey nods grimly.

'Good day to you, Mr Chuffington.' Rosamund bobs briefly.

Chuffington is as spry as ever, while his confederate, Pimlott, a great corpulent jelly of a man, has, if anything, grown larger over the two years since we saw them last. He makes short work of a duck leg, grease slathering his fingers and chin and grunts something unintelligible.

'When last we spoke I believe I advised you all that though we would not seek you out, you would be wise to avoid our eye.'

'We most certainly did not come here on your account, sir, but were given information that a young man of our acquaintance was under this roof,' protests Rosamund.

Chuffington replaces his specs, gazes at Rosamund, making a steeple of his fingers. 'You mistake me, Miss Howlett...'

'It is Mrs Samuel now, sir.'

Chuffington rocks back in his chair. 'Indeed? Well, well. We were not informed.'

Pimlott sets the scoured duck bones aside and wipes the grease from his fingers with a napkin. 'Indeed we were not, Mr C.'

'At any rate you mistake me, Mrs Samuel, we do not presume to find fault with your presence here, quite the contrary. You was expected.'

'You were summoned as it were, and here you are,' intones Pimlott.

'Looked out for these past two days, 'til my glims was raisins,' titters Weggums.

Chuffington's pale forehead creases in a tiny frown. 'Rouse Mr Meathook, if you please, Mr Weggums. And perhaps bring us some few Naples biscuits.'

'What a treat,' rejoices Weggums, clapping hands and beaming at us. 'And ain't it just as I said? A little of patience and you shall be rewarded. Whoever would have imagined Naples biscuits? What a treat.'

Chuffington smiles indulgently as he skips from the room. 'Mr Weggums is the eldest son of a cousin, somewhat addled from having been dropped on his head as a small child. Mr Pimlott suffers him gladly owing to a marvellously charitable nature.'

'In short, he ain't quite right in the canister,' grumbles Pimlott, uncharitably.

'As always, Mr P. has the nub of it.' Chuffington indicates three hard-backed chairs to one side of the double desks. 'Be seated if you please. You will forgive the accommodations, I am sure; they are of a temporary nature and not quite in order. Though we are hard-working, upstanding men of commerce, alas, there are many who nurse unwarranted resentments and might wish us ill and so it behoves us, from time to time, to relocate our place of business.' He rises and approaches a polished dark wood side table where sits a large silver bowl. He ladles a white liquid into a glass beaker. 'Here is a milk punch, which I daresay you will find to your liking, containing as it does a little of brandy and lemons.' He passes us each a beaker of the mixture, which is indeed quite delicious. 'Mr Pimlott will not look at the day without he has a glass or two and you will go a long way to find a more robust constitution than his.'

Pimlott nods by way of acknowledgement, as he sets to work at his gnashers with a small ivory toothpick

Chuffington returns to his chair and briefly examines a ledger before removing his specs and addressing us once more. 'You will be wondering perhaps why we have chosen to seek you out, prodding you from your Portsmouth obscurity like a set of winkles.'

'Your safe harbour, as it were,' adds Pimlott.

Chuffington chuckles. 'Did you catch that? Mr Pimlott is known for his astonishing perspicacity but alas, is seldom credited for his wit. Is that not so, Mr Crockford?'

The clerk, pauses momentarily in his work. 'It is one of the great injustices of the age, sir.'

'Your "safe harbour" indeed. Do not think that because you have removed yourselves to that distant province that you are beyond our reach, or eye. We pay a close attention to certain of our port districts, Pompey being foremost amongst 'em. Since we have a interest in the movement of certain commodities, it behoves us to know, in particular, the comings and goings of the worthier inns where trade might be done: who takes rooms, who dines with whom, what prices are agreed and so forth. Imagine our mystification when we was most recently informed that a certain Mr Facey had reserved a private room at the Keppel's Head for the purpose of hosting a dinner. Bless my soul, what possible reason for such profligacy? On account, it transpires, of a young 'un returning from voyage aboard the vessel *Pandora*. A young 'un, moreover, bearing the name of John Samuel.'

'Rest assured, gents,' asserts Pimlott, still digging away with his little pick, 'those two names, Samuel and Facey, had not been entirely forgot by us.'

'Your young lad, home from the sea, Mr Samuel. An inconsequential snippet concerning old acquaintances, or so I had imagined. But trust Mr Pimlott to find a way to turn such a trifling matter to our favour. For he always will, you know. You see, it occurred to that most fertile of intellects that our Mr Samuel and Mr Facey, once considered so very proficient at their trade, might be persuaded, for a brief time, to place their undisputed gifts at our service. After all, we never forget an obligation.'

'There is no such obligation,' retorts Rosamund. 'You were rewarded handsomely for the release of Mr Facey when last we met.'

Chuffington tuts and wags an admonishing finger. 'I think not, Mrs Samuel.'

'Four thousand pound in notes of hand is no trifling sum,' insists Rosamund.

'Ah, but did we obtain the full four thousand for 'em? We did not. Nor anything like. Mr Crockford?'

Crockford reaches for a ledger, which he solemnly opens. Licking an inky forefinger, he flicks through the pages before finding what he seeks. He runs the finger down the page until it arrives at the entry in question. 'Seven hundred and twenty pound, six shillin' and five pence, ha'penny precisely, Mr Chuffington.'

'There you have it. Them notes on Liston were never like to be paid in full, Mrs Samuel. We dunned, threatened and squeezed but to no avail, receiving only a fraction of their true value. An outcome, I warrant, which shall come as no surprise to you.'

'In short, we was gypped to the sum of three thousand, two hundred and seventy-four pound, thirteen shillings, sixpence, ha'penny,' growls Pimlott.

'What a privilege to observe that colossal intellect at work once again. A prodigy is he not?'

'Indeed, sir,' acknowledges Rosamund, 'an impressive feat of calculus, but how might any of us have possibly known whether Henry Liston would honour his debts or no? He appeared well-britched enough to the likes of us. Caveat emptor, as the Latins might say.'

Chuffington gazes at her, unblinking ice blue eyes behind the specs. 'You are a sharp one, Mrs Samuel. I noted it when last we met. Have a care lest you are injured by your own acuity.' Finally, he smiles, showing a row of small pointed teeth veneered in brown. 'Well, well, that is water under the bridge. We shall not quibble, since it is the matter of your small service to us we must now speak of.'

Rosamund sighs. 'May we first see the boy?'

Chuffington rubs his hands in anticipation. 'Indeed you may. And you will be pleased to note that he is in perfect fettle. Right as a trivet, I should say. Is that not so, Mr P?'

'Could not have expressed it better myself, Mr C.'

'High praise indeed from a man of such intellect and clarity of mind.'

Chuffington reaches across his desk for a small brass bell which he shakes. Within a few short moments an ante room door opens and Pure John is shoved roughly across the threshold. His face is bruised, there is a smear of dried blood on his temple and his hands are bound. Behind him stands the menacing figure of Meathook, who acknowledges us with a brief, unfriendly nod. I notice that the boy wears the trousers and good linen shirt which we acquired for him before he went to sea, no doubt with the intention of making his best appearance for the homecoming.

Rosamund leaps to her feet, intending to embrace the lad.

'Stay,' warns Chuffington. 'This is no time for sentimental reunion, Mrs Samuel, merely the prelude to the matter of our business.'

Rosamund sinks back into her chair. Ignoring Chuffington, she gives Pure John an encouraging smile. 'It is good to see you, John. You have grown since you have been at sea.'

Despite the circumstances, John grins. 'Likewise, it does me good to see the three on you. Though I could wish it were elsewhere than here.'

'Have these mistreated you, lad?' asks Facey.

Pure John cocks his head. 'This lot? Not so much, Mr Facey, sir. But as I turn up Broad Street off the jolly boat, two nasty sods waylaid me and give me a crack on the head what made a night sky of my noggin; first come the stars, then all goes black as the Earl of Hell's riding boots. Next thing, I come to my senses on a old mattress here, which is a most confounding matter when being more accustomed to the swing of a hammock. At any rate, they did give me vittles, which the cracknut brung me...'

Meathook cuffs him across the head. 'Mr Weggums to you.'

Facey rises, preparing to launch himself across the room. Meathook reveals the wicked-looking butcher's knife in his hand, which he now places across the boy's throat. 'Steady, Mr Facey. Your prowess with the mauleys is well known, but I assure you I shall have the lad's gizzard laid open afore you ever think to lay a mitt on me.'

'Enough, gents. This ain't St Giles',' snaps Chuffington.

Facey subsides into his chair at the same time as Meathook lowers his blade. just as we hear a gentle rasp at the door. 'Come,' intones Pimlott.

Mr Weggums enters with a broad grin, flourishing a large plate. Catching sight of Meathook and Pure John, his face crumples. 'Oh dear me. What a blessed pickle. I counted out sufficient for all, being most particular to account for each and every person, and now there are more on us here as there are biscuits to be had. I especially accounted two for Mr Pimlott, well knowing his partiality, but had forgot to add Mr Crockford. And now there are two more persons arrived and I cannot say whether I am coming nor going.' He lays the plate on Pimlott's desk and, with a tearful frown, begins to enumerate the available dainties with his fingers.

'Do not fuss so, Weggums. 'Tis of no account,' advises Chuffington.

Weggums wrings his hands in distress. 'I should like the lad to have a biscuit.'

'Then give him yourn,' grumbles Pimlott, snatching a couple to himself.

'I could never abide a Naples biscuit,' says Rosamund. 'And so, should not thank you for one, Mr Weggums.'

'For goodness sake, sir, take your biscuit and leave,' orders Chuffington. The crestfallen Weggums snatches one away before scuttling out.

As it happens I'm somewhat peckish, having had no breakfast, and quite partial to a Naples biscuit myself, but have no desire to fall foul of Pimlott, who, having made short work of his earlier seizures, now eyes the plate with a predatory glare.

Facey has no such compunction; he reaches across and takes two biscuits, earning a look of pure malice from Pimlott. He crams them both into his mouth, nodding approval as he chews.

'Well, well. Now that refreshment has been taken and our duty as hosts is complete, we must move swiftly to business. It is, in course, evident that this young man is of some consequence to you. Your own son, Mr Samuel? A relative of some description, a natural perhaps? After all, his removal has readily brought you to us today.'

The milk is already well spilled and so I see no advantage in dissembling here. 'As like to a son as makes no difference,' I reply.

'Of sufficient consequence that should he suffer further harm at your hands, take my word, such injury will be revisited upon you fivefold,' announces Facey, spraying pastry crumbs. 'Especially you, Meathook. You and me have unfinished business in any event.'

Meathook sneers, flourishing the knife beneath Pure John's throat.

Pimlott reaches for the remaining two biscuits. 'Like a pair of bantams in a pit, Mr C.'

'Indeed, Mr P. Very like. There will be no further strutting and spitting if you please.' Chuffington takes a tiny sip at his milk punch. 'What hurt is visited upon this young man or otherwise is entirely in your hands, Mr Facey. We offer you a simple exchange: the safe return of the lad in return for your cooperation in a small matter of procurement.'

'What matter, exactly?'

'Naught for which your many skills and experience have not already equipped you. A trivial hoist is all.'

'We have left off that game, Mr Chuffington, when we removed to Portsmouth.'

'Then you must resume your old profession now that you have returned.'

'Believe me, sir,' I interject, 'we should be honoured to oblige you gents in any task. It ain't necessary to trouble yourselves in holding the lad. Certainly, there is the expense in providing board and lodging to be considered.'

Chuffington chuckles, 'I believe we can bear the expense, Mr Samuel, though it is noble in you to consider it.'

'Bring it off and the boy shall be returned to you,' declares Pimlott. He waves a languid hand at Meathook who takes a good grip on Pure John's linen shirt, hauling him towards the door. The lad gives him a good kick to the shin, which is instantly repaid with a solid clump about the ear. 'Mr Samuel will surely come for me,' sobs the boy, 'and then Mr Facey will come for you. Make no doubt, he will scrag you for that, you grass-combing bugger.'

The little fellow is hauled away voicing protests and a further barrage of shockingly foul-mouthed curses, which I can only assume he has learned at sea.

Chuffington tuts, shaking his head. 'Well, you have laid eyes on your young man. He is hale for the moment and so we must move to the business at hand.' Chuffington removes a heavy brass paperweight, a winged lion set upon a plinth, from atop a pile of old newssheets on his desk. He selects one, a copy of Facey's periodical of choice: The Penny Illustrated. 'I wonder if you have heard of the late Edith Belmont?'

'I have not, sir,' I say.

'Nor I,' adds Facey.

Chuffington smooths out the paper before him. 'Well enough, there is no reason why you should have. Mrs Belmont was a woman of privilege and wealth. While she lived, she existed in a sphere way beyond your own. In short, she was a woman of some repute and, for a time at least, welcomed within the highest circles of the land. She was wed to one William Belmont, a nabob serving with John Company in Kolkata. A man of little distinction but some considerable wealth, who indulged his wife, most notably with the gift of the Eye of Brahma.'

Chuffington passes across the paper. Rosamund and me examine it. On the cover is a detailed depiction of an item of jewellery, somewhat like a necklace. Set in the centre is a huge gem, of what type I could not say.

'It is very beautiful,' announces Rosamund.

'The piece is of a type known as a ferroniere,' explains Chuffington, 'something like a tiara, fashioned to be worn around the head. The centrepiece is the gemstone in question, the Eye of Brahma, a black diamond, very rare and of seventy carats.'

'Pilfered from a native temple and reckoned to be cursed,' adds Pimlott with some relish.

'That's as may be, though the owner might believe himself to be fortunate enough given its value. Certainly, the piece caused a great sensation in the salons when first it made an appearance on Mrs Belmont's brow. The periodical is from a while back previous, when the talk was of naught but this dazzling gemstone.'

Facey rubs his hands on the greasy legs of his keks, a sign that he is becoming impatient. 'We have had little enough dealings with you gents in the past, but surely you must be aware that we ain't cracksmen. Items such as this are beyond our simple doings.'

'You are too modest, Mr Facey, it is precisely your accustomed skills that will be required here. Edith Belmont expired some few days past, most inconveniently, since our Mr Crockford had been in negotiation for the purchase of this very stone.'

Crockford nods gravely by way of acknowledgment.

'Misfortunately, a price could not be settled upon afore she carked it,' adds Pimlott.

'There is an eager buyer on the continent but he shall not remain forever on the hook. Gentlemen, make no mistake, we are well aware of your abilities and you may be sure they are what we require and quick smart at that.'

'How so?' I ask.

Chuffington grimaces. 'The Belmont woman chose to be interred with her bauble.'

'So it ain't her flesh that requires hoisting but rather what she wears to her eternal rest,' explains Pimlott.

'I do not say we are unwilling, gents. But curiosity compels me to ask: Why us? You have gone to some lengths to lure us here when there are plenty here in the city who might carry off such a task.'

'Like your confederate, you are modest, Mr Samuel. You have a reputation, sir. Word is that you and Mr Facey are amongst the very best; the thing must be carried off with the greatest circumspection, leaving no sign of tampering. No trace whatsoever, lest the taint of impropriety dissuade our buyer.'

'I am flattered, Mr Chuffington, but it has been two...'

'Do not be,' interjects Pimlott, snatching the last of the Naples biscuits. 'The Belmont woman expired of the Asiatic Cholera and so none else of merit amongst your profession will do it. Not for any amount of tin, nor even in the face of the direst threats.'

'The Blue Death.' I say.

'Indeed the Blue Death. Some four days past. By all accounts she commenced the morning in perfect health and was carried off by evening.'

Pimlott leers and snaps his fingers. 'Gone, just like that.'

'Edith Belmont now lies sealed in the Belmont family mausoleum in St James's Gardens, adorned with the ferroniere and, no doubt, other knickknacks. The remainder is of no account, it is the Eye of Brahma we must have.'

'Fetch it us with all discretion and the boy will be returned to you in good health.'

'But never think to delay. Our buyer is a man of limited patience.'

'As are we,' adds Pimlott.

CHAPTER V

Once dismissed from that grim residence we head eastward down the New Road, pausing by unspoken agreement in the pleasant surroundings of Park Square, where before us stands the white colonnaded majesty of the Diorama building.

Facey removes his hat and scratches at his thickly bristling hair before breaking the silence. 'I believe there is naught for it but to do as they ask.'

Rosamund has never loved our old profession, so I expect an objection. 'Indeed you must,' she agrees, to my surprise. 'There is, in my estimation, no sensible alternative. You can scarcely mount an escalade on that house nor attempt any other desperate measures without John suffer for it. No, the lesser of these evils is that you resume your former occupation with my blessing.'

'I have not brung the tools,' I say. 'Other than for my crowbar.' I pat the specially sewn inner pocket of my jacket where I still keep my small crowbar. These days, I keep the instrument's reassuring weight about me for protection alone. It has not been applied to a slab or vault for two years or more now.

'I do not doubt that may be easily remedied within an hour or two.'

'It may,' agrees Facey. 'A visit to the Fortune of War will do it, brim-full as it is with them as might easily lay hands upon the tools of our trade; a few shilling here and there will be sufficient to equip us for the night's work.'

'We go tonight then?'

'I see no merit in delay; there is no need of a nose around, since we know the spot. You will recall, Sammy, St James's Gardens is the place we took the prodigious fat fellow some three years back. Him that was carried off with the apoplexy?'

'I well recall him,' I say. 'And a deal of trouble he gave us too.'

Facey chuckles. 'Such was the heft of him that the handles on Shields' cart were busted clean off,' he explains for Rosamund's benefit.

'Thank you, Mr Facey, it is sufficient to know that you are familiar with the ground.'

'Entry will be simple enough, though we shall have to cast about a little for the mausoleum. A dark lantern with shutters will suit the purpose.'

'And how do you plan to carry away this ferroniere?'

Facey plants his hat back on his head. 'Why, in the usual manner, Mrs Samuel, in my pocket. Though it seems large enough for a gemstone, it don't look particular heavy.'

'I do not ask on account of its weight but of the contagion it bears. Though you believe this commission to be a straightforward matter, there is a reason why the more judicious men of your profession have refused it, even under threat.'

'The Blue Death.'

'Exactly so. It is a most fearful prospect. All your precautions are for naught if you are not mindful of the true danger, the invisible contagion no doubt lurking within that tomb.'

'We must have vinegar then, and plenty of it,' I say.

Rosamund nods. 'Certainly, and be sure to touch nothing in that place without you employ a rag and I urge you to take a covering for the mouth and nose.'

'Your advice is sound as always, Mrs Samuel, and carries the seal of Doctor Trimble, though I doubt there is vinegar to be had at the Fortune of War. 'Less of course you count the Madeira.'

'I shall see to the vinegar and purchase a good sound jar with a stopper along with some few neckerchiefs to be soaked. In the meantime, go see to your tools.'

Facey considers her for a moment. 'Might I ask you a favour, Mrs Samuel?'

'Name it, by all means.'

Facey shoves his hands into his pockets and jingles his heavy purse. 'I should first tell you that I did not quite like the manner in which we were regarded by our taverner last night.'

'I should say that was evident to all, Mr Facey.'

Facey pulls at the threadbare lapels of his old coat. 'Well, Mrs Samuel, it may well be that I cut a poorish figure in these old slops and I was wondering whether, whilst you are out and about, you might find the opportunity to purchase a newish coat and perhaps a shirt or two on my behalf.'

'Certainly, Mr Facey, I should be happy to.'

Facey glances at me. 'I could not think to put my oldest friend to shame and so you might do likewise for Sammy.'

'Why, Mr Facey...'

'No, no, I will not be gainsaid. Either we are both on us to be primped, prettied and tricked out to the nines, or neither.' With that, Facey extracts a few shillings from his heavy purse before handing it to Rosamund. 'In any event, I have no head for figures and so I ask you to be the official banker of our expedition.'

'I will take it, Mr Facey, and be sure to give you a strict accounting.'

'No need. There is tin aplenty and you will recall your Sammy played his part in the getting of it. No, 'Tis Liberty Hall; you must spend as you see fit, though I make one condition.'

'Which is?'

Facey, who is ordinarily so utterly fearless, appears to be summoning his courage, first gazing down at his boots. 'I hope you will not be offended by the provision, Mrs Samuel.'

'We have known one another for a good while now, Mr Facey, I doubt if there is aught you can say to me which will cause offence.'

'Well then, it is like this: what with me and Sammy topping it the swells in our new coats and such, I believe there would be justice in considering a article or two for your own self. In for a penny, in for a pound, as they do say.'

Rosamund considers this for a moment before slowly nodding. 'There is no possible offence to be taken here, Mr Facey, and since I could never consider bringing discredit to a couple of right Dapper Dans, it seems you force me to contemplate a new dress and bonnet for myself. Now, we must go our separate ways in preparation for the work tonight.'

Facey inclines his great head with a look of great satisfaction before turning, striding away in the direction of Tottenham Court Road. I give Rosamund my arm and we stroll due south down Portland Place, heading for the slop shops and apothecaries of Oxford Street.

'It is a curious thing,' I say, 'Facey has never cared a fig for the opinion of others, certainly not on account of his appearance.'

'I do not believe his concerns have changed.'

'Then why are we all to fit ourselves out in new togs?'

Rosamund smiles softly, giving me a knowing look. 'I do believe your Mr Facey is a more considerate man than he is oft given credit for.'

Our room is furnished with a mirror, albeit small and somewhat tarnished. Nevertheless, it has been put to considerable use today, principally by Rosamund, who is delighted with her new frock, which is of a greenish colour with some species of flower forming the pattern. Now, it seems, it is Facey's turn. His coat is a black moleskin with three buttons and barely worn, though the sleeves are a trifle short. Facey's long, quick reach was one of the many natural advantages which made him such a dangerous contender in his days at the scratch.

'I have bought items for sewing and will let down the sleeves, Mr Facey. But otherwise I should say you look very well in it.'

'Thankee, Mrs Samuel,' says Facey, shrugging out of the garment before handing it back to Rosamund. 'It is very fine, though, in course, it will not be worn tonight.'

'Indeed not, though I hope you will wear the kerchiefs which I have got for you. Well soaked in vinegar, mind.' Rosamund delves into her basket and hands us each a couple of sizeable lawn kerchiefs before producing the stone bottle of vinegar and a thick glass jar, which we purchased this afternoon.

'Very well,' announces Facey, putting on his old coat. 'For my part I have secured a second crowbar, a length of good rope and a little of fresh mortar.' He grins at me, 'You would never credit it, Sammy, but Ricketts still keeps my old pins.' Facey means the two stout teak belaying pins, which we used as rollers when shifting a particularly heavy slab. In the past, a set was always kept ready for him behind the counter at the Feathers as well as at the Fortune of War.

'And how goes life in our former realm?' I ask.

'Not at all for some. It seems Mrs Pidgeon was carried off with an ague two winters past; Stirabout suffered transportation; Bishop and Williams was taken up and scragged.'

'I read of it in the London papers last Christmastime. Those two were ever wont to be reckless.'

'A pair of halfwits and no loss to an honourable profession. Rather than wait on a corpse like proper Christians they made one by heaving some poor sod down a well, thereafter touting their victim for guineas at the King's College.'

'A young Italian lad, if I recall.'

'And a half-dozen more that were admitted to.' Facey shakes his head in disbelief. 'Teeth and Mutton are still at the game. Though few hoists are attempted lately on account of the contagion. It is said that young Eddie Green will stump fourteen guineas for prime flesh, such is the scarcity.'

Rosamund makes no remark, avidly working away at Facey's sleeves with her needle and thread. She has never been queasy but I believe she occupies herself to remove her mind from the perils ahead of us.

'Eddie Green is well, I hope?'

'They say he has come up in the world. Still at St Thomas', he has a post as instructor, no less. Under this new act of Parliament, he has a licence to take on cadavers without the law can touch him. Now, ain't progress a fine thing?'

'I wish him joy of it. Eddie is a decent cove and was ever straight with us.'

Facey shifts the curtain and peers out of the open window. The sky is clear after yesterday's downpour but, thankfully, the moon is on the wane and it will be sufficiently dark for this night's work. 'Time we was about our business,' he says, with a glint in his eye.

The edifice has been constructed in the style of a classical temple, twin Greek pillars in marble supporting a kind of portico into which is carved the name: Belmont. The entrance has been sealed with a large stone block, fashioned to resemble a doorway. Perhaps it has been hurriedly applied, or the heavy rains have washed out the lime, but the mortar seal affixing the edges has been poorly set and comes away easily. The block is almost flush to the doorframe, but we apply crowbars to the narrow gaps and lever away until we are able to heave it a foot or so to one side, revealing an interior blacker than a tipstaff's heart. Facey flips open the shields of his dark lantern and makes to enter when I place a warning hand on his shoulder. 'Kerchief,' I hiss.

Facey nods, producing the large pale square from his coat pocket. I bring out the stone vinegar bottle, removing the stopper before pouring a good quantity onto the fabric. An acrid reek permeates the night air around us and, as I place my own kerchief to my face, my eyes instantly fill. Facey for his part, begins to cough. 'Jesu, Sammy, the cure is surely worse than the affliction,' he whispers hoarsely.

I nod, blinking back tears and fighting for breath. We waft the fabric in the chill night air, waiting for the effects to subside before giving it another try. This time, the pungence is more or less bearable and we secure the damp kerchiefs firmly around mouth and nose. Facey squeezes through the gap; I follow close behind. For a moment or two we crouch inside this cold, dark space, ears cocked for sounds of alarm. We catch the sound of distant, drunken laughter, which quickly subsides. Otherwise, there is only the rustling of the night creatures inhabiting these dreary gardens and our rasping breaths beneath the masks. We are accustomed to being cautious but are not overly concerned by the attentions of watchmen nor even the law, since so few are at the game these days.

Facey nods and raises the lantern, casting an eerie glow over the rows of carved stone tombs wherein some few generations of this family have been laid. Despite the shadows we quickly identify Edith Belmont's resting place by the sheen on the new slab and its hastily carved inscription. I put my crowbar to work once again, raising an edge of the slab by inches. As I lever, Facey employs his brawn and slowly slides it across from the opposing side. When the slab is finely balanced on the tomb's rim, we take an end each and carefully manhandle it to the ground.

Facey retrieves his lantern and directs the narrow beam into the murky interior of the stone casket revealing, like the kernel of a nut, the dark wood coffin inside. Holding the lantern in one hand he reaches in with the other and, with his prodigious strength, raises one end sufficient for me to pass my rope underneath. Between us we haul the coffin out and place it down at our feet. We insert our crowbars under the lid and press down. With a cracking and splintering of wood the lid flies open; the sound is deafening, like the sharp report of a barker echoing around in this cramped space. Facey instantly flips shut the lantern shield and we are plunged into darkness.

Some years back I suffered the terrifying torment of being buried alive. It is not an ordeal I ever wish to repeat and the experience of this pitch-black, cramped space has become something very like. I struggle to catch my breath and in my panic am on the point of wrenching off the kerchief when I feel Facey's calming hand on my shoulder. In the dark I can make out the glittering of his one good eye above the mask. As the pace of my breathing slows, from outside we hear the night creatures recommence their busy scuttling.

Facey flips open the lantern shield and there is blessed light, albeit a single narrow shaft, before pushing aside the casket's lid. He plays his beam across the face of the corpse. Despite the reassuring sight of the ferroniere about her brow, I recoil.

Few, if any, of the undertaker's arts have been employed here. Even in the lantern's insipid glow we can see that her face is a deep, terrifying unwholesome blue. The jaw has not been secured with a cloth bound tight under the chin, as is so often the case; in consequence the mouth has fallen open, contorted in an endless, soundless scream. The rigor which follows death has passed, though on account of the colder weather there is little sign of bloating, and corruption of the flesh is not yet evident; if there be an odour, it is well-masked by the vinegar reek.

"'Twould not take a man of Trimble's learning to know that the cholera took her,' whispers Facey, as he delves into one of his coat's inner pockets. 'Stand ready with the receptacle now, Sammy boy.' He produces his old awl and with great care, in the manner of a surgeon or anatomist, makes ready to apply it to the woman's forehead. I bring out the thick glass jar from my own pocket, quickly unscrew the lid and fill it halfway with vinegar. Facey deftly hooks the ferroniere and lifts away. The heavy diamond rocks back and forth, glittering exuberantly even in this half-light. I hold out the open jar and Facey angles the awl allowing the piece to slide off the blade safely into its temporary home.

'It is done,' I whisper, stuffing the precious jar into the voluminous pocket of my coat. 'We ought be away.'

The corpse is shrouded in a long green gown, simple and unadorned, though of evident quality. Facey plays the lantern's beam across the woman's intertwined hands. Like her face, they are a livid blue, the fingers festooned with a fortune in bejewelled rings; he reaches out a hand. 'Touch naught,' I hiss.

'Them fingers hold a king's ransom, Sammy, shocking waste to leave them fawneys be.' He passes me the lantern and rummages in his pocket for one of the spare kerchiefs. 'A drop of that there vinegar if you please.'

I pour a measure onto the cloth. Carefully avoiding contact with the flesh, Facey wraps the kerchief round Edith's middle finger, which is adorned with a particularly large and handsome ruby ring. He pulls and gently twists but the fawney remains fast on account of the finger's swelling. He grips the fabric more firmly in his fist and gives a sharp pull. We hear the crack of bone and tendon. 'Buggering finger's gone and busted.'

'Leave it be. We have what we came for.'

'Knife,' he whispers.

I pat my pockets for the clasp knife. I am not particular over the removal of Edith's busted digit, after all, I have spent too much of my life hoisting corpses for the eager scalpels of the London Hospitals. I am, however, concerned about further delay. By my estimation we have already been here an hour or more and need a little time yet to return all to order, leaving not the slightest sign of our incursion.

We are startled by the chime of the St James's Chapel clock ringing the hour. It is two of the morning, which confirms my reckoning. 'Time we skedaddled.'

''Tis no easy thing to wrench a finger clean off, Sammy. Even a dead 'un.'

With a sigh I pass him the knife.

CHAPTER VI

Though we had little sleep, we have not lain abed this morning, all three on us being eager to conclude our business. We step out of the hackney before the shabby front door of the New Road residence some time before the hour of eleven. Facey had earlier sent the tavern's boy to inform Pimlott and Chuffington of our success and so we have every reason to be hopeful, though, to be sure, with these men, outcomes are ever uncertain.

The front door sweeps open before I can even raise a hand to the knocker. 'Welcome, welcome, one and all. You are perplexed I see, wondering how I knowed it was yourselves afore you ever thought to knock.' Weggums hugs himself with glee.

'We are indeed,' agrees Rosamund. 'It is a very great mystery.'

Weggums claps his hands. 'Hah, I have been keeping crow and had already spied you from the upstairs window. You are awaited, though you must not expect biscuits today since there are no more to be had,' he informs us sadly. 'Mr Pimlott is at his breakfast, and he don't share.' With that, Weggums darts up the stairs. 'Quick smart and keep a wary eye out for our busted step.'

⁂

We are shown into the same office, which has little changed since yesterday other than for the absence of Crockford. 'You are returned then?' says Pimlott, making short work of a cold pork chop with his teeth. He deposits the gnawed bone onto a sheet of greasy brown paper before bundling it up and wiping his fingers with a kerchief.

'Garlanded with laurels, if your note is to be credited,' adds Chuffington, indicating the chairs.

We sit. Weggums ambles over to the window where he sets to peering, observing the rooftops with the utmost concentration.

'Where is our lad?' demands Facey, without preamble.

'Close by and sound enough for the nonce.'

'Better that we lay eyes on him,' he insists.

'And so you shall, once the Eye of Brahma is in our possession.' Chuffington reaches into a drawer beneath his desk and produces a jeweller's loupe, which he begins to polish. 'You are in no position to quibble, Mr Facey. It is a simple matter: produce the Eye of Brahma and the boy shall be released, unharmed. As we agreed.'

Rosamund delves into her reticule and produces the jar, which she places on the desk before Chuffington. The ferroniere is visible through the glass, curled at the bottom of its vinegar bath like an anatomical specimen.

Chuffington sniffs and frowns. 'Vinegar is it? You see fit to haul our precious gemstone about like a pint of Limehouse winkles?'

Rosamund is not in the least cowed. 'It is for our own protection, sir, and will not harm the piece.'

Chuffington gives her a puzzled stare.

'There may be substance to that notion, Mr C. I have heard that vinegar, and plenty of it, is the very thing for scouring a premises,' rumbles Pimlott.

'If Mr Pimlott attests to its efficacy then I can have no objection, though I have always been averse to the aroma of vinegar,' frowns Chuffington, 'Perhaps you would be good enough to extract our prize and wipe it down.'

Facey gets to his feet and unscrews the lid before producing his awl. He delves into the jar and catches the ferroniere on the narrow blade before hauling it out, the jewel dripping and glittering like a freshly caught mackerel. From his pocket, he produces his kerchief which he uses to dry it off. He hands the piece to Chuffington who briefly holds it up to the light from the office window. Suspended by the intricate gold band, the stone rocks back and forth, scintillating and flashing sparks from its many facets. He passes both loupe and ferroniere across the desk, whereupon his partner screws the instrument into his eye and begins his examination of the stone.

'I spy a gammy pigeon on the ledge across the way,' muses Weggums. 'Whoever heard of a one-legged squab? Should he be caught and roasted, there would only be sufficient dark-meat for one. He is plump enough, to be sure, so perhaps it is he begs his living in corn meal...'

'Thankee, Mr Weggums. I must ask that you take your accustomed station at the second-floor window and keep on a good watch of the street outside.'

Weggums slaps his wide forehead. 'Indeed I should, Mr Chuffington. Forgive me, I have been most remiss in my duty, sir. I was distracted by that most mystifying fowl.'

'Think nothing of it, Mr Weggums.'

Weggums treats us to a neat bow before skipping from the room

Finally, Pimlott exhales, placing the items down on the desk before him.

'Well, sir?' says Chuffington, breaking the silence. 'Is it flawless as they say?'

Pimlott considers for a moment. 'There is but one flaw, Mr C.'

'Indeed?' Chuffington turns to address us with some complacency. 'If Mr Pimlott claims a flaw, then a flaw there must be. Imperfection or irregularity, he will always sniff it out. Do you see?'

Pimlott extends a plump hand towards his partner. 'The paperweight. May I?'

'By all means, Mr P,' agrees Chuffington, holding forth the heavy winged lion, which yesterday sat atop the pile of newspapers. Pimlott inspects it, tracing the curves with a stubby finger. Of a sudden he brings it down with all his might onto the great black diamond, which shatters into a hundred shards.

There is a moment of stunned silence.

'There is your flaw, sir,' rumbles Pimlott.

'By God,' breathes Facey. 'Why do such a thing?'

''Twas no true diamond,' explains Rosamund. 'A diamond would never suffer itself to be crushed by brass.'

Pimlott grunts, giving Rosamund a grudging nod. 'The flaw, Mr C., was that the item was snide, fashioned of glass. Glass and pinchbeck, to be precise.'

'A facsimile, Mr P?'

'Indeed, Mr C. Though we may be certain that the original was a proper stone, attested to by any number of reputable jewellers; there was never question as to its veracity. Our Mr Crockford was most particular in the matter.'

'Then evidently a substitution has been made,' announces Rosamund with a shrug.

'Correct,' agrees Pimlott.

'I see.' Chuffington turns his implacable gaze upon us. 'You think to penny-weight us? Explain, if you please.'

'Surely you cannot believe it is any of our doing?' I object.

Facey retrieves one of the scattered black shards from the Ottoman rug, which he places on Chuffington's desk. 'Gents, we have done your bidding, stomached the dread disease and brung you your stone, hoisted from the very brow of its former owner. Whether it be glass, pinchbeck or any old bit of refuse ain't no concern of ours. Nor that you have to chose to bust it to flinders. Our work is done and I should be obliged to you for the return of our lad forthwith.'

Chuffington sighs and slowly shakes his head. 'On the contrary, Mr Facey. You have signally failed in the task we set you.'

'I believe we were tolerable specific in the terms of our arrangement, Mr Facey,' adds Pimlott.

'There it is,' nods Chuffington. 'You would be unwise to debate terms with Mr Pimlott for he is a phenomenon of recall, and you shall have the precise specifics from him to the very last detail. You always will, you know. Mr P. forgets nothing, most especially when it comes to a matter of business.' Chuffington leans back in his chair with an air of great satisfaction.

'Our terms, precisely,' continues Pimlott, 'were that the lad would be released in exchange for the Eye of Brahma. I recall being most particular on that matter.'

'We brung what was there,' mutters Facey.

'What you have brought us is a worthless bauble, so very far away from being the Eye of Brahma that it ain't worth the mention.'

'Indubitably a substitution has been made,' announces Chuffington, 'and how are we to be certain that you yourselves did not perpetrate this monstrous fraud?'

'Pish,' snaps Rosamund.

'You will keep a civil tongue, if you please, Mrs Samuel,' replies Chuffington. His tone is even but his pale blue eyes glitter with unspoken threat.

Rosamund, who has always been quite fearless, presses on regardless. 'That is quite absurd. We had never even heard of the item till yesterday. Moreover, though it be a copy, I should say there is a deal of work and skill in the making, which would, no doubt, have taken time.'

Pimlott flaps a plump hand at his partner. 'I cannot disagree.' He raises the remains of the ferroniere and examines the links. 'There is a certain artifice here and a knowledge of the original would be required. No, I do not believe the work could be carried off in a single night.'

Rosamund bobs her head in acknowledgement.

Chuffington steeples his fingers, giving Rosamund a thin smile. 'If Mr Pimlott says it is so, then it is so. We shall not hold you to account for the substitution, Mrs Samuel. But, in course, you do remain accountable for the fulfilment of the task.'

'That is neither fair nor honourable. We brought what was there.'

Chuffington chuckles. 'Fair? Gracious, is there some new act of Parliament, Mr P., of which we have been unaware? One which dictates that dealings between men shall cleave solely to that which can be accounted fair?'

'I do not believe so, Mr C. I should have noticed.'

Chuffington shakes his head in wonder. 'In every transaction, Mrs Samuel, there is one party who exhibits the greater need. A ravenous cove may crave a meat pie above the vendor's need to sell. In consequence, your shrewd pieman will ask what price he believes can be got for his viands, something a good way above its cost at any rate. It is simple profit, Mrs Samuel, the jobber's turn, if you will. Fairness don't come into it. Imagine a world where all is fair. Why, no trade would be done. Naught would be made nor sold. No advantage equals no incentive, madam.'

'I understand the notion of profit, Mr Chuffington.'

'But not the practice of business, it seems,' intones Pimlott.

'Indeed not,' acknowledges Chuffington. 'To put it blunt, possession of the Eye of Brahma would be desirable to us, since it shall fetch a tidy profit from our continental buyer. Notwithstanding, our establishment shall get on well enough without it. Your lad, on the other hand, must indubitably retain his life's blood if he is to thrive. He cannot do without it, do you see? And I am certain you would never wish me to allow our Mr Meathook free reign. He don't care for the boy overmuch and would take much pleasure in the unfettered use of his implements.' He snaps his fingers. 'Your need then is the greater by a considerable measure here. In consequence the advantage is ours. There ain't no fairness in it. Nor never was. 'Tis a simple arrangement, and one which still stands. You may take it or you may leave it.'

'I should say you put that most clear, Mr Chuffington,' announces Pimlott.

Chuffington brushes a little dandruff from the shoulder of his customary black coat. 'I am gratified that you should say so, sir.'

Pimlott inclines his great head. 'My partner has been tolerably plain on the matter and so I urge you to seek out the true Eye with all speed. Our patience is not boundless.'

'But where to begin, sir?' objects Rosamund.

'Where else but at the Belmont residence? I should wager one or other of the servants had a hand in it. None else had opportunity. The article has not been touted by the shylocks, or we should have heard, and so the true Eye remains, for the moment, concealed somewhere about that house, you may rely upon it.'

'And are we simply to present ourselves at the door and demand entrance?' queries Rosamund.

Pimlott reclines in his chair, his great bulk producing an ominous creak. 'I believe it was Socrates, a philosophic cove of the ancient world, who declared that necessity is the mother of invention, Mrs Samuel.'

''Twas Plato, sir, but I take your meaning.'

There is a momentary silence. A flush suffuses Pimlott's already florid countenance; his piggy eyes narrow to slits.

Rosamund shrugs. 'My pa was a printer, sir.'

'Did I not say she was a sharp one, Mr P?' smiles his partner.

'You well know that we are not cracksmen, gents,' I interject, by way of distraction.

Chuffington waves a long-fingered white hand dismissively. 'So your Mr Facey has said, and yet you would breach a sealed mausoleum easy as kiss-my-hand. A tomb, a house, where's the difference?'

'There is a world of difference, sir, between the sleeping and the dead,' interjects Facey.

'And so, you must tread lighter than you are accustomed to,' advises Chuffington. 'Our Mr Crockford informs us that the household is somewhat diminished since the demise of its mistress. The heir is a mere squeaker with but a handful of servants remaining. The contagion,' he explains. 'Once it was known there was pestilence in the house, the bulk of 'em quailed at the prospect and packed up sticks. There remains, I believe, the housekeeper and steward along with the cook and a lackey or two. At any rate, there is naught under that roof to affright men of your fortitude and undoubted resolution.'

'One doddering old retainer may raise the hue and cry as well as twenty,' mutters Facey.

Abruptly, Pimlott sweeps the detritus from his desk. 'Enough, Mr Facey. Do not test our patience further. You will fulfil the task we have set for you or your boy's life is forfeit. It is Four and Twenty of Dover Street; a day or two should be quite sufficient.'

Chuffington smiles thinly before producing a gold hunter from his weskit pocket, 'Well, there you have it. Mr Pimlott has spoken. We expect to see you again, two days hence.' He considers the time. 'At twenty minutes after one, precisely. Do not be late. We neither of us can abide a lack of punctuality.'

'Precisely,' smirks Pimlott, folding pudgy hands across his capacious weskit.

CHAPTER VII

The three of us alight from the hackney on Grafton Street, where we walk from the top of Dover Street down towards Four and Twenty, taking the time to consider as much of the street and surrounds as possible. It might appear that the likes of us are quite invisible in this most fashionable region of Mayfair. Elderly dowagers, smart young bucks and gaily attired women pass in wafts of lavender and orange blossom, being sure to give us a wide berth. Not one spares us a glance. And yet they do see us. Though not tradespeople, we have the audacity to stroll their hallowed streets; their opinion of our transgression is only too apparent in the elevation of their carefully tonsured heads and pained expressions.

Rosamund and me walk arm in arm while Facey struts a few paces ahead, glowering at all and sundry like a Seven Dials bug-hunter. Not far from our destination is a flower girl and cart, providing us with an excuse to loiter. Rosamund haggles over the price of a small bunch of purple violets; Facey and me stand behind, furtively examining the frontage of the house. It has been lately built by my reckoning, ascending to four floors with an imposing pillared entrance; fixed to the front door is a wreath of laurel leaves intertwined with black ribbons to mark the recent loss. Despite the filthy air of London, the exterior remains pristine white. There are six tall sash windows spread across each floor, three to each side.

'I see recesses in the blockwork,' I inform Facey in a low voice. 'I believe I might shin up and gain access by one of the upper windows.'

Facey grimaces. 'You might at that, Sammy boy, though there are shutters at each of them windows, doubtless well secured at night.'

'I might unlatch 'em with a strong, narrow file.'

He shakes his head. 'There is a deal of tin hereabouts and so a sharp watch will be set upon these streets, and at all hours. 'Tis a tricky job, even for a proper cracksman. 'Twould take an age while you cling to the front of that house like a limpet in the moonlight.'

'Then the rear?'

'It must be the rear 'less we can make a friend of one of the servants as, I believe, is more commonly done in the housebreaking lark.'

'But any one of those servants may be our quarry.'

Facey screws up his eyes and removes his hat, running a hand through his hair as he is wont to do when perplexed. 'You are in the right of it, Sammy. It is a mazer and no mistake. My belly has been growling like an old mastiff this past hour, what say we take ourselves to a chop house; puzzle it out over a mug or two and a plate of good vittles?'

I can tell that Rosamund is unsettled. She knows Facey too well by now to be bashful of her chipped tooth and must be as sharp set as we are, yet only prods and pokes at the succulent meat before her, from time to time taking tiny sips at her glass of port wine.

'What ails you, my love?' I ask gently.

She sighs. 'I cannot be content with good food and wine while poor John languishes who knows where, his only company a lackwit and a foul, murderous brute. I feel the passing of each moment is like a drop of his life's blood ebbing slowly away. In truth, I blame myself and should have had a better care of him.'

Facey has made short work of his chop and taters and now leans back in his chair with an air of considerable satisfaction. He surveys the chophouse's busy interior, savouring the air, which carries an aroma of ale and tobacco smoke all mixed together with the fragrance of roasted meats. 'Now, Mrs Samuel,' he declares, 'your compassion does you credit. Me and Sammy well know what anguish it brung you when the lad chose to go to sea. But that were the path his heart was set on. I am no authority on such matters but I reckon it ain't always about the coddlin' and the holding on. Oftentimes, it is the knowing when to leave go what counts.'

'There is truth in that,' concedes Rosamund.

'In course, it helps to be sure there is one place in the world where a fellow may always return, knowing he will never be judged. That certainty gives a cove a measure of fortitude and a pride in hisself. Sufficient enough to stick to his path and become all the man he might be.'

I am astounded at this reflection and somehow saddened to hear it from Facey's lips, since his own ma skedaddled, leaving him to fend for himself when he was but a very young boy. He has never had what I would call a true home in all the years I have known him; perhaps it is that very thing which prompts him to speak so.

'And I shall tell you what more,' he continues, 'That young lad well knows that there are three on us in this world shall shift heaven and earth to see him right. And if that ain't sufficient lookin' out for a body, then I don't know what is.'

'Well said, Mr Facey,' nods Rosamund, raising her glass to him before taking another tiny sip. 'So, how best to proceed?'

Facey shrugs. 'There is naught to be done for the nonce since it is clear that an escalade from the front is a forlorn hope. We must kick our heels till dusk. No doubt there will be a wall giving on to the rear of the property, which may be reached from Albermarle Street. Sammy and me will shin up quick as a wink, survey how the land lies and so determine our breach.'

'It is a plan,' I say, 'which is something at least.' I place my hand over that of my wife.

She ponders a moment, before slowly shaking her head. 'And after that, what? Even should you succeed in effecting silent entry, what do you propose? This gemstone will not be set out on display like an item in a raree show. You must somehow search every nook and cranny in the premises from attic to cellar before dawn without waking a soul. No, 'tis an impossibility. Better we return to the New Road ken, keep a good watch on that place and so discover where it is those villains hold our John.'

'Well now,' announces Facey, rummaging in his pocket. 'Since you put it so eloquent, Mrs Samuel, I believe I am of a mind with you. What say you, Sammy? I should, in any case, relish a set-to with that Meathook scoundrel.'

'We are caught 'twixt the Devil and the deep blue sea, it seems. I might consider long and hard afore further provoking the ire of Pimlott and Chuffington. Their viciousness knows no bounds and their reach is long. Should we be so fortunate as to bring it off, I doubt we may ever sleep safe in our beds again. They have eyes, as we know, even so far away as Portsmouth.'

Facey scowls, produces a square of cloth from his coat and is about to wipe the grease from his stubble when Rosamund starts. 'Would that be one of our new kerchiefs at all, Mr Facey?'

'It is.'

'Never use it for a napkin, I beg. A waft of contagion may yet be harboured there.'

'It were well enough soused with vinegar, Mrs Samuel.'

Rosamund's brow furrows as she leans in to peer at the article. 'I had marked it earlier when you wiped down the jewel. It bears a most peculiar smudge, a stain of some description. I wonder how you came by it?'

Facey examines the linen. Sure enough, there is a distinct blue smear across the pale fabric. He grins wolfishly. 'The lady as we took the article from last night, that is to say the dead 'un, had about her a few other pieces and whatnot, which, seeing as she had no further use for, I saw fit to relieve her of one or two items.'

'That does not account for the smudge, Mr Facey.'

'Ah, well, there was a particular valuable-looking fawney on her right hand, which I could not, in all conscience, leave to waste. Since you was so concerned that we took pains to touch naught directly, I first wrapped her digit in this linen, thereby shielding my own flesh. Some force was required in the removal, so it is simply the livid hue of her, which has come away and transferred itself to the kerchief, most like on account of your vinegar.'

'May I?' she says, extending her hand for the kerchief, which she examines closely. 'This was the shade of her flesh?'

'Certainly,' affirms Facey. 'A profounder blue if anything. Clear as day in the bullseye beam.'

'The kerchief has not been employed for any other purpose since?'

'Not a thing.'

'And the stain might have come from no other source, you are quite certain of this?'

Facey nods in affirmation. My wife returns the kerchief, a thoughtful expression upon her face. 'This casts a different light on the matter entirely.'

'How so?'

'Unless I have mistook the words of Doctor Trimble, the pestilence imparts a bluish cast to the flesh from within; it is not, I believe, a mere superficial staining to be sponged away with some little vinegar wash.'

Facey runs his hand through his hair. 'I do not take your meaning, Mrs Samuel.'

I do not know this word "superficial" but catch the gist of her meaning. 'You suppose the colouration to be a counterfeit then?' I ask, more for Facey's benefit than my own.

Rosamund nods. 'I cannot come upon a better explication, Sammy.'

'Either way, it don't hardly signify,' mutters Facey, eying Rosamund's barely touched meat with his single glim. 'Blue, green or piebald, the Belmont woman rests in her earth bath and there is naught to be done about it.'

'You are most welcome to what remains on my plate. It is perfectly flavoursome and, like you, Mr Facey, I cannot abide waste.'

'Obliged to you, Mrs Samuel,' he nods, procuring the chop with his bare fingers.

'It signifies because it may be that Edith Belmont's flesh has been treated to resemble the effects of the dread disease. I suspect this mark to be Indigo, a substance readily available and commonly used in the process of laundering.'

'That being so, how might that knowledge bring us closer to our goal?'

'Death disguised and the gemstone missing, Sammy? Two events which are surely connected. It is a trail of sorts and, in the absence of any other, worthy of our attention.'

'I reckon I have it,' muses Facey, tearing into the chop, 'was the Belmont woman snuffed, then it were done to conceal the filching of this Eye.'

'You are a quick study, Mr Facey.'

'Thankee, Mrs Samuel,' replies Facey, with great complacency, not unlike one of our young pupils having mastered the art of addition.

'And so, you reckon a laundress to be our quarry?' I ask.

'I could not say. 'Tis all supposition and fancy for the nonce. Asides, anyone may lay their hands on a quantity of Indigo. Nor can we be certain as to the manner of the woman's demise.'

'That ain't such a stretch to discover,' grins Facey. 'What we have done this last night we might easily do again.'

Rosamund considers for a moment before reluctantly nodding. 'The discovery of the how is like to lead us to the who, though for such conjecture a true anatomist would be required.'

'Then it is our good fortune, Mrs Samuel, we have many such amongst our acquaintance,' crows Facey, elated by the prospect of a further night's work and, no doubt, mindful of those few sparklers still adorning Edith Belmont's wrists and fingers.

''Tis a deal of risk against an uncertain outcome,' warns Rosamund.

'No worser a risk than we have already took. I am for it, if Sammy is willing,' proclaims Facey. 'I shall roust Michael Shields for the lending of his old cart and what say we deliver to Eddie Green for his judgement?'

I am less sanguine but, for the moment, can offer naught better. 'Eddie it is then,' I concur.

Tonight, it seems, there is nothing for it but we must once again resurrect the dead.

CHAPTER VIII

Strange to say but St James's Garden was this night deserted and silent as the grave. Those who have never participated in our profession might presume that to be the case in the ordinary way of things, but it is not so. There are many perils to be avoided in the vicinity of a boneyard during hours of dark. Mollishers, bug-hunters, drunks, the destitute, bobbies and watchmen, are all accustomed to frequent these places for the purposes of either transgressing or upholding the law. Though we set about our task early, at around the hour of ten, there were few folk, if any, to be seen. For the sake of prudence, we once again secured kerchiefs about our mouths and, with mortar and joints ready breached by our previous night's work, were swiftly back inside the vault. Taking care to avoid directly touching flesh, Facey set about removing the woman's few remaining adornments and, having pillaged to his satisfaction, we parcelled up the corpse, still in its gown, with a length of tarpaulin. After diligently setting all back to rights, we were away back through the headstones afore the expiry of an hour.

Doubtless, Michael Shields and the others of his trade would have chose a skulking, roundabout route for delivery of the corpse, involving manifold side streets and quiet alleys. Since we had elected to shift for ourselves, we designated haste and directness to be our priorities, and so from Hampstead Road headed due south with our cart and its felonious burden, making use of the main thoroughfares of Tottenham Court Road, thence Holborn and over the bridge at Southwark. No doubt fearful of the nocturnal miasmas, denizens of the night were scarce, even in these populous streets, so, we were neither troubled nor delayed during the course of our swift passage. A final turn into the well-named Dirty Lane brought us out onto Borough High Street where we hastily crossed, arriving safely at the side entrance to St Thomas'.

Unusually for men of his caste, the porter is wide awake and, at the sight of us, bustles out from his cabin, wiping ale froth from his moustaches with the back of a sleeve. 'Gents, you is expected. I shall fetch Mr Green this instant.' He belches loudly before disappearing through the arches. Meanwhile, Facey and me rearrange the sacks of old clouts which have been hitherto been piled atop the tarpaulin-wrapped corpse in the event of a brush with the law.

It is not long before we hear two sets of swift footsteps approaching. Eddie Green appears, typically, with hair askew and coatless, instead wearing a leather apron over his linen shirt. 'Mr Facey, Mr Samuel, it is good to see you both. How do you get along, gentlemen?'

'Well enough, sir,' replies Facey, as the two of them vigorously shake hands.

Having set out earlier in a hack to bring notice of our arrival, Rosamund stands alongside of him. She gives me a small smile, relieved, I imagine, that we have carried off our night's work without mishap.

I take Eddie's hand. 'We have been at Portsmouth this past couple of years,' I explain.

'So I have been informed,' grins Eddie, indicating Rosamund. 'I had no notion you were wed, Sammy. Mrs Samuel and myself have been discoursing on matters of natural philosophy; I believe you are the most fortunate of men to have such a wife.'

'My thanks, sir, and well I know it,' I affirm.

Rosamund bobs in acknowledgement.

'Mrs Samuel informs me that you are schoolteachers these days and Mr Facey, a man of commerce. I cannot say how delighted I am at your change in circumstances and yet I hope you will not mind if I say that you have been much missed, since good cadavers have been few and far between, despite this new law. I shall not pry into the circumstances touching the resumption of your former profession, but instead rejoice at my good fortune to be its beneficiary.'

'Then I reckon we might get the karker inside afore it turns to dust,' interjects Facey, as the porter appears wheeling a metal trolley.

'Certainly, certainly,' agrees Eddie, rubbing his hands as me and Facey haul the tightly wrapped cadaver from under the sacks and transfer it to the trolley. We follow as Eddie and the porter lead us through the sandstone archway into the gloomy bowels of the hospital. One of the wheels squeaks objection as it trundles across the flagstone floors. 'My own circumstances are somewhat changed. I am now instructor of anatomy here,' announces Eddie proudly.

'So we had heard. And wish you joy of it, sir,' replies Facey.

'You are become a man of considerable distinction, Mr Green,' I observe.

'I should scarcely say so, not when there is one here tonight far above me in both skill and learning. You shall clap eyes on him shortly.'

The sharp odour of embalming fluid pervades the air, which is surprisingly chilly within these halls; shadows dance from gas-lit sconces along the maze of corridors as we hasten past. Finally, we arrive at a sizeable room furnished with rows of ascending seats arranged in a circular manner, not unlike the cockpits of Westminster. Further additional sconces set about the walls lend a subdued light to the place. In the centre of the room is a long wooden table, behind which stands the familiar figure of Joshua Brookes, in the process of wiping off an array of surgical instruments. A tall, sprightly cove in his later years, yet still an anatomist of great repute, Brookes is known to us, having been a customer on numerous occasions. Two years previous, we were instrumental in reuniting him with the body of his natural son, and, in the doing of it, were able to right a great wrong. Judging by his open, friendly expression, I believe he is still well enough disposed towards us, despite his status as a considerable gent. 'Well, well, Mr Samuel, Mr Facey, how do ye do?' He returns the instrument in hand to the metal table and inclines his head towards us.

'In good health, sir,' I reply with a bow. 'Honoured that you recollect us.'

'Tush, Mr Samuel. I never forget an obligation and remain indebted to you all. Indeed, I had concluded for the night and was on the point of embarking for home when your good wife made her appearance and informed us of your imminent arrival. My felicitations, by the by.'

'Thank you kindly, sir.'

Brookes inclines his head once again. 'Now, I understand that you have brought a fresh subject. We anatomisers face something of a drought at this time, quite deprived of good material, despite the easing of the laws.'

'It is a subject of middle years, sir. Female, and not five days passed,' announces Facey.

'Well, well, let the hounds see the fox, by all means.'

Eddie waves over the porter who wheels forward the squeaking trolley. The man hauls off the parcelled corpse, lays it down along the long wooden table and fetches a lamp from a nearby bench; he makes a small adjustment, intensifying the flame, before placing it alongside. With a dutiful bow to Brookes and Eddie Green, and a brief nod to the rest of us, he removes himself from our company in a gust of ale.

'Mr Green, you shall do the honours,' declares Brookes, as he dons a leather apron. Eddie can scarcely contain himself as he positions himself at the head of the table.

'What is this place?' asks Facey, 'It puts me in mind of a cockpit.'

'A theatre of sorts,' replies Eddie. 'For the edification of my anatomical students. Not two hours previous the space was packed to the rafters, crammed hugger mugger, brimming with young minds eager to learn the secrets of the body's workings. A full house, enticed by the news that the great Mr Joshua Brookes was to make a demonstration. Had you come but an hour or two earlier, we might have made a great spectacle of your glorious, fresh cadaver, 'stead of making do with ancient, preserved bits and pieces. Now,' he says, reaching down for the wickedly sharp scalpel which Brookes had earlier relinquished, 'let us see what you have brought us.' He slices effortlessly through the thin ropes with which we have secured the tarpaulin, then tugs the material away from the head, revealing Edith Belmont's slack-jawed visage. 'Jesu,' he cries, recoiling from the sight, backing well away from the corpse. 'Saving your presence, Mrs Samuel, but by Christ, you have brung us the Blue Death.'

'Forgive me, gentlemen, that I failed to warn you of this,' pleads Rosamund. 'I did not wish you to refuse examination.'

'Which I surely would have done and shall assuredly do now,' objects Eddie, retreating towards the door behind us. 'You should know that the pestilence presents the gravest of dangers, even manifest in a corpse. I must ask you to remove the remains forthwith. You will take the cadaver instantly to our ovens where it may be turned to ashes.'

'I beg your indulgence, a further moment if you please, Mr Green. Not all is as it appears,' pleads Rosamund.

Brookes has produced a silk fogle, which he holds to his face. 'I know you to be a young woman of great sensibility, Mrs Samuel, yet to expose us all to such hazard is beyond belief.'

Facey flourishes his kerchief, exhibiting the stain. 'Gents, in the course of the hoist it so happened I gave the flesh a wipe with a drop of vinegar and this here is the result. I do not pretend to be a man of learning but 'tis my understanding that such an occurrence ain't 'zactly regular.'

'Indeed it is not,' agrees Eddie, intrigued despite his alarm.

'It is our supposition that the impression of the pestilence here is counterfeit,' announces Rosamund. 'The exposed flesh has been stained with a substance, most likely Indigo, to replicate the signature of the Blue Death. Such is my conviction that, should you have a little vinegar to hand, I shall reprise the demonstration.'

'I will countenance no such action,' objects Eddie. ''Tis reckless in the extreme.'

'A moment, Eddie,' interjects Brookes, peering closer at the exposed face in the lamplight. 'Now I think on it, the colouration does appear a little off. A trifle livid in my estimation.'

Eddie considers for a moment. 'If that is your opinion, Mr Brookes, I shall certainly defer to it. I believe there is a quantity of acetic acid hereabouts,' he concedes, fossicking amongst a row of glass jars on a bench at the rear of the stage.

'Forgive me, Eddie. Might I suggest a little sodium hypochlorite?'

'Very well, sodium hypochlorite it is.' Eddie unstoppers a glass jar and pours a little fluid onto a clean rag before holding it out to Rosamund. 'You take a considerable risk, Mrs Samuel.'

'There is no risk to Mrs Samuel,' I announce, stepping forward and accepting the scrap. 'Since that task falls to me.' I am not ordinarily a man of courage but Facey and me have already been in proximity to the corpse whereas my wife has not. And, though my well-being might now rest upon a mere supposition, I rate the hazard small since Rosamund's perspicacity is the soundest thing I know of.

'Just so,' nods Brookes approvingly.

With that, I step to the corpse and, taking a firm grip of the head with one hand, give the cheek a brief wipe with the rag. I inspect the cloth. It remains pristine.

I glance at Rosamund. 'Firmer, Sammy,' she instructs.

I give the flesh a vigorous rub.

'Well now,' murmurs Brookes. 'Most interesting.' Sure enough, the fluid has begun to do its work; the stain, no longer dry, comes away in long streaks onto the fabric, the flesh beneath revealing itself to be the colour of old porridge.

'Extraordinary,' mutters Eddie, approaching the corpse. 'It appears you are quite correct, Mrs Samuel, the superficial flesh has been stained for a certainty, most likely post mortem, but to what end?' He begins to pull away the remainder of the tarpaulin. Facey and me help unwrap. In a few moments the body lies adorned in its gown alone. 'The corpse lacks a finger on the right hand,' muses Eddie. 'Again, a post mortem injury since there is little sign of exsanguination.'

'Ah, yes,' explains Facey, without an iota of shame, 'that is my own work, gents. What you might describe as a perquisite of the profession.'

Brookes purses his lips in disapproval but keeps his own counsel on the matter.

Eddie takes his scalpel and begins to cut away the thin gown. The arms and legs have been stained entirely and the blue colouration extends downwards all the way down to the breasts. Only the remainder of the trunk, where formerly covered by the gown, is revealed to be a commonplace deathly grey.

'There has been foul play here,' announces Eddie. 'Why else take the trouble to disguise the cause of death?'

'That has been my suspicion, sir. Now confirmed,' agrees Rosamund, 'and so I hope you might apply your skills to ascertaining the true cause.'

'We might at that,' agrees Eddie. 'Mr Brookes, should you wish to remain?'

'I should be most happy to assist, Eddie.'

'Assist? By no means, sir. Though it be my theatre, I am not the master here.' Eddie hands the scalpel to Brookes with a brief bow.

Brookes accepts the instrument with an inclination of the head. 'Since you are good enough to say so, might I suggest that we first cast for signs of poison? In particular those of arsenic, which so well duplicate the symptoms of cholera?'

'My thoughts entirely, sir.' It is evident that Eddie is eager to commence but first he turns to address Rosamund. 'Mrs Samuel, our work is not to everyone's taste. Perhaps you would rather wait in my office, where there is a good stove and trappings for the brewing of tea?'

'I am seldom queasy, Mr Green, but own that I do have a fondness for tea.'

Eddie raises an enquiring eyebrow at Facey and me. 'Most considerate as always, sir,' I say, taking my wife's arm.

'Can't abide the stuff,' announces Facey with a grimace. 'If I had the urge to quaff bog water, I should take a stroll out to Romney Marshes and spare myself the expense.'

'It is an acquired thing, Mr Facey. Should you rather ale or some such, you might ask the porter, who is known to keep a few bottles about; you may inform him that I will bear the cost.'

'Obliged to you, Mr Green.'

Without further ado, Brookes leans over the body brandishing the scalpel and begins to make an incision lengthwise down the belly.

Eddie bustles Rosamund and me to the door at the rear of the stage. We step through to find ourselves in a smallish chamber endowed with a random selection of elderly furniture, illuminated by a couple of oil lamps. A pair of threadbare armchairs leak stuffing as though they might at one time have been subjects of Eddie's investigations; the floor is scattered with piles of books and periodicals, while against the walls are dusty display cabinets filled with wax casts of body parts and organs. In the corner is a cheerful stove, which delivers a welcome warmth after the chilly air of Eddie's lecture room. Dust and general air of neglect notwithstanding, it is a comfortable refuge for all that. At the far end of the room is a stand arrayed with a large ewer and bowl along with china cups, pot, kettle and tea caddy. Rosamund fills the kettle with water from the ewer and sets it upon the stove. She turns as I settle myself on one of a pair of scuffed, wooden-backed chairs, leaving the armchairs vacant. 'It seems I have married a foolish man,' she announces.

'How so?'

'One prepared take such risks at the mere supposition of his wife?'

'You are not a woman given to idle fancies.'

Rosamund spoons a quantity of leaves into the pot. 'I chose to marry you, did I not?'

'That was on account of my great wealth and handsome figure.'

'Indeed it was not.' She turns again and, stepping towards me, plants a kiss on my lips. 'You have always been a braver, better man than you believe yourself to be. Though somewhat glocky.'

'I suppose there was a chance, a very small chance that the supposition was false and the poor woman had indeed expired of the pestilence,' I admit.

'Yet, you were fervent to run that risk in my stead?'

'It was not courage, but cowardice; in truth I could never countenance the prospect of life without you, my love.'

Rosamund tuts and shakes her head, though not before I catch the tiny half-smile, revealing that she is secretly pleased. She fusses with the kettle, which has now boiled. 'Though you would always have your Mr Facey to console you.'

'It is no laughing matter,' I retort. 'Besides, I do not feel that to be so. I believe he frets at our small life in the provinces.'

She pours the boiled water into the pot before turning to face me once again. 'I think you are in the right of it,' she replies, in all seriousness now. 'I cannot help but notice how eager he has been to resume your former profession.'

'I too.'

'You are not of a similar mind, I hope?'

'I am not. But it troubles me. No matter the outcome of this venture, I do not reckon those men will easily forgive us, permitting Facey to return to London for a permanence.'

'What's this? I hear my name flung about and hope it ain't being ill-used,' announces Facey, appearing at the door with a couple of bottles under one arm, hat under the other.

'Speak of the devil,' I say, 'and he must appear with a bottle or two.'

"Tis a good London stout,' crows Facey, settling himself in one of the chairs and placing his hat on one of the piles of periodicals on the floor beside him. He takes a great swig from one of the bottles. 'Porter from the porter, no less. A decent enough cove as it turns out, though I daresay he will gouge young Eddie for the price of these here bottles. Still and all, fair is fair; Eddie has a good fresh corpse to dig about in and no push expended for it.' He smacks his lips appreciatively.

Rosamund pours herself a dish of tea from the pot. 'There is a loaf of sugar here. I do not suppose Eddie will object should I use the nippers to add a little to my tea. I have heard it greatly enhances the taste.'

'A shocking waste of tin, to my mind,' observes Facey, taking another pull from his bottle.

'Is there a verdict from our gents?' queries Rosamund.

'The poor woman is unfastened to the guts, Eddie and Brookes still up to their elbows in gore. I have never quailed at the sight of a dead 'un, but should draw the line at casting about 'mongst the scraps and lights in such a manner.'

'And if it should be poison? What then?' I ask.

Rosamund sits in another of the chairs with her tea. 'I have been thinking on it.' She takes a delicate sip. 'It is true, by the by, the savour of tea is much enhanced by the addition of a little sweetness.'

Facey shakes his head, unconvinced.

'Should we discover foul play here,' she continues, 'I fancy a bold stroke might serve. It is a half-formed stratagem, to be sure, but I had thought the two of you might present yourselves to the Belmont household as representatives of the law. Shaved and dandified and in your new coats, you may pass for a magistrate and his tipstaff.'

'Me, a Bobbie?' Facey guffaws. 'I might grow wings an' all.'

'I did not say you would be the genuine article, only that you might briefly pass yourself off as such and, armed with what evidence is furnished by our anatomists, mayhap compel an admission of guilt, or, at the least, induce the signs of culpability.'

Facey runs his hand through his hair, considering. He sighs, "Twould be a mighty stretch, since me and Sammy have spent so much of our lives on the other side of the fence, so to speak.' He shrugs. 'Though I am game. What say you, Sammy?'

Before I can respond, Eddie and Brookes enter the room in a flurry of activity, sleeves rolled up, hands and forearms smeared with gore. The three of us make to rise when Brookes cheerfully demurs, 'There is to be no formality here. Remain seated, I beg you.'

They head swiftly for the stand where Eddie pours water from the jug into the ewer. The two of them sluice down before drying their hands with a small towel. 'I imagine you are eager to hear our findings, but you will forgive me if I first fortify myself. Mr Brookes, sir, should you care for a little of brandy? It is very fine.'

'Certainly, Eddie. And who is to say we have not earned it?'

Eddie opens a small cabinet and produces a decanter and a couple of glasses. He peers about him, grinning. 'Sammy, you have naught to drink.'

'I do not care overmuch for tea, sir.'

'Then you shall share our brandy.'

'I will, sir. Very good in you.'

Eddie pours a glass each for the three of us. I note that he takes the upright wooden chair by me, leaving the remaining armchair for Brookes. We wait while Brookes takes some few small sips at his liquor before delivering the verdict. 'I am not accustomed to mincing words in matters anatomical and since you possess a tolerably robust constitution, Mrs Samuel, I shall speak plain, if I may.'

'Please do, sir.'

'The stomach was opened by means of a series of incisions, which on close inspection immediately revealed the presence of a distinctive yellow smear, or bolus, within the cavity. This is significant, since, during the initial decomposition process, sulphur is ordinarily released within the organ, which is known to react with arsenic trioxide to create arsenic trisulphide. In short, the very yellow precipitate such as we observed: unequivocal evidence of arsenic poisoning, and a large dose at that, the substance having been administered in food, or more probably, drink. The poor woman would likely have exhibited many of the symptoms of cholera before expiring. That is to say, vomiting, blood in the urine, cramping muscles, stomach pain and convulsions. These, in combination with the subsequent colouration of the visible flesh, would have been sufficient to convince any interested parties of the presence of this pestilence. The contagion is so feared that, to my mind, only a cursory examination would have been undertaken before hurried interment.' Brookes leans back in the armchair, long, elegant fingers of both hands intertwined about the bowl of his brandy glass, warming the amber liquid.

'Most economically put, sir,' acknowledges Eddie. 'Not to put too fine a point on it, here is murder proven and a death wilfully disguised. Furthermore, the victim is no commonplace rookery trull neither. No domestic and assuredly no labourer. The gown is of the finest quality, the fingers and hands soft and lacking calluses.'

'What fingers yet remain,' adds Brookes pointedly.

'How ever did you come by this corpus and under what circumstances?'

'Why, in the usual manner, sir,' grins Facey.

''Tis the body of Edith Belmont, sir. A lady of some wealth and station, I believe,' adds Rosamund.

'Great heavens, you do not say so,' utters Brookes with some alarm. 'I read of her passing. Indeed, was distantly acquainted with the lady, having exchanged brief, inconsequential words at a soiree a year or two ago, though in course, she is quite unrecognisable in her current pitiful condition. You are correct in saying she was a woman of elevated position, Mrs Samuel.'

'In which case we must now, in course, consider our obligations to the law,' adds Eddie.

'We should rather you did not for the moment, sir.'

'It is not a matter for debate, Mrs Samuel. A coroner must be called while the evidence is still practicable. The precipitate will degrade within a day or two. Rest assured, I shall not reveal how the body came into our possession.'

'That is not our primary concern, Mr Green. Only, there is more to this than meets the eye, sir. I must implore you to grant us a little time to unravel these events. And unravel them we will, I assure you. The guilty shall not escape justice.'

Eddie gazes at his brandy before shaking his head. 'I cannot, Mrs Samuel. Certain as I am that you have good reason for your request, I cannot, in all conscience, oblige.'

'A young boy's life is at stake, Mr Green. I may not say more. But, should you involve the law in this matter, his life will be forfeit, I am certain of it.'

Eddie shakes his head emphatically. 'Forgive me, Mrs Samuel, but it is…'

'Stay, Eddie.' Brookes raises a placating hand. 'At times there is a world of difference between what is lawful and what is right, as I have had occasion to discover for myself. That aside, you may wish to first consider the implications of letting it be known that we have tonight, anatomised a woman of considerable standing. If it were understood that we had cut about the gentry, there would be a scandal the likes of which you could not imagine.'

Eddie goggles, his normally pale countenance suffused with red. 'Jesu, I would lose my place here, and that would be the least of it.'

'Undoubtedly,' Brookes sips at his brandy with the greatest composure. 'Your licence permits the anatomisation of the poor and destitute; Edith Belmont is very far from that description.'

'Then I am caught on the horns of dilemma, sir.'

'I am not. We retain a due respect for the law, Eddie, yet know it to be a blunt and heavy-handed instrument, and so men of our profession do not always choose to follow its strictures to an exactitude.' He smiles wryly. 'We must make such exception here. Mrs Samuel has declared that she will see the thing through and that is quite sufficient for my part.'

'You put a deal of trust in us, sir.'

'As I did once before and did not have cause to regret it; you did me a considerable service. Now, how do you propose to proceed with your recent knowledge?'

Rosamund sighs. 'I do not know precisely, sir. Only that we must somehow gain entry to the Belmont residence, albeit by subterfuge, since we believe this to be the handiwork of a servant.'

Brookes nods gravely, 'Alas, all too common an occurrence.'

'I had thought Sammy and Mr Facey might pass themselves off as men of the law and so be admitted.'

Eddie guffaws. Even Brookes permits himself a small smile.

'You have not clapped eyes on our new coats,' objects Facey, somewhat offended.

There is a silence while Brookes revolves the glass in his long fingers, cogitating. 'Forgive me, Mrs Samuel,' he announces, 'I do not mean to say your stratagem is without merit, but it occurs to me that there may be an alternative method, one with less risk and perhaps more efficacy.'

'We are all ears, sir.'

'It would require a degree of resource and resolution.'

'My husband and Mr Facey have never lacked those qualities.'

'True enough. Though it is you I speak of, Mrs Samuel. How should it suit was you able to place yourself inside of that household? To make inquiry from within the very corpus, as it were?'

'How so, sir?'

'A gleaning from the London Pages, my dear, a week or so past. An advertisement inviting application for the role of governess for the Belmont household, and I had remarked it as perhaps, a suitable position for the daughter of an old friend. The role may yet be unfilled and, with the passing of Edith Belmont, likely now most urgently required.'

'You propose I offer myself for that post?'

'You are a schoolteacher are you not? Moreover, I know you to be a woman of gentle disposition and manners. In short, a tolerably convincing candidate.'

'And what of a character, sir?'

Brookes waves a languid hand. 'You shall have it, if you are agreeable. You recall Mr Bamfield, my man of business?'

'Certainly I do, sir.'

'I shall send for him, first thing in the morning, and make all necessary arrangements. A very little deceit, I own, but for what is, perhaps, a worthy cause.'

Rosamund finishes her tea and sets the cup down by her chair, taking a moment to consider. 'They do say that more flies are caught with honey than vinegar. Yours is a subtler, superior stratagem by far and so I am obliged to you, sir.'

'Your obligation must be to justice alone and, in due course, you shall disclose your determinations to the proper authority. Does that satisfy you, Eddie?'

'I believe it does, sir, though this enterprise is not entirely without risk.'

'Certainly,' agrees Brookes. 'You would be well advised to tread carefully, Mrs Samuel; should you procure the position and gain entry to that household, be mindful that you likely share a roof with a shrewd and cunning poisoner. And so, since you are agreeable, I can only commend your courage and wish you Godspeed.' Brookes raises his glass.

We each of us raise glass or bottle.

In all honesty, I cannot say I am best pleased by this new prospect, but once her mind is set upon a path, my wife is not easily persuaded from it. As we toast, I stealthily drop my free hand to the arm of my chair and touch the wood of it, for all the luck that might reside there.

CHAPTER IX

The minute hand of the long-case clock in the tiled hallway is all but at the hour of one when Rosamund and me enter the Whitefriars Street offices. We are instantly ushered into the chambers of Mr James Haverford by a severe, gaunt-looking factotum. Here is a very different picture to Eddie's chaotic domain. Haverford keeps a well-appointed, oak panelled room furnished with thick rugs, bookshelves and lustrous leather armchairs; all in its place and not a speck of dust or grime to be seen. On the gleaming desk before him is a blotter and an open letter, which, from what I can discern, has been written in a fine hand and previously sealed.

Despite fervent protestations I have been entirely unable to prevail against my wife's determination and so we find ourselves, in accordance with Bamfield's instruction, now attending upon the Belmont family attorney.

I remove my hat and make a leg while Rosamund treats the man to a decent bob, as befits two highly respectable personages tricked up in their finest. I have been groomed and dandified like some West End swell in spotless linens and my new fitted coat, while Rosamund is clad in her new green frock and straw bonnet. Only my old boots are worthy of disdain and, though they have been given a burnish, remain shamefully scuffed and dilapidated.

The factotum gently closes the door as Haverford acknowledges us with the slightest inclination of his head before indicating a couple of chairs. Though not so gaunt as his factotum, the lawyer is similarly severe with high, starched collars, cravat folded to an exactitude, austere black coat and glossy black hair parted precisely down the centre. The chime of the hallway clock is perfectly audible even with the door closed, yet he produces a hunter from his waistcoat pocket for confirmation of the hour. 'Miss Howlett, I take it? You are punctual I perceive.'

'I endeavour to be so, sir. Might I introduce my brother, Samuel, who has kindly appointed to stand as chaperone?'

Haverford nods, 'Quite right, Miss Howlett.'

'The city is disconcertingly large, and somewhat fearsome.'

The man flicks an invisible spot of lint from his coat lapel before referring to the letter before him. 'Of course, I understand you are more accustomed to the gentler environs of the provinces?'

'I am, sir.'

'You were formerly governess to a family in Titchfield with a connection to Mr Joshua Brookes?'

'Indeed, sir. I believe the lady of the house was second or third cousin to Mr Brookes.'

Haverford examines the letter once again. 'I have not had the honour of Mr Brookes' acquaintance but, through the good offices of my esteemed colleague, Mr Bamfield, have received a note in his own hand—in his own hand, mind—in which he has requested this interview and speaks of you in the highest possible terms.'

'I am most obliged to Mr Brookes, sir.'

'Very proper. This character is quite impeccable, and from a man of considerable stature, but forgive me, what reason should you have to leave such a worthy post?'

'That position is no longer extant, sir. Alas, the entire family were taken by the Red Plague, which is to say the Smallpox, not two months past. In consequence I found myself with neither employ nor a written character.'

'Which would account for the intervention of Mr Brookes?'

'It would, sir. Mr Brookes was in the habit of visiting the family from time to time. He was kind enough to notice me and, on one occasion, was good enough to share with me an opinion on a matter of natural philosophy.'

'Great heavens, what singular condescension.'

'I am mindful of it, sir,' replies Rosamund, gazing down at her lap.

'And now we must all cower from the Blue Death it seems,' he sighs. 'If 'tis not one multi-hued pestilence, 'tis another.' Haverford indicates his face. 'I note that you, yourself, do not remain unscathed.'

A flush suffuses her face. To my mind, the slight scarring of her complexion has never marred her true beauty. Nevertheless, she does not care to be reminded of her brush with the Smallpox from many years before I knew her. 'I do not, sir, though it was long ago. I am salted.'

Haverford peers down his long nose at her and sniffs. 'You are no ornament, Miss Howlett, I must own. But in addition to your undoubted enthusiasm for natural philosophy, are you versed in the gentle arts?'

'I play the pianoforte and can sketch as well as paint.'

Haverford fussily lines up the letter with the edge of his blotter. 'And your own family, what of them?'

'Pa was a printer, sir. A most respectable man of trade.'

'And you, sir,' says Haverford, addressing me. 'What is your profession?'

'I have the honour to be a clerk, sir, at Pink's pickle factory of Bermondsey,' I reply. It is an establishment I have passed on many occasions and have always been partial to the name.

'A fine, steady line of work,' he acknowledges, giving my boots a dubious glance.

Boots notwithstanding, it seems we have made a favourable impression here. I should imagine the man would be a deal less enthralled were he to discover that but four days previous I was smuggling contraband rum and, only this last night, hoisting Edith Belmont's corpse from out of St James's Gardens.

'Excellent. I have a mind to oblige Mr Brookes as well as the estimable Mr Bamfield, and your propitious arrival has saved the expense of another advertisement in the London Pages. In short, given your evident suitability and testimonial I see no reason to prolong this inquisition. I act on behalf of the Belmont family, now sadly reduced, by which I mean reduced in number to a sole heir: a young boy, William, but six years of age. His father was lost to typhoid some few years back, whilst on foreign service and, sad to say, his poor mother lately expired most unexpectedly, leaving him now an orphan child.' Haverford looks sour. 'There is only an uncle, one Titus Galton, connected to the family by marriage rather than blood. No doubt the matter of young William's disposition shall, in due course, come before Chancery. For the moment we must manage as best we can.' Haverford coughs, tentatively clearing his throat before resuming. 'Ah, I do feel obliged to inform you that, as is the case with so many of our recent mortalities, it was the Asiatic Cholera which carried the late Mrs Belmont off. Does that afright you at all, Miss Howlett?'

'Like most folk of any sense, I fear it. I have heard its appearance is very sudden.'

'Died on Wednesday, buried on Friday. Solomon Grundy ain't in it. Certainly, the cholera is shockingly swift, yet I may assure you that once the deadly miasmas are exhausted there is no further danger. Indeed, it fell to me to see to Edith Belmont's final wishes, attesting that she was interred with some few artefacts of great value to her. I was in proximity to the open casket for some while and yet you see me hale, do you not?'

'I do, sir. And am much reassured by it.'

'I take it you have no ties, that is to say you are able to commence immediately?'

'I am, sir.'

'Shall we say, twenty guineas per annum?'

'Most generous, sir.'

'And now I suppose you might wish to know something of the boy? His temperament, wits, or the lack of 'em? Matters of that nature?'

'I should, if you please.'

For the first time Haverford smiles, albeit thinly. 'I could not say, having never set eyes on the lad. In the cruellest quirk of fate, only lately did young William arrive in London to live reunited with his mother.'

'And prior to that, sir?'

'The boy has spent his life thus far ensconced in the family estate in Hampshire under the ministrations of a nurse.'

'May I ask what is become of the lady?'

'Time, Miss Howlett. Old age. It had become necessary to sell off the estate and, owing to her infirmity and considerable years, the woman had no wish to remove herself to the metropolis. Besides, the boy is of an age as to no longer require a nurse and so you will by now have considered that, given the circumstances, a governess is most urgently required. The housekeeper, Mrs Parkes, is a sound, capable woman but it can be no part of her duties to see to the bringing on of a six-year old boy.'

'Then I should be eager to commence the work.'

'I am gratified to hear it. I take it then that you would have no objection to commencing immediately? That is to say, this very afternoon?'

Rosamund glances at me briefly. 'I had not thought to be so swiftly engaged, sir.'

'Lost time is never found again, Miss Howlett. You will of course wish to gather your effects and so forth; might I suggest you present yourself at number Four and Twenty of Dover Street, at,' Haverford checks his Hunter, 'let us say, four o'clock, precisely? I shall send a message to Mrs Parkes to expect you.'

CHAPTER X

Though I am much in need of sleep, having enjoyed so little of it since we arrived in London, I passed a broken, fitful night. With Rosamund gone, we decided to save the expenditure of further tin and make do with a single private room in the Bolt-in-Tun. We top and tailed it, but with Facey's prodigious snoring and him letting farts all night, it has been very far from restful. If I am honest though, in large part my agitation is likely due to the absence of my wife. It has been two years now since I have lain without Rosamund by my side and I cannot say I care for it.

'I can tell you are straining the canister once again, Sammy Boy,' observes Facey as we head down the grand thoroughfare of Piccadilly to the Green Park where we are due to meet with Rosamund close to the hour of eleven. 'A penny for 'em.'

'I was considering how Rosamund might enjoy these many bookshops, and all in the one street.'

'You was fretting on your missus, bookshops or no.'

'True enough. I am anxious for her safety.'

'We shall see her shortly, right as a trivet I should wager, gemstone in hand and the entire mystery tied up neat as a butcher's parcel.'

'Let us hope so.'

Facey nods sagely. It is a source of considerable satisfaction that my greatest friend has such confidence in my wife's capability, though I am still uneasy over her situation. Should she rouse even the slightest suspicion, there is a myriad of ways a poisoner may do his work. It is a crafty, cowardly business and I should have preferred a little more time for cogitation and due consideration of our stratagem, but in course, Haverford was insistent that Rosamund be put instantly to harness like a dray-horse.

Facey and me stroll in silence to the wrought iron gates leading onto the park where we are accosted by an orange seller, a handsome woman of middle years with a great mane of red hair under a mob cap, a healthy complexion and the look of the country about her. 'Sweet oranges, sirs, and only tuppence apiece.'

'You warrant them sweet, Mrs? I cannot abide a bitter orange,' warns Facey.

'Up from Kent this very morning and sweet as a kiss. China oranges, sir, none of your Sevilles here, which is only good for Shrub and preserves.'

'Then I will take three and, if they are not as you say, be sure that I shall return for a reckoning.' He hands her a silver sixpence and selects three plump oranges from her basket.

'Certainly you will return, sir, once you have tasted. You will beg forgiveness for doubting my honour afore you take three more on 'em.' She throws him a flirtatious wink.

'I'll warrant your honour is beyond reproach,' retorts Facey, grinning. He hands me two of the oranges, pockets the other and cheerfully tips his hat to the woman. He has always enjoyed the banter of the London streets.

In the distance I spy a large oak not far from the ornamental pool and, standing beneath its canopy I am relieved to discern the unmistakable figure of my wife holding a small boy by the hand. I wave and hurry towards her.

I approach and am on the point of embracing her when she gives me a warning look, flicking a glance in the direction of the young boy. 'Why, Mr Samuel,' she says, 'and Mr Facey, what a surprise. How good it is to see you.'

I make my bow. 'Likewise. It is Miss Howlett, I believe?'

Facey is sharp enough to pick up on the charade and treats Rosamund to a formal nod.

'This is William Belmont, my young charge. Kindly pay your respects to Mr Samuel and Mr Facey if you please, William.'

The boy is whey-faced and somewhat gloomy of countenance, though that is scarcely surprising, given his recent circumstances. He is dressed in coat and knickerbockers, both of which appear a little too large for him. He gives us a formal bow. I smile down at him; the mournful expression does not alter a whit.

'Now then, young Juggins. Have you spied the Tyburn Pool yet?' asks Facey. The boy is silent and gazes disconsolately at the ground before him. 'I have here a plump orange and intend to make a coracle of the peel. You shall have a piece if you like,' he continues, producing the article from his pocket.

'I cannot believe an orange to be at all seaworthy, Mr Facey,' says Rosamund.

'A half of the peel must be removed with the most especial care for it to float. No leaks, mind. It is fortunate that I have brung my new clasp knife, which shall suit the purpose admirably.'

At the news of a knife the boy's head slowly rises. He peers at up Facey, eyes half closed against the bright sunlight.

'Should you care to assist in these here naval larks then, young Juggins?'

The boy nods slowly. Rosamund releases his hand and away he trots, endeavouring to keep pace with Facey's long strides in the direction of the great stone basin.

With William's back to us, I take the opportunity to embrace my wife before clasping both her hands. 'You are quite safe, I hope?'

'Perfectly sound, my love. I am endorsed by Mr Haverford and so none in the house may object nor perceive my presence to be untoward. Though I do suffer exceedingly from the want of a husband.'

I smile, giving her hands a squeeze before releasing her. Though it is not much past eleven and the air retains its chill, the sun's rays are sufficiently ardent for us to settle ourselves comfortably upon the grass by the oak. I hand Rosamund one of the oranges.

'An orange, what a treat,' announces Rosamund. 'I have not had one in an age.'

'It is sweet, I believe, though it seemed to me that the seller was more than a little sweet herself on Facey.'

Rosamund chuckles. 'He is a fine man for all his absent glim and bluster. A companion would be no bad thing.' She carefully peels her orange before popping a segment into her mouth.

'I would not be the one to say it. Though I should wish him more content with his life.'

Rosamund gazes over at Facey and the boy. The pair watch intently as their orange peel vessel bobs precariously across the pool, propelled by the light breeze. 'It seems he has made a friend of William. No easy task, since the boy is so quiet and sombre for one so young.'

'The sudden loss of a ma is no small matter.'

'Perhaps, though he scarcely knew her. By all accounts there were few maternal instincts in Edith Belmont. The boy was kept at Chilcomb Hall, which is to say, the family's Hampshire Estate, while Edith remained ensconced at the London residence. In his entire six years of life she visited on no more than a handful of occasions. I can scarce believe it is the lack of such a mother which troubles him.' Rosamund selects another segment and smiles at me. 'I have made a friend of sorts,' she explains. 'Nellie, the maid of all work, who seems an open, good-hearted soul with a deal to say.'

'You do not rate this Nellie worthy of suspicion?

'Not her, she is very young and likely finds it a sore trial recalling how to button her own boots of a morning.'

'And the others?'

''Tis a reduced household. The footman was dismissed a week or so prior to Edith's passing. I am told that the housemaid and laundress had quit their stations for fear of the pestilence; the housemaid, in mortal terror, took ship for her native Ireland. There remain but Mrs Parkes, the housekeeper; Mr Jenkins, butler; the cook, a Mrs Stride; and in course, young Nellie. We breakfasted together, all but Mr Jenkins, who, it seems, is indisposed. Mrs Parkes seems an honest, capable woman; a little sharp with Nellie, though I believe that is ever the case with a housekeeper and her underlings. Mrs Stride was so occupied with her pots and pans that I was able to form no opinion on her.'

'Facey and me must shortly return to New Road and give a good account of ourselves. Should you rate this laundress a likely culprit with her stocks of Indigo? Perhaps in cahoots with the footman?'

'For the moment, I believe we may leave the woman aside, Indigo or no. She was took up for drunkenness and debauch some few days after her departure and lies beyond our reach at the Giltspur Compter.'

'Then the footman? Sufficient disgruntled to poison his mistress?'

'I could not say, not yet knowing the full circumstances. Though I believe Nellie retains a fondness for the man. She is the one lively presence in an otherwise gloomy abode. Mayhap it is the pall of cholera which oppresses the spirits but it seems an unhappy, brooding place. The reception rooms which ought to be full of light and life are dismal, the furniture shrouded with dust sheets like so many spectres. It is on account of renovation work, put in train by the mistress of the house, and so, there is something melancholy about its continuance: the completion of a room for a cheerful purpose, which Edith Belmont shall never now see nor enjoy.'

I reach for her hand. 'You must promise, my love, that the instant you sense aught amiss, you will flee from that place.'

To my chagrin, Rosamund quickly withdraws her hand. 'Have a care, Sammy, the boy has eyes and a working tongue, though seldom used.' We gaze across at the pool, where young William is occupied, working away at a small stick with the clasp knife, overlooked by Facey. The knife is wickedly sharp and Rosamund and me should never dream of trusting our young charges at the John Pounds school with such a tool, even for the sharpening of quills.

Rosamund shakes her head and places another orange segment into her mouth. 'I am scarcely discomfited, Sammy. Asides, whether I like it or no, I must see the thing through for our John's sake. The moment opportunity arises I intend to examine every last room to its utmost particular. I shall make a game of it with William.' She finishes the final segment and wipes her fingers with the fogle she produces from her sleeve. 'I have not yet mentioned one other person of significance, though not of the household: Titus Galton.'

'I have heard that name, though I cannot place it.'

'You heard it from the lips of Haverford. According to Nellie, this Galton has been much in evidence since Edith's passing. He is the late William Belmont's cousin, not long returned from India. Word below stairs is that he intends to make William his ward. By all accounts, he is a puffed-up man much inclined to live beyond his means,' she adds meaningfully.

'Then here is motive aplenty.'

'Though he may be the prime mover, we may not rule out a confederate within the household.'

'Well, it is all grist to the mill for those men at New Road. I count it progress and we must hope they agree for John's sake.'

'Time we was getting along, Sammy,' announces Facey, stumping towards us with the boy in tow. 'I heard St James's strike the half hour a while back and them two coves are sticklers for timekeeping.' I jump to my feet, giving my wife an arm before we brush ourselves down. Facey gently nudges William towards us. 'Here is your young sprog who has performed fine service this day. In consequence, I rate him able seaman.'

William nods solemnly.

'And by what authority do you rate him so, Mr Facey? What is your own rank in this Tyburn Pool navy?'

'Why, admiral, in course.' Facey grins suddenly as though struck by the most wondrous notion. 'Admiral of the Orange.'

'Just so,' agrees Rosamund.

William is silent, raising a tiny hand for Rosamund's consideration. A little blood oozes from the forefinger. Rosamund quickly binds it with her fogle before giving Facey a look of mild reproach.

CHAPTER XI

Poisoned, forsooth. Whatever is the world coming to, Mr P?'
'Not one, but two gentlemen of anatomy have so attested. Employing the most advanced methods of natural philosophy, they were able to confirm the presence of arsenic.'

Chuffington frowns. 'And now in consequence have brought it to the attention of the law, no doubt. You are foolish, Mr Samuel, to have involved outside parties, especially those of gentlemanly status for whose protection all laws are made.'

This is rich coming from Chuffington, who disregards the law entirely and has for his own protection the likes of Meathook and sundry other brutes. 'No representative of the law has been made aware of these circumstances, sir.'

'How so?'

'The gentlemen concerned are themselves circumscribed by the terms of their licence and constrained by the scruples of their own profession.'

'Speak plain, Mr Samuel. We have no patience for sophistry.'

I believe I put that pretty well, having rehearsed my explications on the short journey here, and so am disappointed by the response. 'The new anatomical licence allows only for the anatomisation of the poor and destitute.'

Pimlott nods his slow approval. 'I see it, Mr C. These gentlemen may not let it be known that they have gone and diced up one of their own.'

'Precisely, sir.'

'Well, that is something at least. So, the blue tint of the cholera was replicated by means of your humble household Indigo?'

'We believe it so, sir.'

Chuffington cackles, a peculiar noise, like the crackling of twigs on a small fire. 'That is quite splendid. What say you, Mr P?'

'Ingenious, Mr C.'

'There is a certain stubborn owner of a Highbury brick field who I predict may, likewise, shortly succumb to this Blue Death.'

'Alas, I fear that may well be the case, Mr C.'

Chuffington adjusts his spectacles, his mood changing abruptly, his mouth becoming pinched and waspish. 'And so, Mr Samuel, what is become of our Eye?'

'As to that, we must beg a little more time.'

Pimlott drums his pudgy fingers on the arms of his chair. 'Are we to understand then that you have expended these two days past merely to ascertain that Edith Belmont was carried off by arsenical poisoning? Though the method is to be applauded, its discovery is not. We care not a whit that the baggage was done away with, Mr Samuel, only that you fetch us our gemstone, and that right quick.'

'We believe it likely in the possession of the murderer, sir.'

'Then you must lay on hands on the miscreant and squeeze 'em,' he replies, 'without a shred of mercy.'

'We cannot, sir, since we are yet uncertain of the culprit's identity.'

Pimlott sighs. 'I take it you have not made a full search of the property as we so advised?'

'Mrs Samuel has obtained lawful access to the residence in the guise of governess. She intends to conduct a scrupulous search of the rooms just as soon as soon as opportunity presents.'

Chuffington nods. 'Resourceful, Mr Samuel, but necessarily slow. You are too fastidious by half. I urge you to make use of your wife's presence there to effect an entry and immediately apply the sternest possible measures to each and every remaining occupant of that house.'

'I have often found a well heated poker applied to the glim is sure to unlock a secret or two,' announces Pimlott, as though suggesting a stroll in the park. 'An eye for the Eye, as it were.'

Chuffington gazes at us in apparent wonder. 'Did you catch that?'

'We did, Mr Chuffington,' mutters Facey, taking umbrage on account of his own absent glim.

'An eye for the Eye, forsooth. I believe that to be one of the very best things you have said, Mr P.'

Pimlott inclines his head, chin sinking into roll upon roll of bristled fat above stiff white collars.

'My wife acts in the belief that honey catches more flies than vinegar,' I interject, afore Facey can inflame matters.

Pimlott claps his meaty hands together. 'Give your flies a good swatting and be done with, Mr Samuel.' He brushes them together, removing imaginary residue. I can see though that he is somewhat put out by our unenthusiastic response to his previous quip.

Facey angrily slaps a palm on the leg of his keks with a sharp retort. 'Well, that simply ain't our way, gents.'

Chuffington smiles thinly. 'You forget, Mr Facey, you are a man of some reputation and 'tis scarcely for blenching at the application of force.'

'Where it be warranted, sir. Though I have never delighted in it, unlike some.' He glares at the two of them. 'What you propose is not to my taste. Not for worlds.'

'It ain't worlds at stake here but the well-being of your youthful acquaintance. He is untouched for the while, and his treatment has been kind enough, but that shall change should you insist on defying us and dragging your heels. Why must you cavil and stall?'

'There are two other noteworthy parties who do not reside beneath that roof. It is possible that either may have had a hand in the affair,' I interject.

'Other parties? What other parties?'

'A disgruntled footman, dismissed not long afore the death and a connection of the family, a gentleman of sorts. Moreover, there is the presence of constructors in the house during daylight hours to be considered.'

Chuffington gives me a sour look. 'Your cogitations, Mr P?'

Pimlott's chair creaks alarmingly as he adjusts his great bulk. He produces a pocket watch from his weskit, frowning at the dial. 'I am in dire need of sustenance and have no desire to draw out this debate.

Regrettably it appears that the application of swifter, more forthright methods may well prove fruitless in the circumstances; however,' he raises a chubby forefinger in the manner of one of those antiquated marble statues, 'the presence of constructors is fortunate and serves to expedite matters most handily.'

'A cuckoo in the nest, Mr P?'

'Precisely, Mr C.'

Chuffington rubs his hands. 'Excellent notion.' He chuckles, enjoying my evident confusion. 'We have dealings with a good many London constructors; in respect of materials, provision of labour and so forth. When occasion arises, it is often our practice to insinuate a dubber or snakesman 'mongst the common working crew.'

'Just so,' nods Pimlott. 'Such a one will ferret our Eye quick enough.'

'So, it seems, we shall have no further use for you, nor the young lad.'

'You will return him then?'

'Oh, dear me, no. I scarcely think that equitable, Mr Samuel. Not when you have so wretchedly failed in your task.'

'We have not failed, sir,' I plead. 'It is only that the task is not yet complete. If the Eye is to be found in that house, we shall be the ones to bring it you.'

'Your thoughts, Mr P?'

'They are no snakesmen, though the lad's well-being remains a most powerful inducement.' Pimlott fingers his lower lip in consideration before finally nodding. 'I am sharp set, Mr C, so, by all means, let these proceed, for the nonce, with their slinking and sneaking about.'

'Very well, Mr Samuel, a reprieve.'

Pimlott adjusts the soft white folds of his cravat. 'I see no difficulty in ascertaining who it is undertakes works on the Dover Street premises. Crockford shall make immediate enquiry and tomorrow morning there will appear a fresh pair of working men set to commence their labours.' He indicates the two of us. 'You may thereby enter that house and, alongside Mrs Samuel, employ your cunning and insinuating ways to discover the culprit. Search every room, every inch of that premises and do not consider returning without our Eye.'

'As always, to the very nub of it, Mr P.'

Pimlott smiles contentedly, for all the world like a vast baby having wolfed up its pap.

'And what of the foreman of these works?' queries Facey.

'There shall be no difficulty there, I assure you.'

'There you have it, Mr Pimlott has brought his prodigious intellect to bear and found a way. He always will, do you see?'

'You shall have a further…let us say, four days. Not a minute longer, else we give the lad over entirely to the tender mercies of our Mr Meathook.'

At that, Chuffington produces his own pocket watch, which he examines. 'Very well. Mr Pimlott, as is his way, has been more than generous with the time allowed to you. It is now eight and twenty minutes after three, precisely. We expect you here at this very hour, four days hence with our gemstone. Not a moment later, mind, or it will go the worse for you.'

Pimlott grunts, pushing down on the arms of his chair with some force, his face becoming puce with the effort. For a moment I am hopeful that he is prey to a bout of apoplexy until he straightens his knees, rising finally to his feet. 'I believe I shall take a dish of tripe with some few scallions,' he announces.

CHAPTER XII

A compact fellow of middle years in a pressman's hat made from an old newspaper waits on the pavement outside the Dover Street residence. He wears a full-length, paint-stained apron and puffs away on a clay pipe; at his feet, a large toolbox, a few crusted pots and some rolls of paper. He nods with little enthusiasm in our direction as Facey and me amble towards him.

'Standford,' he grunts, without the offer of his hand. 'You are the new labouring men, I take it?'

'Mr Facey and Mr Samuel, at your service,' announces Facey, tipping his old beaver like a West End swell.

'Airs and graces butter no parsnips with me, young man,' he sniffs, 'only good, honest labour, and you will commence by shouldering my tools and such. I do not know you, and it is only at my guv'nor's express bidding that you are here.' With a gesture to follow, he sets off around the side of the house. We dutifully collect his materials and equipment from the pavement and trail behind.

The servant's entrance is opened by a very young maid with frizzed unruly hair, the colour of straw, erupting from beneath a mob cap. Her eyes protrude like an ornamental fish and she goggles at us, having no better expression to offer. 'Oh, Mr Standford, I had thought to see you here at your accustomed time. Only Mrs Parkes is most concerned that advantage is not taken of our mistress's passing.'

'Tis none of my tardiness to blame this morning, Nellie, but these new working men what I have been awaiting on for the longest time.'

'I shall inform her that you are arrived and you are to commence your work as soon as please, Mr Standford.' Nellie gives us a brief bob and scuttles away to her duties. Standford waves us inside and we follow him along a short corridor from whence we ascend a narrow flight of back stairs. On the first floor, there is a further bare corridor from which we emerge onto a lavishly decorated landing. We cross in the direction of a pair of grand double doors just as Rosamund and young William are on the point of descending the main staircase. My wife shows no indication of alarm at our presence other than for the quizzical raising of an eyebrow as we pass by.

Standford opens the double doors and ushers us through into what I take to be the drawing room, or more properly, rooms, since in actuality it comprises two adjoining spaces, the first of these being what I have heard called an anteroom. Although impressive—the wooden floor is polished to a high gloss and a glittering chandelier descends from one of the high corniced ceilings—it is as Rosamund has described, somewhat oppressive with its shuttered windows and the many dust sheets shrouding the furniture.

We follow Standford to the furthest wall, where there is a sizeable area of bare plaster surrounding a seam of ugly, exposed brickwork, at variance with the pale green papered walls surrounding us. We deposit tools and pots on a canvas tarpaulin at our feet and lay our hats upon one of the shrouded articles of furniture before shedding our coats. Standford runs a stubby, calloused hand across the bricks before turning to face us. 'Now then, "Misters" Facey and Samuel, Nellie will shortly arrive with the water, you shall prepare the plaster mix.' He indicates a row of small hessian sacks stacked against the wall.

Facey gives me a look then shrugs before opening one of the sacks. He pours the contents, a quantity of white dust, into an empty bucket. I gather up one of the other sacks and make ready to add it to the bucket, when Standford calls out. 'You do not propose to measure out your Gypsum powder then?'

'I prefer to do the thing by eye,' responds Facey. 'Though I have but one glim, 'tis a most discerning one when it comes to the estimation of Gypsies' powders.'

Standford puts hands to his hips, throws out his chest and frowns. 'As I thought. You have no notion of the work whatsoever. I am not so green as I am cabbage looking and know full well how yous come to be here. My guv'nor, who is a honest gent, has had yous foisted on him at the insistence of two men of influence. And now, in turn, it falls upon me to bear the brunt. I can do naught about that, but I cannot pretend to like it. You should be aware that a pair of fine labouring men are today without honest work or means in consequence. Both with families to feed and one of them with a babbie on the way. All to make way for a pair of loafing scoundrels up to some skilamalink business. No, it ain't right and I ain't afeared to say so.'

Facey drops the empty sack, slowly and deliberately brushing his palms together to remove the dust. He takes a pace forward, looming over the man. 'Now then, you are a oldish cove and I should reckon decent enough, so I shall let you have that one, gratis. Do not imagine though that further insult shall pass without chastisement.'

Standford, previously puffed like a bantam cock, now subsides unhappily. 'That don't make it right,' he mutters.

'That is not in dispute, Mr Standford,' I say, feeling some pity for the fellow. 'You must know that those same two gentlemen have placed us here for their own purposes. I may not give the reasons, but suffice to say, it is not from our own choosing.'

Fetching his coat, Facey delves into a pocket and produces his purse. 'Since we must keep company 'til our tasks is done, it should go easier for all should we remain friends. It ain't needful for you to pay us daily wages, which may be kept aside for your true labouring men. Asides, I cannot reckon we shall cover ourselves in glory in the matter of Gypsy plasters and so forth.' He tips the purse, producing a couple of silver half-crowns. 'Here is something in addition, for the keeping of your men and the trouble we have put them to.'

Standford nods gravely, accepting the coins. 'It seems I have misjudged you, gents. I spoke in haste, but you will consider that by your association with them two gentlemen what I mentioned, I believed you to be of similar disposition.'

'That is understandable, Mr Standford, but we are very far from being like to those men in every aspect,' I say.

'I see that now, Mr Samuel, and take back them earlier words, what were rashly spoken.'

Facey claps the man on the shoulder, raising a small cloud of dust. 'Well said, Mr Standford.' The man staggers a little, since Facey has ever been unmindful of his own strength.

'Gents, now that we are on more amicable terms, might I beg a favour of you?'

'Name it,' smiles Facey, tucking away his purse.

Standford gazes down at his boots, somewhat discomposed. 'Though you be acting under duress, should you be grafters or cracksmen, might I beg you to delay the larceny till my commission is completed? There is the reputation of my firm to consider.'

'That is not our purpose,' I assure him, 'merely the gathering of information.'

'I am relieved to hear it, gents.'

At that moment Nellie bustles in through the double doors toting a bucket full of water. 'Here is your water, Mr Standford,' she calls, lumbering quickly across the room, 'which it has all but pulled my arms off in the lugging, since I has first to fetch two pails for Mrs Stride's doings, a pail for the new gentlewoman, then Mrs Parkes and old Jenkins, then return to the pump for yourn. An' all afore breakfast. "The pitcher will go to the well once too often", as the Reverend Spotswood was accustomed to say. An' ain't that the good Lord's truth? Though I don't rightly collect its meaning.' She drops the pail at our feet with relief, slopping a good deal of it across the tarpaulin.

'Thankee kindly, Nellie. You are a kind, hard-working soul, to be sure.'

Nellie gawps at the three of us as though we might have grown two heads apiece. Her reverie is broken by the sounds of approaching footsteps. We turn as one to see an imposing figure standing at the double doorway, a tall, heavy-set woman with greying hair in a severe black gown. An intricate silver chatelaine pinned to the waist, from which dangles a variety of keys, instantly marks her for the housekeeper.

Impossibly, Nellie's eyes widen, she throws us a brief bob and scuttles away in the direction of the doors.

Ignoring Nellie, the housekeeper strides towards us, Rosamund and young William in tow. 'Mr Standford,' she says, 'I trust you have not been distracted by our maid of all work. She is inclined to lollygag and run her tongue. You must send her about her duties should she be tempted to dawdle here.'

Standford tugs his forelock inclining his head a little. 'I shall, Mrs Parkes. Though she has, only just now, kindly brung water for the plasterwork.'

Mrs Parkes indicates Rosamund, who stands respectfully behind her, William's small hand tucked in hers. Rosamund gives me a small, secret smile. 'Here is William Belmont,' announces Mrs Parkes, 'now master of this house, accompanying him is Miss Howlett, new governess.'

Taking our cue from Standford, we tug forelocks with all due deference. 'At your service, Miss,' announces Standford.

'Miss Howlett has a notion that the observation of your work may be in some way edifying for her charge. I trust this will not be an imposition, nor unduly delay the business at hand?'

'By no means. Honoured, Mum.' There is a pause while Standford collects himself. 'Only, might I ask: had you given further consideration to the brickwork?'

Mrs Parkes frowns, giving him a steely glare. 'I have not and do not propose to reprise our former conversation on the subject. You shall complete the plasterwork, hang the paper and there will be an end to it. It is typical of your sort, Mr Standford, to pretend to find fault in the work of others for the purposes of further gain. Though this house is without its mistress, I shall not permit any to take advantage of that state. The matter is closed. We shall not speak of this again, I hope.'

Mrs Parkes turns on her heel and departs with a clicking of heels on the bare boards.

''Tis a pity to spoil a good ship for a ha'porth of tar,' sighs Standford, running his hand across the bare brick once more. 'Whoever done this don't know their end from their elbow, saving your presence, Miss. 'Tis a put-up job and a shame.'

Rosamund and me exchange a meaningful glance before she addresses Standford. 'Should you be kind enough to explicate the purpose of these works, for our benefit, sir?'

'Certainly, Miss. This here was formerly a chimbley which, I am informed by Mr Jenkins, was crumbling from deep within the flue and could not be lit for fear of conflagration. Now, a busted chimbley is of no use to man nor beast. When the wind is up you shall have a shocking draft and no comfort, blowing as it does all the 'cumulated soot of years throughout the house. In general, they is costly things to put right and it is often less trouble and tin to simply brick 'em up, 'specially when there is already another that will serve.' Standford indicates the substantial fireplace bordered in marble near the double doors.

'Yet, I take it you are not quite happy with the work here.'

'Not so much, Miss. Though 'tis none of my doing. The lady of this house, God rest her soul, had the work begun by some shocking unhandy party of no skill nor craft whatsoever. Now it falls to me to complete the thing. Which I am a plasterer and paper hanger by trade. Misfortunately, some of these here bricks of the breastwork have not been proper levelled and I shall have to take back the edges with a chisel afore applying my plaster, else it should resemble the Highlands of Scotch land.'

'There shall be no imprint nor sign of the recess then when your work is complete?'

'Not a whit, Miss. Not if I know my trade. None might ever guess there was a chimbley breast here once my paper is hung.'

Rosamund nods, addressing her charge. 'Here is conjuring for you, William. Mr Sandford shall make these bricks quite disappear.' The boy blinks owlishly, gazing up at her. 'I wonder if William might be permitted to aid you in some way?'

Standford considers for a moment. 'When I have mixed my plaster, the young gent may give it a stir, if he be so minded.' With that, Standford crouches over his sacks and begins to measure out the powdery substances into a clean bucket. He adds a quantity of water from the pail before rummaging in his tool chest for a small wooden baton, then begins to blend the thick mixture afore beckoning William over. 'Here is no easy task, young sir, requiring as it does a mighty arm. Mr Facey will lend a hand when you tire.'

'Set to then, young Juggins,' chivvies Facey.

The boy takes the baton, giving Facey a small, uncertain smile of recognition and, applying every ounce of his strength, begins to stir with great concentration.

'Now then, Miss...'

'Mr Standford,' I interject, 'I doubt those bricks will level themselves.'

Standford gives me a puzzled look. He peers at Rosamund, then back at me before the penny drops. 'Ah, I see which way the wind blows and do not have to be told twice. *Tacet* it is then, Mr Samuel,' he says, tapping the side of nose before stepping over to his toolbox from which he produces a hammer and chisel.

Rosamund and me step away, positioning ourselves out of earshot, close by one of the shuttered windows. 'Sammy, how...?'

''Tis Pimlott and Chuffington's doing. They grow impatient, demanding resolution afore the expiration of four days, else it is all up with our John.'

Rosamund casts her gaze in the direction of Standford, who is now carefully tapping away at the brickwork. 'And this foreman?'

'Like us, he must do as he is bid; he seems a decent enough fellow and will not peach, if I am any judge. Facey and me shall begin by tearing down this brickwork. If the gemstone is in the chimney breast, as I suspect it may be, we shall have done with all this and our John restored to us safe and sound.'

'And if it is not there?'

'Why then, I suppose we must reconsider.'

Rosamund shakes her head. 'You wager all at one throw, Sammy, by tearing down all at a single stroke. Once that milk is spilled it cannot be unspoiled. Better you take a more circumspect approach, stealthily prying away a single brick at a time. That way, should there be naught to discover, you may more easily conceal the disturbance and we shall be none the worse for it.'

'Very well, my love. We shall be like mice, silent and unheeded, whilst we gnaw away at our hole in the wall.'

'Then it shall be my task to keep the cats away.'

At the sound of fast approaching footsteps, we separate. Rosamund settles herself at a shrouded pianoforte close by. She lifts an edge of the dust sheet, opens up the keyboard and begins to softly finger the keys. I retreat to the area of the works just as a breathless Nellie enters through the double doors. She casts her wide-eyed gaze about the room before spying Rosamund at the pianoforte and making her bob: 'Miss, I am to inform you that Mr Galton is come and desires to see the young master this instant, if you please.'

The words are barely out of her mouth when we catch the steady clump of booted feet from behind her. A tall, splendidly attired cove strides into the anteroom. 'No need to stand on ceremony in this house, Nellie. You must know I am blood, not some Johnny-Come-Calling to be left kicking his heels in the hallway.' The speaker sports a striking set of bugger's grips extended to the jawline and clasps a fine, glossy beaver in one hand, an elegant ebony cane in the other. He peers about him, a sour look on his sallow countenance.

'Here is Mr Titus Galton, Miss,' announces Nellie, hesitantly. Galton peers across at Rosamund who rises from the pianoforte seat and offers a formal bob to the man.

'Miss Howlett, sir. Governess.'

Galton swallows, causing a prominent Adam's apple to make its appearance above an immaculately tied cravat. 'Governess, is it? I had not been informed.'

'I was appointed but two days previous by Mr Haverford, sir.'

Galton sneers. 'Haverford, is it? Well, I may tell you, Miss Howlett, I ain't much pleased to hear it. There are altogether too many women about the boy as it is. He is become a milksop and, by my reckoning, requires the firmer guidance of a masculine hand.'

'I cannot speak to that, sir. Only that I might assure you that I will perform my duties diligently as I am able.'

The cove nods, somewhat mollified at Rosamund's respectful demeanour. 'And your charge, what is become of him?'

'He is over by the working men, sir. I shall fetch him for you.'

Instead of responding, Galton simply strides towards our little group, where William and Facey still crouch over their pail. 'Stirring mud, is it, William? I daresay there is little edification to be had from that pursuit.'

Facey, who has been crouching alongside of William, rises and, taking the boy under the armpits, gently hoists him to his feet.

Galton removes a cream-coloured calf-skin glove and offers his hand. 'Well, well, William. Shall you greet your uncle?' The boy dutifully shakes with a doleful expression. Galton sniffs. 'I am to take you in hand, young man, for you are to become a sportin' gent. Ain't that prime? I intend for us to be the firmest of friends and so tomorrow, we take a barouche to the Park together. Should that please you?' With no reply from the boy forthcoming, he addresses Facey. 'Who is foreman here?'

Standford bustles over, 'I have that honour, sir. Standford is my name.' he announces, raising his paper hat.

Galton flaps a languid hand in the direction of the repairs. 'And how long afore this work of yours is completed?'

'Within the week, sir.'

'I intend to reside in this house and cannot abide disorder. Moreover, I have a mind to use these rooms for cards and whatnot. I should rather see it fit for company in a day or so.'

'Alas, 'tis beyond mortal power to make a plaster set quicker than it so chooses. I cannot hang paper 'til the plaster is proper dry and set hard, sir.'

Galton fussily dons his glove. 'Apply yourself, Standford, and you shall have a guinea to speed the effort.'

'Do my best, sir.'

Galton treats me and Facey to a cursory inspection. 'Your labourers seem handy enough brutes and may apply themselves to the porting of my dunnage.'

'By all means, sir,' nods Standford, eager to please.

Galton airily waves his cane in the direction of the double doors. 'You men shall fetch my effects from the carriage outside, transporting them to the master bedroom on this floor with all speed. You may use the main staircase. Touch naught, break naught or it shall go ill for you. Quick as you like now.'

I give Facey a swift warning look to quell any objection. Instead, we tug forelocks like the obedient, unthinking brutes he imagines us to be and set to our task in a clatter of boots.

CHAPTER XIII

The master bedroom is more properly a boudoir, being as it is, or was, the late Edith Belmont's private sleeping chamber. The walls here are panelled in a pleasing pale blue colour, the edges picked out in white. There are any number of mirrors and looking glasses, all of which have been covered, veiled in black crêpe, in recognition of the former occupant's passing. It is fortunate that the day is dry and we have not muddied our boots, since a large white rug covers much of the floor. A delicate light-wood dresser and chair is set by the window and there is a large armoire against one wall, both of which are worthy of examination, though the most promising prospect is a walnut writing desk by the door.

Facey and me lower Galton's twin leather trunks to the floor. I pull the door to, being sure to leave it just a little way ajar and we begin our search. Facey makes for the desk while I rifle through the dresser.

'Locked,' announces Facey, moving swiftly to the armoire.

With Edith Belmont gone there has been no reason for Nellie to set a fire this morning, so I run my hand around the inside of the chimneypiece; without success. I turn my attentions to the small cabinet at the bedside, upon which lays a novel by Godwin, a few small bottles of scent and an ornate silver candlestick. A hectic search of the interior reveals naught of interest. Ignoring book and bottles, I raise the candlestick, and there, beneath its hollow base, discover a small tasselled key.

Sure enough, in moments, I have the writing desk open. It is full of trivial keepsakes, bills and sundry demands, but nestled amidst that nest of paper is a lacquered casket of a size to contain the ferroniere.

There is no lock to the casket; I lift the lid to reveal a bundle of letters bound in a thin red ribbon. They are endorsed by Captain the Honourable Lawrence George Squires and amongst them is a bound strand of auburn hair. I do not need to peruse the contents of these missives to know that they are private declarations of affection to the former lady of this house, and so I return the bundle to its container.

There is naught of further consequence in the desk, other than for a couple of loose sovereigns, which Facey pockets. I close the lid just as we are alerted to the approaching sound of heavy top boots on the boards outside. Facey and me instantly step across to the trunks and begin fussing with them, shifting them across the floor as though we have just this second placed them down.

Galton, now without hat or cane, throws the door wide, satisfied to see his property safely delivered. 'Obliged to you fellows. You may take yourselves to the scullery and obtain refreshment, should you have a mind to.' The man steps inside and, like a gazehound spying game, his eye falls with a predatory gleam upon the desk. I have not had sufficient time to secure it and the key remains in the lock. He approaches and raises the lid; in his eagerness to explore its contents Galton has failed to notice the softly dangling tassel. He discards the piles of bills, casting them about the floor before lifting out the casket. As he removes the letters, he is reminded of our lingering presence. 'What do you still do here?' he snaps.

'What do *you* do here, Mr Galton?' comes an angry female voice in echo. It is Mrs Parkes, now standing at the open doorway.

Galton pockets the letters before calmly turning to face her. 'I am minded to reside under this roof, since a London club is such a costly place to berth. This chamber should suit me very well, Mrs Parkes.'

'By what right do you say so, sir?'

'By my blood ties to the boy. Furthermore, you must know, the Belmont estate is entailed to me.'

'Then you have no rights at all. Your expectation lies a good way in the future, if ever. For the moment, all things are in the hands of Mr Haverford.'

Galton sneers. 'Haverford, that prissy ink smudger.'

'I demand that you quit these rooms, sir, else I shall send to Mr Haverford, informing him of this egregious trespass and urge him to bring on a magistrate with all despatch.'

'You forget yourself, Madam.'

'I recall only my duty to this house.' Mrs Parkes' left hand clasps at the keys hanging from her waist. Whether it quivers in anger or trepidation, I cannot say, but it sets those keys to rattling.

'I am a gentleman and you would do well to remember it.'

'Then you will comport yourself so and abide by my wishes.'

Galton, exasperated, kicks at the bills and papers littering floor. 'I'll not bandy words with a housekeeper and so will take my leave. Mark me, I shall return tomorrow to call upon my young relative. Be assured, Madam, you will not obstruct me in this.' With that, he sweeps majestically past us; we hear his boots thundering away down the corridor.

Mrs Parkes now appraises us, white-faced, hands on hips. 'You men ought never have been present for that disagreeable exchange, nor do you have any business in this part of the house.'

'Beg parding, Mum,' I say, coming it the labouring man and touching my forelock, 'only we was charged with shiftin' the gent's dunnage.'

'Then you must return to your proper labours at once.'

'Beg parding, Mum,' echoes Facey, 'we was pledged a mug of ale from the scullery in return for our efforts.'

This is not, in course, precisely true. There is a sharp intake breath and, for a moment, I am anxious that Facey has overegged the pudding. 'Mr Galton is not master of this house and has no right to make such a promise. Ale, forsooth.' Mrs Parkes rattles her keys in irritation. 'Very well,' she announces finally, 'you shall follow me down to the scullery and Mrs Stride will see what there is to be had.'

Mrs Stride turns out to be a well-looking woman, of about thirty years. There are tiny lines at the edges of her eyes but these, I would say, are from smiling and laughter, which she is wont to do as often as not. She has laid out for us a plate of buttered bread and a jug of pump water and, with the departure of Mrs Parkes, seems so pleased by our company following introduction, that she settles herself at the scullery table alongside of us. 'By no means stand on ceremony, gents, but take your fill,' she announces. 'It were these very hands churned that butter from best Wiltshire milk.'

'Very fine it is too,' announces Facey, between bites. 'All it lacks is a bottle of London porter to wash it down.'

'Here is good Adam's Ale, fresh out the George Street pump this very morning.'

'I have been advised to avoid London water at all costs, Mrs Stride. And that from a guinea-a-day physician.'

'Tush, Mr Facey, I never heard such stuff.'

''Tis gospel, as Mr Samuel will attest. The water of London in all its forms is to be shunned on account of the contagion.'

'From your mouth to the good Lord's ear. What stretchers you do tell, Mr Facey,' Mrs Stride chuckles. 'Lord love you, it ain't the water but the miasmas, which is to say the bad airs, what steal up nights from the marshlands and river. Asides, whoever heard of a gentrified physician jawing away for the likes of us? No, not for ten guinea a day.'

'You are not afeared then, Mrs Stride? We hear this house has been touched,' I remark, searching the woman's expression for sign of guilt.

'I fear the pestilence, Mr Samuel, and who would not, when it was the mistress here was took, not even a fortnight past? Though I have heard tell that miasmas are wont to rise upwards and, since I am accustomed to reside below stairs entirely, rate myself safe as any in this city. In course, some of those in the attic rooms took fright and fled and none can blame them.' Her countenance remains open and honest as a newborn babe's; either she imparts straight truth or performs with such veracity as might cause a sensation on the Adelphi stage. 'Will you not take a further slice, Mr Facey? Working men must have their vittles.'

'I cannot, Mrs Stride, good as it is. Not when I have a thirst on me sharp as the Reaper's scythe.'

Mrs Stride clucks her tongue. 'Since you are so insistent in spurning our noble water, it may be that I have some few bottles of porter beer put by, which I take myself from time to time, for the constitution, you understand, since a drop of porter is said to strengthen the blood.'

Facey grins broadly, throwing me a wink as Mrs Stride opens one of her cupboards, returning to the table with a couple of brown bottles. 'I am testament to that, Mrs Stride. At the scratch I was never a day without my porter, which, I swear, ingrained these arms with such vigour as none could stand against 'em.'

The woman sits and pours us each a mug. 'A pugilist then, Mr Facey?

Facey takes a long draught before smacking his lips with some satisfaction. 'Indeed, I was. Brought on by the great Tom Canon hisself.'

Mrs Stride brings a hand to her open mouth. 'You never was?'

'No stretcher,' I affirm. 'With my own eyes I have seen him put down a horse with a love tap from that right hand.'

'Then you are, yourself, a dark horse, Mr Facey. Even I have heard of Mr Tom Canon from the late Mr Stride, who was an enthusiast for such sporting pursuits.'

'Late, is it? Then I am sorry for your loss.'

'Oh, Lord, do not be. Mr Stride was a venerable gent, a deal older than I. He passed many years back when I was but a slip of a thing. Truth to tell, I barely recall his face, though I believe it was often kindly.' She refills Facey's mug.

Facey reaches over, flexing his great right arm. 'Should there be any doubt, you may give it a squeeze and assure yourself that this arm yet retains its authority.'

'For shame, Mr Facey.' Mrs Stride bats him away, though her eyes crinkle with amusement. ''Tis a mercy Mrs Parkes is off about her duties.'

Facey settles to his porter, giving the woman an appreciative glance over the rim of his mug.

'A forbidding woman, your Mrs Parkes.' I remark, by way of casting my line.

'A true ogress,' adds Facey.

Mrs Stride chuckles. 'It is mostly show. In the main, she is a decent enough, good-hearted sort. It is well known that housekeeper and cook will often cross swords on domestic matters and struggle for precedence over each and every detail. Not so with Mrs Parkes and me. We have long ago come to an accommodation: all above stairs is her domain, below, I have the final word. She has been a loyal servant to this family these five years or more and was much affected by the passing of our mistress. She presents herself as stern, since it falls to her to manage a rudderless ship: a much-reduced household, absent both master and mistress and but a wee boy remaining, and him not yet attained the age of reason.'

'Surely that task falls to your steward?' I press.

'In the ordinary way of things. But Mr Jenkins was alus partial to his wine and, if anything, was even more afflicted by the mistress's passing than Mrs Parkes. We have seen little of him since, though our chambers are close and I hear him at nights.' Mrs Stride taps her mug and winks. 'In his cups, you understand.'

Facey shakes his head in disapproval, like the most censorious of temperance reformers, before swilling the last of his porter. 'Obliged to you, Mrs Stride.'

'Now, you might call me Bessie, if it please you. Though, more properly, it is Elizabeth, which, being a regal sort of moniker, might easily be took for the putting on airs and graces, and so I am content enough with my simple Bess.' She fills our mugs with what yet remains in the bottle. 'Nor might I bemoan of it, since I should mention I once heard tell of a gent with the baptismal name of Friendless who, though he would never change that appellation, was driven into a rage whensomever addressed so. And thus, it proved prophetic, since none thereafter desired to keep company with him.'

Facey guffaws, all but snorting his porter.

Mrs Stride claps her hands. 'G'arn, look at me, rattling on like Lady Muck-a-Muck with naught better to do. It is only that so few mouths remain in this house and my labours become so modest that I may fritter the morning yarning away in my scullery over a mug or two, though I doubt your gaffer should be much pleased by your long absence.'

'I shall remove the sting from Mr Standford's disapproval by fetching up for him these last remnants of our bread and butter,' announces Facey.

'Then I should first wrap them in a little of brown paper if I could but lay my hands on some.' Mrs Stride rises from the table and fossicks amongst a jumble of tins and jars scattered about on a dresser. 'I find my scullery has become adrift in a ocean of noxious substances.'

I give Facey a meaningful glance. 'Noxious, you say?'

'Quite deadly, I should hazard. These here jars are bursting with the most foetid dust and putrid spices from the Indian continent, which have been foisted upon me by Mr Galton. Him who takes the most scandalous liberties on account of some distant connection to the young master. The merest reek of 'em would make you cat up.'

'Galton has been sent packing this very hour by your Mrs Parkes,' grins Facey.

'And thank heaven for that. Him, without two farthin's to rub together, lordin' it over the household if you please, assertin' meats ought be prepared in the most heathen manner. In this house, you may have your joint boiled, baked or roasted with a little salt and that is feast enough for most folk.'

'Though likely you have not seen the last of him,' I say, 'for he has declared his intention to return and take the boy on spree.'

'His aim, no doubt, to 'sinuate himself into the younker's good graces, though what that fellow may do or don't do outside of my kitchen ain't none of my concern.'

'I reckon the boy could use some cheer,' remarks Facey, getting to his feet. 'It is is a solemn cove for one so young.'

Mrs Stride glances over in surprise. 'I know little of the young master, him being only lately installed here. You have had sight of him then, gents?'

'He came to view the works, though he don't say much.'

'Well, then you know more of him than I. I clapped eyes on him but once at the family estate in Chilcomb. Some three years past it was, when extra hands was needed to prepare for a grand dinner-giving. I was packed off to that place for a day and a night, and there expected to play second fiddle to a country cook who could not tell a rump from a rib; I do declare all her doings was as like to charcoal as don't make no difference, not if it was ever so. On that occasion the boy was brung down to us in the scullery for a slice of duff or some such, by his nurse what saw to his bringing on. I only recall him as being petulant and desirous of having his own way in all things.' At the dresser, Mrs Stride finds a scrap of her paper and briskly makes a tidy package of the remaining hunks of bread and butter. 'In course, it may be that the years have improved him somewhat,' she says, handing Facey the parcel. 'Though yet a child, I suppose he is master of this house and so I should not expect to find him below stairs, nor should I venture above.' She pauses for a moment, eyeing the parcel in Facey's hand. 'But that don't preclude them as needs to stopping by for a sup of something at my table if ever they have a mind to.'

'Thankee kindly, Bessie Stride,' says Facey, 'though I must warn you, the hangin' of paper can be mortal thirsty work.'

Ordinarily, it might be accounted a liberty, but, since there is no servant to accompany us, we make our own way up the rear staircase finding ourselves back at the drawing rooms with ease. At the doors, I place a hand on Facey's arm, pausing him for a moment. 'You recall that we are here to fulfil a pressing task and it ain't to inspire the fairer sex with our brawn and killing airs?'

'Cheese it, Sammy. 'Tis a tolerably handsome woman there.'

'That's as may be, but a pleasing appearance don't disqualify a deceitful heart.'

'Handsome is as handsome does, Sammy boy,' he replies with an incorrigible grin.

I release his arm and he struts into the room ahead of me, brandishing Standford's little package. At the far wall we find our gaffer hard at work. Alerted to our presence he takes a step back and turns to greet us, trowel in one hand, plastering tray in the other. 'Well, gents. Here is progress, and on my ownsome to boot,' he announces proudly. 'And what have you to say to that?'

In point of fact, we are entirely speechless. In our absence, he has managed to apply a complete layer of plaster, entirely obscuring the brickwork.

CHAPTER XIV

We arose early this morning and hot-footed it to Dover Street where, to our vexation, we were constrained to kick our heels for an age in the street until the trade door was finally opened to us by a still-sleepy Nellie. Our purpose: to breach the chimney place without interference.

On entering the drawing rooms, we find our intentions further frustrated by the presence of Mrs Parkes, standing close to the far wall, inspecting the new plaster. She turns, treating us to a wintry smile. 'Here is a fine pair, eager to be about their labours.'

'We is arrived early to inspect the plaster, Mum,' I explain, removing my hat and coming it the labouring man once again. 'If it ain't set just right, it must be catched soonest else it ain't worth spit.'

'And how might that be judged?'

''Tis mostly by the hue of the thing, Mum,' I explain, though, in course, I have no clue on the matter.

'I see,' nods Mrs Parkes.

We stand in silence, waiting for the woman to depart but, for some reason, she will not. Facey and me shrug off our coats and rummage about the sacks and pails, conveying the impression of industry. In the event, I am grateful for the arrival of Standford, who bustles in toting his tool box. He gives us a puzzled glance before lifting his paper hat to Mrs Parkes. 'Good day, Mum.'

'Good day, Mr Standford. I find you have made progress.'

'Certainly, Mum.'

'You will forgive my intrusion, I am sure, but since the proper regulation of the household falls to me, I should wish to know that all is in order here.'

'You may be assured on that account, Mum. I warrant my work as fine as any in the city.'

'The plasterwork sets as it should?'

'Certainly, Mum. Well enough to hang paper within a day or two.'

'And what shall you be about in the intervening period?'

Standford indicates the remaining wall with a sweep of his hand. 'Why, scraping, Mum. All this old paper surrounding my new plaster must be removed. Every last speck scoured, else you shall have hillocks and hummocks 'neath your fine new decoration. Once we have took it back to original plaster, the whole of it will likely require a coat of skim.'

Mrs Parkes considers before giving Standford a curt nod. 'Very well. I am satisfied and shall leave you to your scrapings.'

'Can't leave well alone, that one, but she must be constantly peerin' and pryin' into every little thing,' grumbles Standford, once Mrs Parkes has quit the rooms. '"What progress do you make? Leave them bricks be. Has the plasterwork set as it should?" Kindly kiss my arse, Mum.' Having exhausted his indignation, Standford turns to us. 'Gents, I shall not inquire the reason for your early appearance for it ain't none of my concern. Though since you are here, and it don't require more but a little elbow grease, I might ask that you lend a hand to scrapin' at the wall.'

In return for our blank looks, he sighs, indicating his open tool box. 'The scrapers, gents, are them articles with the straight edges.' He picks one out. 'Kindly observe while I remove a section.' With that, he sets to, inserting the straight blade beneath an edge of old wallpaper whereupon a small strip comes away. It seems simple enough and so we take an implement each and commence our labour.

112

It may be that only an hour or two has passed yet it feels more like ten. Facey and me are sopping with perspiration and my right arm is afire. I step away from the wall to perceive that all this effort has uncovered a bare patch of an area no greater than a decent-sized portrait, so it is a relief to see Rosamund as she quietly enters the room.

'Well, gents, we have earned a respite and I believe I shall take a spell outside for a suckle on my pipe,' announces Standford, giving Rosamund a respectful nod as he passes.

Facey downs tool and sets to stretching out his back. Rosamund chuckles. 'Honest labour is it now, Mr Facey?'

'Such toil, Mrs Samuel, and for a mere six or seven pennies a day. It ain't hard to see why a cove without my own high moral character might choose to stoop to a little skulduggery.' He casts his one glim about the room. 'The younker ain't with you then?'

'He is not, Mr Facey. Mr Galton called for him this morning and they are for Hyde Park and the Serpentine. He has brought the boy a sailboat.'

Facey sniffs, in some dudgeon, no doubt, that his orange peel coracle has been so effortlessly superseded.

'I am of a similar mind, Mr Facey. No doubt, Mr Galton ingratiates himself with the boy for his own pecuniary advantage. I cannot find much to like about that man, though I daresay it may do William some good and perhaps bring him out of himself.'

Facey smooths back his sweat-dampened hair and tucks in his shirt. 'Now then, I believe I might allow the pair of you a private moment together and likewise step out; I find this unaccustomed labour has brung on a prodigious thirst.'

We watch as Facey stumps from the room.

'He makes for the scullery,' I say, 'we have had dealings with Mrs Stride and it seems that she and Mr Facey are not altogether displeased with one another.'

Rosamund nods. 'I met her this morning at my breakfast. Affable enough, she is, though she must necessarily remain in our watchful eye, notwithstanding Mr Facey's partiality. After all, who should have better opportunity to administer a noxious dose than a cook?'

I nod in agreement, though I have no intention of raising the notion with Facey. 'For our part, I must tell you, my love, we are set back on our heels,' I indicate the fresh plasterwork. 'A circumspect approach will no longer answer. We must have all down and be done with it.'

'Stay. For a little while longer at least, Sammy. Knocking through that wall shall be our final stroke should all other avenues lead to naught. I have come upon other fish to fry and begin to think it an unlikely place of concealment.'

'How so?'

'Consider. How might the article ever be retrieved should it lie there bricked and papered up for all eternity? Better to keep it closer to hand.' She digs into the pocket of her frock, producing a sheaf of flimsy papers, which she passes to me. 'Or placed in hock perhaps?'

The papers are signed pawnbroker chits on an establishment in Cork Street. 'How ever did you come by these?'

'My chamber is below stairs, sharing a corridor with Mrs Stride and Mrs Parkes. Mr Jenkins has a room set apart at the furthest end. Last night, about the hour of nine, I heard a heavy male tread pass by. Peeping through the merest crack of my door, I caught sight of a figure I took to be Mr Jenkins, candlestick in hand, making his unsteady way toward the wine cellar. The rattle of keys, confirmed it so, since only the butler may have possession of them. He entered the cellar and, once he had locked the door behind him, I crept into his room.'

'A shocking risk, my love.'

'Pish, Sammy. *Fortes fortuna iuvat.*'

'I am well aware you only spout those dusty phrases to vex me, knowing I do not have the learning.'

'True enough,' she gives me her slantendicular smile. 'At any rate, it did not take long since there was little to examine in that room. Few enough possessions, to be sure, 'less you count an army of dead bottles scattered around the floor. As I crept about the place with naught but the intermittent glow of a lucifer to guide me, I caught the squeak of a loose board beneath my foot. It was the work of a moment to prise it up and, concealed in the cavity below, I came upon those chits.'

I examine the paper more closely, inspecting the dates. 'All from the self-same Cork Street office, though some go back six months or more.'

'More than a few are recent. It may be the ferroniere was represented as an article of glass and pinchbeck, cheap paste stuff. And now it lies in the broker's keeping, hidden in plain sight, as it were, till it may be redeemed and sold by this Jenkins.'

'Or the Cork Street cove is party to the business. It would not be the first time the fruits of a larceny came to be in the hands of a pawnbroker.'

'I may not come and go at will, so that must be for you to gauge. Question this broker with care, keeping a sharp eye for signs of evasion.'

'I shall lose not a moment,' I announce, fetching my coat and hat.

Rosamund hands me a full purse from her reticule. 'Here are a few of Mr Facey's shillings. Should we be so fortunate as to have hit upon our gemstone and the broker unknowing of its true value, you will require the tin to redeem it. If not, you shall need funds for the chophouse.'

'You are very good to me, my love. We was obliged to miss our breakfast and, what with having to scrape away fiercer than a Irish wake fiddler, I am sharp set and should welcome a nice cut of pork.'

Rosamund tuts. 'Not for filling your belly, Mr Samuel Samuel, which grows soft enough to be sure; do not think I had not remarked it. It is to Miller's chophouse on Regent Street that you go. According to Nellie, who is sweet on him, there you will find the former footman, now a waiter at that place. Name of Walter Price, and it may be that he is embroiled in some way. Certainly, his abrupt dismissal is grounds for bitterness. A little of that silver may loosen his tongue.' She gives me a softer look. 'Though should there be opportunity for a bite, I dare say Mr Facey will never begrudge the use of his shillings.'

Suspended from the shopfront above the pavement are the triple brass balls proclaiming the business of this Cork Street jerryshop. I peer in through the double bay windows, which are remarkable for their spotlessness, wondering for a moment if I might catch sight of our ferroniere. It is, of course, a far-fetched notion and I am scarcely disheartened by the absence. There is, instead, a great variety of assorted objects and, not just any old jumbled tat, but of evident quality. There are musical instruments, not the knackered old fiddles as one might find at the stalls of Shoreditch, but glossy, chestnut-hued violins, violas, a flute or two and some species of brass horn buffed to a mirror shine. There is silver plate, even the solid stuff, in abundance: creamers and coffee pots, lacquer or silver-backed grooming sets, snuffboxes and the like. It is, without doubt, a good cut above any jerryshop I have ever known.

A little bell tinkles sweetly above my head as I enter. Within, all is order and artful display. To one side of the counter stands an enclosed wooden booth, there to offer customers a little privacy when signing away their chattels. On the counter itself are a number of small glass cabinets displaying jewellery and precious objects. As I approach, eager for a closer look at these items, a sharp-eyed, grey-haired fellow emerges from the back rooms.

'How do, Uncle?' I say, employing the familiar cant for men of his profession.

The cove compresses his lips as though I have just hawked on his waxed floorboards. 'I decline to answer to that appellation, sir. This ain't Wapping, nor it ain't one of your two-a-penny slopshops neither. I might hang out the brass balls but that is all there is in common; we are alike to them places as chalk to cheese. My name is Worth.'

Of a sudden I am conscious of my unkempt appearance; old keks and coat lightly peppered with scrapings and plaster dust. I remove my hat. 'Forgive me, Mr Worth. I have a small matter of business, if you please.'

Worth appraises me with evident disapproval. 'It may be that you have lost your way. You find yourself in Mayfair, sir.'

'I have a ticket or two to redeem,' I reply, reaching into my pocket for the chits. I quickly sort them to the most recent before handing them across the counter. 'You will find them endorsed by this establishment. 'Less in course, you are correct in your assertion that I have lost my wits and taken a wrong turn entirely in a city I know as well as the back of my own hand.' I bring out the full purse and give it a rattle.

'Now, now, sir. It may be that I spoke a little chuff just now and you will never mind it. Certainly, a little tin on the incoming tide is always welcome here.' He examines the tickets and nods. 'A moment.' He steps into the backroom while I examine the jewellery on display. Necklaces, in the main, and a few rings but none with stones larger than my fingernail. There are one or two ferronieres, these being quite the thing just now, but they are set with pearls and pretty dwarfish ones at that.

Worth returns with a handful of small items, which he places on the counter. There is a neat little silver snuff-box, an ivory-handled toasting fork and a shiny red leather box, each accompanied by its own handwritten tag affixed by a piece of string. For a brief moment I am hopeful of the box until Worth opens it. 'Six mother of pearl dress shirt studs. All just so and right as a trivet.' He squints, casting his gaze toward the ceiling as he begins to enumerate without recourse to pen or paper. 'Now then, that is six shilling advanced for the studs, interest at one halfpenny per two shilling per month for two months, or part of, which come to thruppence. Eight shilling laid out on the snuffbox and that with two month of interest, which is to say, tuppence. Fourteen shilling and five pence to pay for the two items. The fork, but three shilling advanced, interest one penny. In all, seventeen shilling and sixpence, if you please.'

I slap my forehead. 'Forgive me, Mr Worth. What a blockhead I am.' I hand over the remaining two tickets. 'I had come to redeem a sparkler, though paste and of little value. I do not recall when it was pledged.'

Worth gives me a queer look.

'It is of a type known as a ferroniere, a lady's headband with a jewel suspended from the centre. 'Tis only a Brummagem thing, to be sure, but of considerable sentiment to me. The ornament has been fashioned from glass to resemble a great black diamond.'

Worth guffaws. 'By God, you describe the Eye of Brahma. And don't I wish I had it. I should have packed sticks long ago and even now be taking my ease on a fine estate, shying golden guineas across the boating lake for sport.'

'You have knowledge of the piece then?'

'Who don't? It being the wonder of the season a year or two past. The very idea that such an item might be pledged. The copy alone is worth a handsome sum.'

'A copy, you say?'

'I do say. And well I know it ain't yourn, nor never will be. What sauce, sidling in here like butter wouldn't melt. You overreach, my friend, in the hopes of redeeming the Eye of Brahma like I am the flat of the world. I will tell you what it is, cully, though you have my tickets, I do not reckon they are come by honestly. You are a dipper most like, chancing his arm for what he might discover. G'arn, afore I bring down the law on you.'

I do not believe for a moment that Worth intends to carry out his threat, him being so assiduous over the reputation of his establishment.

Rather than leaving, I open my purse and shake out some few of the coins. 'Three shillings should you tell me where this copy is to be found.'

Worth moistens his thin lips, innate covetousness striving against a sense of righteous indignation. 'Four,' he announces finally.

'Very well, four it is.' I count them out into my palm. 'And you will return me the tickets first.'

'You may keep them with my blessing, though they are of no value to you since you would not be wise to cross this threshold in the future.'

'I have my reasons,' I say, pocketing the chits.

'Well then, as for the copy, 'tis no great secret, to be sure. Being as how the Brahma jewel had created such a stir, even made mention of in the broadsheets, a enterprising fellow hereabouts fabricated a facsimile. Not from life, mind, but from its close depiction in one of them illustrated papers. It was displayed in the window of his establishment as a form of advertisement, exciting great admiration from the public, with crowds three deep on occasion.' Worth holds out his open hand expectantly. I drop the coins into it. 'Bailey and Skinner on Jermyn Street, jewellers,' he smirks, 'as any hereabouts might have informed you, gratis.'

I pocket my purse and clap on my old hat. 'Good day to you then, Uncle,' I say pointedly, turning on my heel.

'Go practice your wiles elsewhere, cully, 'gainst less downy birds than I,' calls Worth to my departing back. 'And you might try the Devil's Acre, where I have heard there are great strings of emeralds and rubies hanging from the trees.' A disagreeable mocking laughter follows me out in harsh contrast to the bell, which gaily tinkles my departure.

CHAPTER XV

For a while I am undecided as to whether I ought head direct for this jewellers or take myself to the chophouse. For one thing, I am shabbily attired and would doubtless make a poor impression upon a refined Mayfair jeweller, even were I to gain admission; for another, my belly is growling like a brickyard mastiff and so enjoys the final word on the matter. I head south, threading my way through the knots of unruly, perambulating bucks of Vigo Street, having had my hat knocked off but twice, and thence onto Regent Street and to my destination.

'Now then, old cock. I have been informed you was inquirin' after me.' A youngish cove in the long white apron of a waiter, sits himself opposite at the communal table. Though he is clean shaven and of pleasing features, there is a pugnacious look about him and his high forehead is beaded with perspiration.

I set down my fork. 'If you be Walter Price, then I should appreciate a moment of your time.' I reach into my coat and retrieve a couple of shillings from the now depleted purse. I place the coins on the table, covering them with my hand.

Price eyes me warily. 'You have the advantage of me, cocky. A show of silver is all wery well, but you could be a bailiff's man for all I know.'

I smile. 'Do I have the look of such?'

'I own you do not, being a trifle stunted for such work,' acknowledges Price.

'My name is Samuel Samuel. Builder by trade and a simple working man. You have naught to fear in exchanging a word or two with me, and two shillings to be gained.'

Price nods and reaches across for my tankard. 'Wery well, Mr Samuel, the waiting lark is hot work and I am quite parched. Since we are such good friends, you will not object if I take a pull at your table beer.'

I had purchased a quart of the stuff alongside my plate of beef and it is a liberty, to be sure, but if it serves to loosen his tongue, I see it as fivepence well spent. Thirst quenched, Price wipes his mouth on his sleeve. 'Now, old cock, I am at your service.'

'It is like this, Mr Price, I have a nephew, a fine lad, honest and of good length and appearance, who desires to become a footman. I should wish to hear more of the business from a cove what knows his onions.'

Price narrows his eyes. 'Fart-catchers are ten a penny in this great city and yet you seek me out by name, though I do not know you from Adam.'

'I should have mentioned earlier, I work alongside Mr Standford.'

'That name means naught to me.'

'We conduct renovations at number Four and Twenty of Dover Street.'

Price nods slowly. 'I was footman there these last couple of years, though I cannot now recall the house with much fondness.'

'And yet, you are well spoke of by the remaining servants, which accounts for my being here.'

It seems I have the measure of the man. The bait I have cast has been swallowed whole; Price preens, eager to hear more of himself. 'I do not doubt it, though I do say so myself.' Price leans across the table, lowering his voice. 'I reckon you are a cove what can keep a confidence, Mr Samuel.'

'I am, Mr Price.'

'Well, now, it was known as I had been marked out. Noticed, sir. A position of far greater eminence was in the offing, that is to say, a certain titled gent had his eye on me for a post in his own household. A wery great household indeed, sir. Of such eminence that I am precluded from naming it. I might only say, never think of your tuppenny baronets neither.' He winks. 'Enough said, old cock.'

'I could wish such expectations for my nephew, Mr Price.' I push the coins across the table.

Price scoops them up without a second glance and they disappear into the pocket of his apron. 'It ain't no mystery, Mr Samuel.' He rises to his feet and, raising his long apron a little ways, reveals black breeches, buckled to the knee above white stockings. ''Tis all down to these manly calves, sir. Did you ever see the like? Such profile, such definition. Michael Angelica ain't in it.'

'Indeed not, Mr Price.'

'A footman ain't worth his wittles without he displays a manly calf. You just pass that to your nevvie.'

'I shall, though in all honesty, he cannot lay claim your physical advantages.'

'I ain't hardly surprised to hear it, sir, though I do say so myself. Such perfection don't come easy though, but must be worked at. I raise myself up onto my toes six hundred times a day, Mr Samuel, no matter how fagged I am. Up and down, up and down. Three hundred of a morning and three hundred at night. Should your nevvie be persuaded to do likewise, why then, there you have it. He is on his way.'

'I am much obliged to you, Mr Price, and shall earnestly entreat him to do so.'

Price sits himself once more and reaches across for my tankard, which he takes a good pull at before clearing his throat. 'I 'spect you are curious, old cock, as to how I find myself in these current circumstances, so far beneath my merits?'

'Certainly, Mr Price. 'Tis a mazer right enough.'

'I shall tell you straight, though you will find it shockin'. I was let go.'

'You do not say so?'

'Dished, cocker. And what is more, without a character to boot.'

'By what terrible injustice, sir?'

'Dismissed out of hand by Edith Belmont, mistress of that house, as was.'

'She who was took by the cholera?' I ask, taking care to note his expression.

'The wery same. Carked it, but a few days after I was sent packing. And good riddance, I say. There is the Lord's swift justice if you like; may she rot in her eternity box.'

I shake my head in wonderment as Price continues to make free with my tankard.

'All on account of a beefsteak, if you can credit it,' he says, wiping his mouth again.

'How so?'

'Well, cocker, owing to Edith Belmont's debts, the Chilcomb estate of Hampshire was obliged to be sold off and the servants all let go, so there was naught else for it but the sprog William, that is to say the son and heir, what was accustomed to live there, must be brung to London. The old nurse at Chilcomb, being so wery ancient and decrepit, declined to make such a journey, and so it fell to me to fetch the boy in a hired carriage. In course I made no objection, it being something of a spree. What's more, a decent purse was given for a morsel and a wet, for it is a tolerable longish run.'

I nod my encouragement, while taking a bite at the day-old slice of bread which has accompanied my plate of thin, indifferent beef. Though at a scandalous tuppence a slice, with an additional penny for butter, it is not to be scorned.

'I rated the sprog a poor sort of younker, and a shocking grumpkin on account of a head-cold. No good company for man nor beast, what with all the mitherin', coughin' and the snot flyin'; first, the shades must be up, then, no, the shades must be down and I don't know what all. I was not in the least sorry for the change of hosses at Hook, where we was able to step inside of the White Hart Inn and partake of refreshment. A syllabub was brung out for the young 'un, on account of his years and indisposition, which he set about with a will. I, myself, took a beefsteak and a few taters. Well, it was not so wery long afore the sprog had ate up his syllabub and drank off his milk and water, for he was not stinted. No, not at all. Now, whilst my attention was momentarily distracted by the exchange of a few pleasantries with the pot wench, the bugger betook it upon himself to hoist the beefsteak off my plate and by the time I remarked it, had ate it up entirely. It were a wery meagre beefsteak, to be sure, but even so.' Price shakes his head in wonderment before drinking off the last of my table beer.

'Can you credit it, Mr Samuel?' He shoves my empty tankard back across the scarred oak table. 'Now, the sharin' of a bottle or a wet 'twixt them on friendly terms is one thing, and don't signify, but I should never dream to trespass on another cove's plate. You will take notice, Mr Samuel, that whilst we have shared a companionable sup, your own wittles, the plate of beef what you have not quite finished up, lays entirely unmolested. Who should ever, ever be so froward as to transgress 'gainst another man's wittles? An Englishman's plate is his sovereign territory, his comestible castle, if you like. Touch it at your peril.'

'A most admirable principle, Mr Price. And I am gratified to hear it,' I say, quickly forking up the last of my meats.

'Ain't it though?' He is momentarily distracted by a sudden gale of laughter from the end of our long table, where three coves of the middling sort, tradesmen most like, share a bottle and smoke their clay pipes. There are other similar groups scattered about the room but not so many as I should have expected at this hour, likely on account of the contagion.

'It occurs to me, Mr Price,' I say, 'that you were the injured party in this matter of the filched beefsteak and yet were deprived of your livelihood on its account.'

'Wery true, Mr Samuel. Being a Englishman through an' through, it fell to me to serve the boy out. I give him a good clump for his sauciness and so, having thoroughly boxed his ears, we resumed our places in the coach.'

'The boy made some objection to this treatment, I take it?'

'Not 'alf, cocky. With him blubberin', grindin' his gnashers and ragin' at me, there was not a moment's peace to be had all the long road back to London. In course, once at Dover Street, the brat, still in high dudgeon, made free to peach directly, bellowin' indignation to the world and his wife. Word swiftly carried to his ma, the mistress of that house, whereupon it was the cold pavement for old Walter Price, never a chance to make explication, nor even a character to soften the blow.'

'Very harsh, sir.'

'The grievance of the world, old cock, though I do say so myself.'

'I collect you were not downcast then to hear of Mrs Belmont's passing?'

'In all honesty, I cannot say the world is a worser place for it. A snappish, touch-me-not mistress, who, on her wery deathbed gave no thought to her servants or their prowision, though made plenty enough for herself. It was her wish that she be laid out in her box festooned with her sparklers. Of sufficient walue, I have been informed, for a whole army of footmen to comfortably retire on.'

'Such stuff, Mr Price.'

'No word of a lie, sir. I have it direct from the lips of Nellie, the slavey, who, on occasion, steals away from her duties and comes awisiting.' Price taps his nose. "Twixt gents, Mr Samuel, I believe she is somewhat taken with these fine calves of mine.' He winks and smiles with what he imagines to be a killing air. 'Any gate, it were all done in a tearin' hurry on account of the pestilence what carked 'er; so they lays her out in one of the downstairs rooms for the briefest respects of the fambly and what have you. Nellie, being a curious sort, poked her head in, and there was Mrs Belmont, in her box, afloat in gold and sparklers like the Queen of Sheba. A great stone at her head, the size of a dove's egg and blacker'n old Boney's heart. In such state was she carried to the boneyard as though she might buy her way into heaven. And that ain't hardly likely. Not her, cocky. In course, you may think me a unfeelin' sort but I cannot rightly say my heart bleeds for it.' The man leans back in his chair with an air of considerable complacence. 'And why such stipulation regardin' the disposition of them sparklers, would you imagine?'

'I could not say.'

'Why, for spite, sir. Pure and simple. 'T'was so that none other might ever bask in the splendour on 'em. In particular, one Sophia Sidney, Baroness De L'isle and Dudley, no less. A wery great lady who had her beady glim on that great black gemstone; I heard it said that her people had made approach and offered a king's ransom but the mistress would never part with it, leastways, not when it come to the Baroness De L'isle and Dudley.'

Price smirks, basking in my rapt attention.

'And why should that be so?'

'Well now, cocky, my mistress were not exactly what you might call the forgivin' sort and, though her sparkler was good enough for the baroness, it seems that Edith Belmont herself was not quite the thing, for the baroness had, on particular occasion, wery publicly declined to notice her. In short, she had been cut, sir. Snubbed by that wery grand lady before all of London society. And so the mistress resolved that the neither the baroness nor any other of her ilk might ever possess her precious diamond. Not in life and most assuredly not in death.'

'What a tale, Mr Price. I should like nothing more than to while away the hours with you over a bottle or two, but alas, we are both honest, hard-working men with duties to attend.' I get to my feet.

Price gives a nonchalant shrug. 'Mr Miller, him what owns this place, gives me reign to come and go as I please on account of the fine figure I present, all them other waiters being crook-backed, stunted creeturs. It is his great good fortune to have such a ornament to his establishment and well he knows it.'

'Just so, Mr Price. A pleasure to make your acquaintance, sir.'

Price rises. 'Your nevvie might follow old Walter Price's adwice to the letter and he shall not go far astray, though I do say so myself.' With that, Price strikes a pose, hoisting apron and making a leg as I head for the door.

'Price,' bellows an angry red-faced cove from over by the counter. 'I do not pay you to stand about like a great Jack-Pudding. Shift your arse, you idle sod, for there is dinners to be brung.'

CHAPTER XVI

In Dover Street, close by the house, I come upon Standford, perched on the edge of a horse trough, placidly smoking his pipe. He gives me a friendly nod. 'Why, Mr Samuel, you have been out and about, I find.'

'I have, Mr Standford, and you will forgive me and Mr Facey for our neglect of your wall.'

'Never mention it, Mr Samuel. You have your own business to attend, which is none of mine.' Standford tamps his pipe with a great blackened thumb and gets to his feet. We head for the trade door, which has been left on the jar by means of a small wooden wedge, where he gives me a wink. 'I manage the door so as to come and go for a pipeful without alerting the dragon.'

We ascend the back stairs and are at the point of crossing to the drawing rooms when I hear a sharp hiss. Rosamund stands in the entrance hall below urgently waving me to join her. Standford merely shrugs and goes about his business as I hotfoot it down the main stairs. Rosamund takes me by the hand and hurries me into a side room, before closing the door behind us.

The room is a small library of sorts, furnished with handsomely-bound, book-lined shelves, set about with brightly patterned Turkey carpets and a few small tables displaying intricate carvings of wood and Indian ivory. The farthest corner has been partially enclosed by means of a painted screen behind which there is a well-upholstered leather armchair, side table and a green-shaded lamp. A book, titled "Charlotte Temple", lies upon on the table.

Rosamund releases my hand. 'Mrs Parkes and Jenkins are occupied above just now shifting Galton's dunnage from out of the master bedroom. She is quite crabbed over it and will not let it lie so we are safe enough to talk here, for a while at any rate. This place has become my refuge,' she explains. 'Now, my love, quickly, you must tell all.'

I briefly recount the events at the jerryshop before handing back the tickets. 'You should replace them afore Jenkins notes aught amiss, though, since the objects were likely the belongings of his former master, I doubt the pledges will be ever be redeemed. It appears this Jenkins is no saint.'

Rosamund wrinkles her nose, unimpressed. 'Nor such a great sinner neither. A few trinkets pilfered over time, the steward's perquisites, you might say. No, Sammy, for the moment, Mr Jenkins' light fingers are neither here nor there, not when compared to this momentous news of a facsimile.' She looks at me expectantly.

'It is at a jewellers on Jermyn Street.'

Rosamund frowns. 'You did not think to fly to there with all speed?'

'I should have been given short shrift attired as I am, even if granted entry. I went directly to the chophouse.'

'Where no doubt, you partook of a mug of ale and a chop or two.'

'I did no such thing.' Rosamund scrutinizes me with her unblinking grey eyes. I have never been much at dissembling with her and my bland, guileless expression swiftly collapses. ''Twas a plate of beef.'

Rosamund tuts gently. 'And between gorging yourself and quaffing ale, were you at leisure to speak with this Walter Price at all?'

'I was. It is true that he was dismissed by Edith Belmont and so nurses a grievance on that account.' I shrug. 'Though I rate him a decent enough sort; a blowhard and a dunderhead but I saw no great wickedness in him.'

Rosamund squeezes my hand. 'Well, it is all of a piece now that you have come by this new information. It seems you have hit upon the scent, Sammy. You must uncover all you can of this facsimile and I warrant you shall find it has been lately sold. If that be the case, do all in your power to discover its buyer. For without a shadow of a doubt, there lies our quarry.'

'And if this jeweller will not say?'

'Press him, Sammy. Use what silver remains; if that does not answer, then allow Mr Facey his turn.'

'Perhaps it were better that you...' My utterance is cut short by the sounds of violent battering at the front door.

'Hush now, it is Galton returned with the boy. I must be about my duties.' She pushes me behind the screen. 'You ought not be discovered in this part of the house. Remain here till the coast is clear.'

I wait, keeping an ear cocked at the commotion in the entrance hall. Instead of subsiding, the hullaballoo only increases in volume and stridency. From the hallway I hear an angry male voice combined with a lower, more placatory tone followed closely by the sound of purposeful footsteps echoing along the passage in the direction of this room. Of a sudden, the door is thrown wide.

'Who the devil is this Titus Galton fellow, and what does he mean by his presence here?' roars the angry voice.

'It is true that we enjoy the pleasure of Mr Galton's company from time to time, but he is not currently in residence with us, sir.'

'I received a note requesting a meeting with him here at this address. A very great presumption is it not?'

'I could not say, Captain. I only know that Mr Galton is cousin to the late mistress, though a distant relative, to be sure. I believe a cousin by marriage, sir. Not by blood.'

'That don't give him the right to set up shop here, do it, Jenkins?'

'It does not, I fear. Mrs Parkes has some pretty sharp words to say on the matter, sir.'

'I suppose he believes himself to have some claim on the place, does he? Ain't there a proper heir? A squeaker of some sort?'

'Just so, sir. Young William Belmont, lately up from Chilcomb.'

'Thought as much.'

'Mr Galton has been out today in company with the young master and is expected to return shortly. Alas, our drawing rooms are in a sadly dilapidated state and so you may wait on him here, or perhaps the morning room?'

'Never trouble yourself, Jenkins. I am perfectly content here. I have always admired Mrs Belmont's taste in literature.'

'As you wish, sir. And might I offer you refreshment at all?'

'Obliged. I shall take brandy, if you please.'

I hear the squeak of Jenkins' shoes as he departs the room. The screen which serves for my concealment, is a construction of two parts, comprising twin hinged panels set at an angle, and so I am able to peer through the narrow gap at the room beyond. The newcomer, it transpires, is a military gent, tricked out in white breeches, glossy hessian boots and a red coat with orange facings, trimmed with the gold lace and epaulettes which mark him for an officer. His cockaded hat rests on one of the occasional tables. Still in a state of considerable agitation, he prowls back and forth across the room. An imposing figure with his rigid, military bearing, the man is impeccably groomed and sports luxuriant moustaches curled upwards at either end. He pauses and, for a terrible moment, I fear he might have heard the pounding of my heart. There is little I might say to excuse my presence here and, should I be discovered, might very well be taken up and hanged for a common sneak thief.

It is only that his eye has been caught by one of the carvings. He raises the intricately worked elephant and examines it closely, fingering the detail. After a moment, he replaces the piece and steps over to the shelves, where he makes an examination of the books. I can only hope that the volume on the table by me will not interest him sufficiently to draw him over.

'I have brung the decanter, Captain,' announces Jenkins, to my relief, toting a small silver salver upon which is a full decanter and single glass. This steward is a squat, broad faced figure with thinning silver hair, protruding watery blue eyes and thick, moist lips. He manifests the florid complexion of a tippler, resembling nothing so much as a great rubicund bullfrog. Trembling hands holding out the salver confirm his enthusiasm for the bottle.

'Very good in you, Jenkins.' The captain tosses off the bumper of brandy in one and refills his glass.

There comes the sound of two sharp raps on the door knocker. 'That will be Mr Galton returned with the young master, I make no doubt. I shall inform him of your presence here, sir,' advises Jenkins.

'Well enough,' nods the captain, knocking back his second glass. He sets the empty receptacle down on the side table, plants his feet apart and clasps his hands behind his back in readiness for his meeting. In a matter of moments Galton strides into the room, careful to close the door behind him before making his bow. 'Captain Squires? Honoured, sir.'

Squires neglects to return the courtesy. 'Honour, sir. You speak to me of honour? What the devil do mean, sir, requesting a meeting in this house, which is none of your place?'

Galton gives the slightest shrug of his shoulders. 'You are intemperate, sir, but I shall satisfy you. I have an interest in the Belmont estate, which is to say, it is entailed to me; furthermore, I am the current heir's uncle and guardian.'

Squires sniffs. 'Well, well, that ain't none of my concern. I believe you are in possession of certain property, which rightly belongs to me.'

Galton smiles. 'You refer to the parcel of letters.'

'I do, sir. They are mine and I demand their return forthwith.'

'Those letters were in possession of the late Edith Belmont and are, in consequence, part of the estate.'

'A grubby lawyer's quibble, sir. I cannot agree. They are a private and personal correspondence, writ by me and indorsed by my own hand. They must be returned.'

'And so they shall be, Captain. Shall we say five hundred?'

'We shall not, sir. Not a penny shall you have for them. I insist they are my rightful property.'

'Come now, Captain, a few hundred ain't such a stretch for items of this nature. Though I do speak in guineas, mind, not pounds. I am a reasonable man and should desire to do right by you. I should not, for example, wish to imagine such a correspondence falling into other hands.'

'You go too far, sir.' Although he presents a stolid, unmoving figure to Galton, from my vantage point I observe Squires' hands behind his back clasping and unclasping in agitation.

'Sir John Oswald is not a man to suffer loose morals amongst his officers, I believe.' Galton smirks.

'You infernal blackguard, to have read a gentleman's private correspondence.'

'Why, certainly I have perused them and might only say you are fortunate that my dear cousin, the late William Belmont, is no longer with us, else we should be considering a case of criminal conversation.'

'You will not relinquish my property then?'

'Not for a penny under five hundred guineas.'

'You are a damned scrub, sir, and no gentleman.' Squires takes a step forward and, reaching forth, takes Galton's long nose 'twixt thumb and forefinger and sharply tugs. 'There's for you, sir.'

Galton steps back, a shocked expression on his face, his snout already beginning to suffuse with colour.

Squires reaches across and retrieves his hat. 'You know where I am to be found, sir; I am perfectly willing to give you any satisfaction you choose to ask for.' With that, he strides past his adversary and throws wide the door, revealing Jenkins standing solemn in the passage outside. The butler gives him a deferential nod.

'Thankee, Jenkins,' announces Squires briskly, 'but I shall show myself out.'

With that, Jenkins steps softly into the library. 'Is there aught else I may do for you, Mr Galton?' he asks, with a knowing smirk.

'I have no doubt your ear was to the keyhole this whole time and will be aware that I am to give the captain a meeting.' Galton ruefully rubs his nose. 'Mr Jenkins, might I speak frankly with you?'

Jenkins licks his lips, otherwise remaining impassive.

'Now I ain't precisely master of this house, as Mrs Parkes is so considerate as to remind me. But I ain't so very far from it neither, and should appreciate your willing assistance in this affair.'

'I am at your service, Mr Galton, and should be pleased to assist with aught that lies in my humble powers.'

'And I may count on your discretion, I hope?'

'I am a trifle deaf, sir.'

Galton nods his approval. 'I shall not forget it, Jenkins.'

The butler inclines his head. 'You are very good, sir.'

'Now, I must engage a second to act on my behalf without delay and so should wish to send a note. Is there pen and paper to hand?'

'In the morning room, sir. There you will find pen, ink and paper aplenty. I shall charge Nellie to run out for a messenger when you have done.'

'Excellent. I recollect that at one time my cousin had a pretty pair of pistols. Were they sent home with his effects at all?'

'Indeed they were, sir. Holland and Holland and exceedingly fine pieces too. The late mistress had no liking for firearms and so they are stowed in the attic.'

'I will tell you, Jenkins, I have not been out since India and, if I am to meet with this Squires in the morning, should desire to have my eye in.'

'I shall fetch them down, sir, while you are about your note.'

The pair quit the room to attend to their business, but only when both sets of footsteps have entirely receded do I emerge from my corner. Cautiously, I peek my head out of the doorway. Satisfied that the passageway is quite deserted, I hare off up the backstairs.

Back in the drawing rooms I find Facey in good spirits and smelling strongly of porter. I have only this moment apprised him of our doings and we are preparing to head out for Jermyn Street when Galton enters through the double doors. For the sake of appearances, we quickly retrieve our scrapers and join with our foreman in prodding away at the wall.

'You men there, how should you like to earn a sovereign?' drawls Galton, striding towards us.

We stand mumchance, reluctant to be diverted from our sortie to the jewellers.

'Come now, Mr Standford, I daresay you are able to spare your men to do me a great service.'

'As you wish, sir,' agrees Standford with little enthusiasm, having had no assistance from either of us for the best part of the day.

The garden to the rear of the house boasts a paved terrace giving on to a grassed expanse set about with ornamental shrubs. Here and there are stone or marble statues: coves in a shocking state of undress, holding urns or posed in deepest cogitation, no doubt wondering who was it filched their keks.

Jenkins is already on the terrace when we arrive in train with Galton. He holds a brass-cornered, dark wood case in his hands and has set out a couple of dark green bottles and a dozen or so champagne saucers on a stone plinth nearby.

'Now, men,' announces Galton, 'there is a shooting ground at Battersea Fields where gentleman sometimes meet over affairs of honour. D'ye know of it?'

'I do, sir,' grunts Facey.

'I have a matter to settle there in the morning. Pray, present yourselves at that place at first light tomorrow. You are to stand ready in the event I am brought down and must immediately carry me from the field. I am to be returned to my carriage with all speed, no shilly-shallying. Is that understood?'

I knuckle my forehead. ''Tis, sir.'

Galton nods. 'I should like to know that I have two able-bodied types to see to me. If I am killed outright, well, then it don't much signify; never fret though, you shall have your sovereign from my second.'

He nods at Jenkins who opens the case, revealing a pair of perfectly matched pistols along with compartments for the powder flask, rods, oil, brush, balls and percussion caps.

Galton selects one of the weapons, holding it up to his eye. 'I saw a good deal of these affairs in India, Jenkins. And it is all very well to have a medico present and so forth, but do you know, the one thing I remarked was that the swifter the ball was fittingly extracted the better the odds. I have a decent sawbones in Onslow Square who can be relied upon to get the thing done, provided I am carried there at all speed.' Galton begins loading the first of the pistols. 'It ain't exactly in the code duello, but that don't say it ain't to be done neither.'

'An eminently sensible precaution, sir,' intones Jenkins.

'Know you aught of a barker, Jenkins?'

'I am tolerably familiar with a fowling piece, sir. Mr Jenkins senior was gamekeeper on the Dyrham Park estate.'

'Was he though? Well, well, first unstring the wine, then shall you be good enough to load for me.'

Jenkins places the case down on the plinth, picks up one of the bottles and begins to untie the hemp string securing the stopper. It opens with a muffled pop. He carefully fills a half dozen of the glasses; tiny bubbles ascend the amber liquid, sparkling and scintillating in the late afternoon sunlight. Jenkins offers the first to Galton who drinks it off in one. He hands the empty glass to Facey, at the same time indicating a statue at the far end of the garden with his pistol. This specimen is an oldish, bearded cove with a high forehead. He stands as though expounding on a matter of great significance, hand extended, palm upturned. 'You will set this upon the hand of Aristotle, if you please.'

'Harry Stottle it is, sir.'

'Aristotle. I believe yonder figure is likely he, though it may be Plato; any gate, one of them tiresome philosophical ancients whose endless twaddle was beat into me all throughout my schooldays.'

Facey duly trots across the expanse of grass. Galton pulls the hammer to full-cock before allowing his arm to drop. The moment Facey balances the glass on the outstretched palm, Galton brings his arm up to the firing position. There is a sharp report and Facey takes a step back just as the statue's razzo explodes in a shower of dust and chips.

Galton grimaces, 'Philosophise that, you old windbag.' He hands the pistol to Jenkins in exchange for a full glass. 'She fires somewhat high and to the left, I believe.'

'They have not been used in an age, sir. No doubt you will find 'em truer when the barrels have warmed.'

Facey hastens back towards us and, from his expression, I can see that he is in a towering rage at being so used. By my reckoning it is a mite too early to tip our hand and so, for the nonce, we must endure whatever indignity comes our way without complaint for our John's sake. I shake my head as he catches my eye, a stern warning to make no objection.

'We shall see,' Jenkins passes across the second pistol, which he has expertly loaded despite the tremor in his hands. 'You may take a saucer for yourself, Jenkins,' announces Galton, raising the cocked pistol. Jenkins falls upon his glass, quaffing greedily. Evidently the tantalising proximity and abundance of the wine has thus far been a sore trial to him.

Galton fires. This time the ball is true; the glass shatters into a thousand shards. 'There. Now, that is more to the point,' crows the man, taking another glass to himself. Jenkins hands me his empty and nods in the direction of the statue. The pistols must now be reloaded but even so, I am at pains to get the thing done afore the next ball comes streaking down the garden.

And so it continues, Facey and me running back and forth, up and down the lawn, replacing the targets until both bottles are quite emptied and the dozen or so champagne saucers lie all about as so many tiny, glistening fragments.

Jenkins returns the pistols to their case along with the powder flask and ramrod.

'Now then, you men will recall your duty on the morrow, I hope?' announces Galton, slurring a trifle.

'We shall, sir. The shooting ground at Battersea Fields, first light, if'n you please.' I reply, knuckling my forehead.

I believe Galton's impetuousness at the trigger is his way of showing out, a demonstration of his facility with these deadly tools. And well he might, for though he has drunk off those two bottles, he missed the mark but twice. Certainly, I should not give much for Captain Squires' chances come the morning.

CHAPTER XVII

It is yet full dark when we arrive at Battersea Fields but we are scarcely strangers to guiding ourselves by the light of a moon, gibbous as it is. The ground hereabouts is marshy, being low and close to the river. Much of the acreage has been given over to shots, strips of land set aside for growing vegetables and, in particular, Battersea's succulent asparagus. There is lavender here too, cultivated for the flower girls of the metropolis. We catch its distinctive scent as our boots traverse the plots before striking the footpath which leads on to the Red House Tavern. In silence, we head down the private road, following it to the shooting ground, an enclosure bounded by a low yew hedge, ordinarily employed for more innocent pursuits, the potting of pigeons and suchlike. It is here that we spy the orange glow from a couple of bullseye lamps, signifying the presence of a waiting landau with closed hoods. One of the horses whinnies and stamps in the darkness as though in some way mindful of the coming encounter.

Facey and me settle ourselves on the ground over by the hedge. I bring out a few cuts of cold meat and bread wrapped in a kerchief, saved from last night's dinner at the Bolt-in-Tun. Facey produces a bottle of porter from one of his voluminous pockets and we make a tolerable breakfast whilst awaiting the dawn.

By the time our bottle is emptied a thin smudge of hazy light can be seen across the horizon, throwing the Red House into silhouette. At the same moment we hear sounds of a second carriage approaching. The carriage brakes and two men promptly emerge. I recognise the tall, upright figure of Galton. His companion is shorter and, even in the near dark, I observe that his form is lacking somewhat in the way of symmetry. The driver remains upon his perch, a hunched figure bundled in his voluminous coat.

Alerted by the arrival of the carriage, two figures now disembark the waiting landau. Squires and his companion, likewise a military man, judging by the cut of his garb.

The antagonists remain at a remove from one another whilst their seconds converge. There is an exchange of handshakes. Galton's man shakes with his left; I perceive on account of he is absent an arm.

The sun's arc peeps warily over the London skyline, soft light imparting a gradual clarity to the scene like the protracted raising of a theatre curtain. As the seconds converse in low voices, Galton peers about him and, catching sight of us, strides across. 'You men are present, I collect, and punctual. Commendable, most commendable.' He strokes his side whiskers, seemingly without a care in the world.

The seconds conclude their discussion. 'Gentlemen,' calls the military man, looking to Galton and Squires, 'might there yet be any possibility of an accommodation between you?'

'By no means,' replies Galton.

Squires merely shakes his head.

'In that case,' nods the military gent briskly, 'there is nothing for it but we must be about the business.' He addresses Galton in a formal, stentorian tone. 'Sir, I have the honour to be Captain John Akroyd of the 35th of Foot. Your friend, Mr Lambert, having been good enough to call upon my principal, has requested Captain the Honourable Lawrence Squires to appoint with you here at this hour. My principal, being the gentleman so called upon, has elected pistols, a single shot to be discharged from an agreed distance; such undertaking to be considered a sufficiency in providing satisfaction. Do you so concur?'

'Certainly,' agrees Galton in an offhand manner, as though he could not care one way or another.

'Well then, let us be about it.' Akroyd returns to his landau where he leans in the open door to collect a wooden casket very like the one brought out yesterday. 'Mantons, gentlemen, matched and cased,' he announces, before heading off through the small wicker gate leading into the shooting ground.

Galton follows, while his one-armed second bustles over to us. 'I take it you are the labouring men engaged by Mr Galton?'

'That we are, sir,' agrees Facey.

'I must tell you, your presence is somewhat irregular and so you may not enter the grounds alongside on us but must remain here, quite still. Do not call out nor interfere in any way. Is that understood?'

We nod. We neither of us have witnessed an affair of this sort before and are curious as to the manner of its unfolding.

'Any gate, you shall not have much longer to kick your heels,' advises Lambert. 'The matter will be decided one way or t'other in a few minutes. Now, should Mr Galton be brought down, you may approach. Indeed, you must do so without delay and convey him to our carriage. It is for that reason alone you have been engaged, since I might be of little assistance myself; you will, no doubt, have observed that I lack for a wing.'

'How came you to be so, sir?'

'With John Company back in '24. Took a ball in the elbow at Yangon. Nothing to be done, d'ye see? A smart young physician whipped it off at the shoulder easy as butter. No mortification, nor fever. But swift, damnably swift. Afore you can say, "knife". And that's the trick. Alacrity is all.'

'Understood, sir,' nods Facey obligingly.

Lambert, content that we have understood his stipulations, turns and hurries away to join those on the field. We give a civil nod to his coachman who remains impassive up there on the bench, evidently disinclined to converse.

Since, for the most part, our hedge is sufficiently low, we are able to observe the events with ease. A couple of heavy sabres, or hangers, have been thrust, point first, into the ground to mark out the distance. Galton and Squires stand away from one another, though in perfect unconscious reflection: hands behind their backs, in contemplation of the rising sun. No doubt each man seeking to convey an attitude of perfect complacency or, at the least, an absence of trepidation. Meanwhile, the seconds set about the loading and priming. Akroyd holds out the pistols while

Lambert, despite his missing limb, inserts powder, ball and wadding with laudable speed and dexterousness.

Once the preparation has been completed to the satisfaction of all parties, Akroyd retains the weapons as Lambert produces a silver coin from his pocket. The coin is flipped into the air and the two attendants inspect the outcome. It seems fate has decreed that Squires is to have first shot.

The principals select their pistols. Thus armed, they stride to their marks as indicated by the upright sabres while the two seconds walk sedately back in our direction, taking position but a few yards from our place at the hedge.

'You did not choose to bring a medico, Mr Lambert?' queries Captain Akroyd in a low but audible voice.

'We did not, sir.'

'No matter. Should events go against your friend, there is one to hand.'

'Indeed?'

'Hunkered down in my landau, prepared to assist after the fact but declining to witness an event which might lay the rest on us open to a criminal prosecution.'

'Understandable. Quite understandable.' Lambert produces a watch from his weskit pocket and checks the hour. 'I believe we might commence proceedings, Captain.'

'Gentlemen,' calls Akroyd. 'You are both content with arrangements?' The protagonists duly indicate their assent. 'Then you may proceed at your convenience.'

We all of us watch in profound silence as Squires slowly raises his pistol. Not ten paces from him Galton stands quite still, side-on, head held high. The man is a conceited, avaricious fellow, perhaps even a cold-blooded murderer, but none can say he is a poltroon.

Squires sights and pulls the trigger followed by the tiniest of delays as the flint strikes frizzen, igniting the priming powder. There is a loud report at the same instant that Galton's glossy beaver is plucked from his head as though by an invisible hand.

There is no perceptible reaction from either man: no disappointment on Squires' side, no sign of glee nor satisfaction from Galton. Galton's pistol remains at his side, pointing to the ground.

'By God, sir, your man means to delope,' hisses Akroyd.

'I doubt that, Captain. It ain't his way.'

It seems that Galton is only drawing out the moment, perhaps in the hope that Squires' resolution might crumble. If so, he must be disappointed. Squires remains impassive, evidencing a degree of fortitude similar to that of his opponent. Galton's arm now slowly ascends to the point of aim. Once again, there is the slightest of delays as he pulls the trigger. The pistol discharges, emitting a flash and a puff of smoke as the ball's impact takes Squires somewhere about the chest. He staggers back a pace before dropping heavily to the ground.

Akroyd turns to Lambert with a pained expression. 'I wonder, sir, might you be good enough to fetch our physician?'

'By all means, Captain.'

Akroyd hurries over to his man as Lambert strides briskly past us towards the hooded landau. Galton lets the pistol fall and stands for a moment, observing his handiwork.

From this distance it is impossible to see how severe the injury might be but Akroyd crouches over his friend, cradling his head and shoulders. For his part, Galton collects the errant hat and claps it back on his head. 'Obliged to you, Captain Akroyd,' he says, with a curt bow before striding from the field.

Having been rousted by Lambert, the elderly physician emerges from the landau toting a black leather portmanteau. He hastens through the gate, tipping his hat to Galton on the way.

Lambert returns to his own carriage, awaiting his victorious companion. 'Wish you joy of your success, Titus,' he calls out to the approaching Galton.

'It ain't all jam, Georgie,' grimaces Galton, removing his hat. He puts a hand up inside and pokes a finger out through the hole in the crown. 'That ball has done for my best beaver. Forty shillin' and all in tatters.'

'Still and all, I fear you may have done for Squires entirely.'

'Shame. The man owes me five hundred guineas, damned scrub.' Galton catches sight of us lurking by the hedge. 'You men may drink to my preservation.' He digs into pockets of his coat before coming up empty. 'Have you a shillin' or some such on you, Georgie?'

'Certainly, Titus.' Lambert tosses me a silver shilling. Most likely the very one employed to open the proceedings.

'It ain't a sov, but then your assistance was not required. So, 'tis a shillin' for naught but loafing and who should say fairer than that?'

'I should say a sovereign was pledged us regardless of outcome,' rumbles Facey, his one good eye narrowing. I believe he is still smarting from Galton's casual disregard for his life and limbs at yesterday's practice.

Galton glares at him. 'How dare you, fellow? You are impertinent.'

'That's as may be,' retorts Facey impassively, 'but it don't change the fact that you pledged to stump a sovereign.' Facey gives him a mirthless smile. 'Though I should be happy to have that blighted titfer of yourn and call it squares.'

Galton purses his lips. 'I take it you refer to my beaver in that wretched thieves' cant?'

'The very article, sir.'

Galton eyes him a moment longer before shrugging. 'You are a saucy wight, to be sure, and shall, no doubt, find yourself at a rope's end soon enough. But you shall not vex me. Not this morning of all mornings.' He removes his hat and shies it at Facey. 'I may never be seen in company with such a ravaged item and so you are welcome to it. Adorn yourself, by all means, and so ape your betters.'

'Very good in you, sir,' grins Facey, retrieving the item from the grass. He removes his battered old stovepipe and claps the new beaver on his head. It fits him remarkably well.

'Well now,' drawls Galton, 'I should welcome a stiffener or two, Georgie. What d'ye say?'

'A capital notion.' Lambert looks to the driver. 'The Oriental, if you please, Thomas.'

The man remains hunched on his bench like a bulky ancient statue, though I have no doubt he has eyed this morning's proceedings as avidly as we have. More so, perhaps, given his elevated view. 'Aye, Mr Lambert, sir,' he replies, touching the brim of his hat with the whip.

The pair climb back aboard and the carriage sets off, skilfully turning about in the narrow road.

Facey fusses with his new hat, adjusting the brim until it sits to his liking. 'A fair bargain, I should say. Ain't I elegant, Sammy?'

''Tis Beau Brummell come again, Facey, yet whilst you stand here primping, a gent yet lies upon the field, mayhap in peril of his life.'

'That ain't none of our concern. We was contracted to Galton and, when last I looked, he was quite able to see himself to his carriage.'

'You do not think we are under obligation to assist? For decency's sake.'

Facey gazes at me before shaking his head. 'You will do it whether I accompany you or no. You are a soft-hearted one, to be sure,' he sighs.

The pair of us hurry through the wicker gate into the shooting ground. Ahead, Squires still lies recumbent on the ground, the physician crouched over his motionless form, digging away at his chest with a set of steel retractors. Squires' fine red coat has been laid open and the linen shirt beneath is now all but entirely soaked, stained a reddish purple by an ocean of gore. A trail of blood oozes from the corner of his mouth, coating his fine whiskers.

At the sight of us Akroyd rises to his feet, urgently waving us over. 'You. A hand here, this instant,' he bawls. 'You are Galton's men, I collect?'

'We are no man's men,' growls Facey. 'And might choose to assist of our own preference were you to bid us civil.'

Akroyd, to his credit, looks somewhat abashed. 'The captain is in extremis, and mayhap I spoke sharp. You will forgive me in the circumstances, I'm sure.'

'We shall, sir,' I reply, 'and you shall tell us how we might serve.'

'The ball has lodged deep in the captain's chest and it seems our physician cannot operate without he has his table and full panoply of instruments and unguents. We must bear him away at all speed and there shall be five shilling for your assistance.'

'We'll take naught for our labours but do it out of decency's sake alone,' announces Facey, giving me a sly look.

The physician is far too elderly and decrepit to be of use in the matter, but betwixt the three on us we hoist the stricken man by the arms and legs and bear him swiftly to the landau. We lay Squires sprawled across the floor without troubling ourselves over his dignity or comfort since he is quite insensible. The physician settles himself upon the bench inside while Akroyd climbs up onto the driver's perch. It seems that he is a gent who prefers to manage his own conveyance and indeed, he whips up the horses and expertly steers the landau in a tight half-circle. He salutes us, touching the whip to the brim of his shako. 'My thanks. Gentlemen you may not be, but you are honourable men and I take this most kind in you.'

It is said that apparel oft proclaims the man and who am I to dispute it? As we stroll through St James's Park, passers-by smile and nod; there is even the odd tip of the hat. Certainly, such courtesies are not occasioned by our merits but on account of our outward appearance. Having swiftly returned to our Bolt-in-Tun for a change of clothing, we are as pink, glossy and trim as the vigorous application of razor, brush and clean water are capable of, tricked out in our new coats, fresh linens and clean, artfully tied neckcloths. In short, as fine a pair of swells as can be imagined, should one discount the sight of my old boots.

'A honourable man, Sammy. It ain't every day I am called that,' announces Facey with considerable complacency.

'Is it such a virtue though, this notion of honour? What kind of men are these that hold their lives so cheap as to risk all in the preservation of it?'

'There was virtue enough in the manner those men stood to a oncoming ball, aye, even Galton, who is a blackguardly fellow on the whole.'

'Rather for the maintenance of their reputation than out of any great virtue. And all in consequence of the mere tweaking of a snout. Amongst our kind such assault might be answered, perhaps with a little interest to account for the insult. But to take another's life for the yanking of a neb is beyond all justice.'

'I should not gladly endure such a provocation.'

'And would instantly repay with the mauleys, no doubt. Your foe might cop a mouse or some such but his life would not be forfeit.'

Facey considers. 'True enough. I am not accustomed to overly chastise.'

'Men such as these have so much, yet it seems to me that the more a man possesses, the less regard he has for it, that he would fling away all for a trifle.'

'These folk may not hold their place in society without they protect their reputations, Sammy.'

'They have twisted the principle into bloody-minded self-interest. And I thank the Lord that he has, in his wisdom, chose to make me a man of inferior class and one without such precious regard for a show of honour that I would stoop to such murderous barbarity for the preservation of it. I hold myself to be a man of some modest virtue, a decent enough cove by and large. But not honourable. Never call me a honourable man, Facey. I do not give a straw for honour if that be its bloody expression.'

'Sammy, I shall tell you what it is: I cannot rightly fathom a word you say with your virtues, principles and notions. It is all one to me. But it has put you out of sorts, which is what comes of overmuch cogitation and that ain't good for the health. Though I 'spect there ain't no help for it since you always was inclined to be a deepish file.'

By this time we are on Jermyn Street, and I spy the hanging shingle proclaiming the small but well-kept establishment beneath to be Bailey & Skinner, jewellers. The shopfront comprises twin sets of mullioned windows on either side of a black-panelled door. Like those of the jerryshop, the panes are entirely spotless and so, most easily discernible through such costly even glass, is a display of valuable-looking pieces arrayed on small velvet cushions. A huge blue diamond necklace forms the centrepiece.

Though scarcely topping it the gentry, having primped and put on our finery, our strategem is to pass for tolerably well-to-do commercial types. I make a last adjustment to my neckcloth and look to Facey. He grins, 'Never concern yourself, Sammy. I am the very model of gentility. Ain't I just?' He has scrubbed up tolerably well and, to be fair, even with that leather eye patch, looks almost respectable in his new coat and elegant beaver.

I lift the gleaming brass knocker and let it fall. The door is unbarred then opened a little way by a smiling, oldish cove in tail-coat and stirrup pantaloons. We both on us remove our hats. 'Good day, sir,' I say. 'Might we impose upon you to discuss a matter of business?'

The cove briefly inspects us and, satisfied that we do not have the look of prigs or palmers, ushers us inside. The place is light and airy, being white-walled with well-sanded floorboards, and the air has a pleasing aroma of charcoal and beeswax. There is a counter, but other than for the pieces in the windows, little else on overt display.

'A matter of business, you say, gents?' echoes the cove, taking his place at the counter. 'No imposition there. I am all for business, provided it be something in the line of precious stones and metals. I have the honour to be Barnabus Skinner, joint proprietor of Bailey and Skinner. "And what of Mr Bailey?" you ask. "There cannot be a Bailey and Skinner without there be a Mr Bailey". Never fear, Mr Bailey is in excellent health and right as a trivet. He is accustomed to remain in our workshop to the rear, where he daily performs prodigies of alchemy and artifice, leaving the privilege of securing patronage and commissions to my humble self.'

'Well, Mr Skinner, I must say your proviso fits my bill tolerably fine, since what I seek is by way of a gift for my wife-to-be. In expectation of my forthcoming nuptials.'

'Indeed? May I offer my felicitations?'

'Very good in you, sir.'

Skinner ducks behind his counter and emerges with a tray of rings. 'Now, sir, I believe a ring is most frequently expected in such circumstances and, it so happens that Bailey and Skinner, purveyors to the nobility of precious ornaments, are pre-eminent in the supplying of such felicitous articles. In short, you are in luck, sir. Luck, I say.'

'Alas, the ring is already spoke for, it being a family token passed down to me and so such trinkets, however virtuous, will not answer. Now, I shall tell you how it is. We are in the mercantile way, lately up from Portsmouth, and I had high hopes of securing a very particular piece, which might serve to wipe the eye of all comers within our small but select provincial society.'

'A singular item then, a nonpareil?'

'There you have it, sir. Something unique, perhaps. I have heard tell, even in the depths of Hampshire, of a ferroniere. At any rate, a facsimile of a most priceless gem, with which you had saw fit to grace your window not so very long past.'

'The Eye of Brahma, you mean?'

'I do, Mr Skinner. And should give a pretty penny for it for the sake of my nuptials.'

'Forgive me, gents, but I cannot oblige.'

'But we have come all the way from Portsmouth, sir.'

Facey produces a heavy purse, which he slaps down onto the counter. 'For his nuptials, sir,' he asserts. 'His nuptials.'

The cove remains expressionless. 'You may insist upon your nuptials as many times as you please, it don't change the circumstance one iota.'

'How so?'

'For a while Mr Bailey's fabrication, paste and pinchbeck though it was, made quite the sensation. Them folk who might never hope to have sight of the original were able to view our own modest copy in this very window and you would never credit the crowds that came to gawp. But time is the great enemy of novelty and wonder. In due course the lustre faded and appetite staled. The metropolitan public are fickle, gents, fickle. They must constantly have fresh curiosities to marvel at, and so you now behold in our window its successor, a copy of the famous French Blue. I own that after six months on display even the Blue is now beginning to falter a trifle in popularity and so I can let you have it for just ten guineas. Such uproar it shall stir in Hampshire, I assure you.'

'You are kind, sir, but I am set on the Eye of Brahma.'

'I no longer possess it, sir. Strange to say, had you but come a fortnight previous you might have had it from me and most welcome. Once the French Blue had replaced it in the window, it languished beneath our counter here, my wealthy patrons, knowing full well that it was but a pale imitation of the original, none were willing to give a price that might even cover its cost to make. And so, there it lay, gathering dust a twelve-month or more. And then—let me see now–' the jeweller inspects his ledger, 'then, only this Thursday last, a gent come along and would have naught but the Eye of Brahma. Five guineas he give me for it. And now, in such a short space, here you are with that very same urgent desire for a piece I imagined I might never be rid of. And if that ain't a rum turn I don't know what is.'

I lower my head, feigning considerable disappointment. 'I had my heart set on the Eye and should never wish to disappoint my intended.'

'She is a dairymaid, sir. A great ox of a girl with a fine complexion and only somewhat lacking in teeth,' adds Facey, to my great exasperation.

'It is irregular, I know,' I persist, 'but I wonder if there might be a way for me to meet with this buyer. I should be prepared to offer him double what he gave for it, nay, even treble.'

'I should be only too willing to oblige you, sir, only I have no notion of his identity. I may say he was a respectable-looking fellow, not a gentleman precisely, but respectable, most like in trade or the mercantile way, similar to yourselves, gents, though less inclined to converse.'

147

'Might he have been a steward by profession at all?' I ask.

'He might at that. A dignified, sober personage.'

'And a trifle short in stature, perhaps?'

'Neither short nor tall but of the middlin' sort.'

'Should you call him inclined to stoutness? Somewhat puffed like a toad?'

'Not in the least stout. Thinnish, if anything, and naught of the toad about him. If he were to put me in mind of any creetur I should most likely say heron, on account of he was somewhat stooped.'

'I see,' I say, a little taken aback.

'Now, sir. I cannot tempt you to a cameo brooch or a fine necklace wrought of South Sea pearls and considered the very latest thing?'

'Alas, no.'

'I see you are set on the Eye and Mr Bailey might certainly make another, 'twould only take a fortnight or two.'

'Too long, sir,' announces Facey. 'This wedding cannot be postponed without its cause becoming overtly evident, if you take my meaning.'

'Ah, I understand perfectly. Then I shall tell you what, if it should help, when I laid eyes on him, the cove in question did have something of a distinguishing mark, a great wen or carbuncle on the one side of his neb. I recall it quite distinctly now, since it put me so much in mind of a red garnet.'

'Thankee, Mr Skinner. You have been most considerate.'

'Known for it, I am, sir. And, should you find your man, that is to say, were it to transpire that I have, in my own small way, contributed to your forthcoming domestic bliss, I should never take it amiss were you to raise a glass to old Barnabus Skinner at your forthcoming festivities.'

'Certainly we shall be sure and raise a full bumper to you, sir.'

We quit the shop and head back in the direction of Dover Street, in all honesty, not a great deal better informed than we were before, and I am only too aware that there remains so little time to come upon a resolution. I had thought for a wild moment that it was Jenkins we had brought to earth, but evidently the anonymous purchaser is neither butler, footman, nor even Galton, but another fellow entirely, and now we must return to Rosamund with an ever more tangled web. These thoughts, in conjunction with the bloody events of the morning, have pressed upon my spirits. 'It pleases you then to make of me a lecherous seducer of toothless dairymaids?' I say, unable to curb my ill-humour.

Facey guffaws, quite unabashed. 'I imagined a little of colour might serve to egg the pudding, Sammy. In point of fact I had thought to throw in horsehair wig and gammy leg but reckoned that might be coming it a touch strong. Come now, Sammy Boy, there is little enough joy to be had in our present circumstances. I had thought to bring you some cheer.'

Facey is in the right of it, I was ever inclined to stand upon my fragile dignity and it makes me pleased to be displeased. I am become a humourless, priggish cove, which I should never desire to be. 'I am only concerned for the reputation of this poor dairymaid of yours,' I explain. 'I shall have to do the decent and tell her I am already spoke for.'

'No great loss on her part, I reckon,' grins Facey.

CHAPTER XVIII

A nd how did you rate His Majesty's levee, gents?'

'The customary collection of rogues and hangers-on, though Sailor Billy sends his best respects to you, Mr Standford,' I reply, as we remove our fine togs, being careful to place our hats, fine new coats and neckcloths on a shrouded table, well away from the dust and detritus of the workings.

Standford chuckles. Evidently the foreman has been hard at his labours, the wall behind him has been stripped of its old paper, the entire surface evenly covered with a coat of skim. True to his word, it is now impossible to detect where the chimney breast might once have been. 'It appears I am honoured to have the most dandified labouring men in the metropolis. A gold-headed cane apiece and I should have taken you for a brace of viscounts at the least. I almost dursn't ask for your assistance in the paper hanging.'

'Forgive us for our shameful neglect of you, Mr Standford. We have found ourselves twixt pillar and post all the morning.'

''Tis of no matter, Mr Samuel, and I suppose there may be some advantage to it, since should the work not be to my liking I shall have none else to blame but my ownself.'

'A most sensible philosophy,' agrees Facey, just as Nellie scuttles in through the double doors. She hurries through the anteroom towards us with her customary expression of startlement and makes a brief bob to Standford. 'Your navvies is sent for, sir,' she announces breathlessly.

'Not myself?'

'Never you, sir, but these pair of labouring men, if you please. Mrs Parkes desires to see them without delay in the scullery.'

We descend two floors by the rear stairs and enter the scullery behind Nellie where we find Mrs Parkes and Mrs Stride awaiting us. Jenkins is seated at the table with glass and brandy decanter to hand. Mrs Stride appears apprehensive and there is a severe expression on Mrs Parkes' face. I wonder briefly if we have done aught to reveal ourselves. 'Thank you, Nellie,' says Mrs Parkes brusquely, 'and let me not keep you from your duties.'

Nellie reluctantly turns and heads slowly back towards the backstairs, evidently drawing out her progress in the hopes of catching some juicy tidbit.

'Mr Jenkins informs me that you men were present at a certain infamous event this morning, having been so engaged by Mr Galton,' announces Mrs Parkes. 'Since the matter touches this household I should very much like to know precisely what occurred, if you please.' She indicates the table. 'Sit, and take refreshment should you be so inclined.'

Facey and me seat ourselves opposite to Mr Jenkins. 'There is plum cake, gents,' advises Mrs Stride, 'and small beer.'

'I should prefer porter,' declares Facey, not in the slightest abashed. Mrs Parkes gives him a look of disapproval and tuts.

'It so happens I do have a little of porter beer put by for the fortifying properties in it,' says Mrs Stride, giving Facey a brief wink.

'By all means, let the fellow have his porter for the Lord's sake,' grumbles Jenkins.

'Well, sirs?' insists Mrs Parkes, as Mrs Stride produces a black bottle from her cupboard and pours out a couple of generous mugs.

'Thankee, mum,' says Facey, emptying his draught in one, which Mrs Stride refills on the instant. 'We was present first light at Battersea Fields in accordance with Mr Galton's instructions, where he was waited upon by Captain Squires to resolve an affair of honour.'

'This much we know. And how did the affair conclude?'

'Captain Squires was brought down by a ball in the chest. I cannot speak to his condition.'

'And know you what caused the quarrel?'

'I believe it was aught to do with letters, Mum,' I say, 'that was in possession of Mr Galton.'

'I see,' nods Mrs Parkes. 'Here is the sorry end to a squalid chapter, Mr Jenkins. The wages of sin is surely death.'

'So it is often said,' nods Jenkins gravely.

'And what of Mr Galton?'

'Untouched, Mum, and right as a trivet.'

Mrs Parkes sniffs. 'Would that it were otherwise.'

'Really, Mrs Parkes,' grunts Jenkins, refilling his glass from a nearby decanter.

'My thanks to you men, I shall not impose any further on your time. You may remain and finish your refreshments before returning to...' Mrs Parkes' instruction is interrupted by a violent hammering at the front door on the floor above us, followed by the sound of raised voices.

Jenkins drains the contents of his glass and slowly hauls himself to his feet. 'No rest for the wicked, I fear.' He makes his unsteady way over to the staircase and all but collides with Nellie in her headlong panicked descent. The young girl stands there speechless, wringing her hands, staring wildly.

'What ails you, girl?' snaps Mrs Parkes.

'The gentleman is here, what is to say, Mr Galton. He will not suffer to wait in none of the upstairs rooms; I believe he may be the worse for drink.'

'The worse for drink, is it?' roars Galton, slowly descending the stairs, one hand to the bannister, the other clasping his hat and cane. 'I rather think I am the better for it.'

Nellie scuttles away to cower behind the stolid figure of Mrs Stride as Galton advances into the scullery. Other than for the hat, which is a fine silk D'Orsay, he wears the attire of this morning, though now somewhat dishevelled.

'Mr Galton, how may I be of service?' bows Jenkins.

'I am not come to exchange words with you, Jenkins, but with Mrs Parkes here.'

'Indeed, sir, but might I suggest you should be more comfortable in the morning room?'

'By no means, Mr Jenkins. And where is my nephew, if you please?' Galton brusquely waves aside the butler.

'He is currently engaged in the library with his governess and not to be disturbed,' announces Mrs Parkes. 'I do not, in any case, believe you to be in suitable condition for his company, sir.'

'Your opinion is of no account. I will see my nephew when and in what condition I please; you shall not succeed in your machinations, madam.'

'I cannot pretend to know what you mean, Mr Galton.'

Galton places his hat and cane upon Mrs Stride's butcher's block, reaches into the pocket of his coat and produces a letter, which he brandishes in a rage. 'I speak of this, Mrs Parkes, received just now at my club. A blackguardly missive from that Haverford creature. No doubt sent at your behest.'

The rest of us look on in silence. Mrs Parkes remains with her arms crossed and returns Galton's look of fury with a penetrating gaze. 'It is true that I have been to visit with Mr Haverford, as I warned you I would, in view of your previous incursions. That note is none of my words; I am not, after all, intimate with the finer points of the law, but I own I have an inkling of its contents. In short, Mr Haverford insists you have no right to trespass beneath this roof. Indeed, it appears you have no rights at all in the matter of the Belmont estate.'

'The estate is entailed to me and I will have what is mine,' bellows Galton.

'You are mistaken, Mr Galton. Although Mr Haverford acknowledges that you were named in the late William Belmont's will, there is no fee tail, only the remote possibility of inheritance upon the demise of the current heir. I understand that such a bequest may be altered when young William Belmont reaches the age of majority.'

'I am the boy's only living relative and so master of this house in all but name, Mrs Parkes.'

'Young William Belmont is master of this house and all it contains under the charge of Mr Haverford. That is the law, sir.'

'I shall settle that soon enough; I intend to make an application to Chancery this very day for guardianship. I am the boy's blood, forsooth.'

Mrs Parkes nods, well knowing that she has had the better of the disagreement. 'That is your prerogative, Mr Galton. In the meantime, it is not fitting for you to be here amongst us in the scullery. Should you wish to see your nephew, I may not interfere, but would ask that you wait in the morning room, as is seemly, while the boy concludes his learning.'

'Come, sir,' says Jenkins, indicating the stairs. 'Might I see to some refreshment while you wait?'

Galton flings the crumpled note at Mrs Parkes, his face flushed and suffused with hatred. 'You think to turn me out like some tinker? You shall do no such thing. It is you who are dismissed and shall quit this house this instant without so much as a character.'

'Those words carry no weight, sir. At this time, the proper regulation of this household falls to Mr Haverford and he alone.'

Galton advances. I would swear he is at the point of laying hands on the woman when Facey very deliberately sets his mug down on the table, rises to his feet and places himself in the man's path. Though the two of them are of equal height, Facey is the broader by far. 'Sir, you have been asked to remove yourself and, seeing as you is a gent, ought comply whether or no you are in the right of it.'

Galton gazes at him with a hazy, perplexed expression as though suddenly met with a talking dog. 'I know you,' he declares, 'the labouring man. What the devil d'ye mean by addressing me so?'

Facey sighs heavily, 'I have addressed you respectful enough, Mr Galton, and should have thought you had had sufficient quarrel for one day.'

Galton eyes him coldly. 'I do not quarrel with you, you scoundrel; I cannot, since you are not my equal, nor nothing like. You are insolent and will pay for it. I swear I shall have you horsewhipped.'

'You must do as you see fit, sir,' replies Facey, with a small, ironic bow.

'Very well,' Galton briskly retrieves his hat and cane, 'I see there is no profit in remaining, though I shall be sure to return tomorrow for the sake of my nephew. Do not think to frustrate me in this, Mrs Parkes.'

'I shall not, sir. I have already said as much.'

We watch in silence as Galton stomps back up the stairs, the anguished Jenkins at his heels. Facey returns to his seat as little Nellie peers out from behind Mrs Stride. 'Lord, I had thought we was all to be murthered where we stood, Mrs Parkes.'

'Nonsense, girl,' snaps Mrs Parkes. 'The man was drunk and raving. An odious spectacle to be sure, but scarce one of mortal danger.' Despite her assurance she is white-faced, trembling faintly as she labours to master her inner turmoil.

Mrs Stride hastens to fill Facey's empty mug. 'Were it not for Mr Facey I imagined that Galton might strike you down, such was his intemperance, Mrs Parkes.'

'Tush, Mrs Stride. Such wild exaggeration.' She eyes Facey with disapproval. 'Mister Facey is it? I must inform you that it is none of your place to interfere in matters of this house. You will kindly devote your attentions entirely to your labour for Mr Standford and to that alone.'

Facey shrugs. 'As you wish, Mum.'

'Mrs Stride, I shall withdraw to my chambers and would ask only that a plain mutton broth be brought me around supper time, if you please.'

'Certainly, Mrs Parkes,' replies the cook with a bob.

Mrs Parkes turns and heads away along the narrow passage to her rooms. When she has quite disappeared Mrs Stride pours the remainder of the porter for herself and Nellie. The two of them join us at the table. 'Such doings,' sighs Mrs Stride, shaking her head before gazing fondly at Facey. 'There's gratitude for you. I, for one, am mindful of your gallant intercession, Mr Facey, even if certain other parties are not.'

'I was put directly in mind of a great fierce Grizzled Bear what I seen one time at the Royal Menangerary,' pipes up Nellie, emboldened by the porter.

'Not a fearsome lion at all?' smiles Mrs Stride.

'No, mum, 'twas a oldish bear. Which his name, if I recollect, was Martin.'

CHAPTER XIX

On account of his height, Facey has been charged to set himself at the apex of the folding steps. He hoists the upper edge of our patterned paper to the line of the ceiling while I crouch on the floor below guiding the lower edge to the skirting board. As the pasted strip attaches itself to the wall, Standford applies a soft brush over all, ensuring that we leave no unseemly bumps or imperfections. It is tedious, back-breaking work and, though Standford is pleased to finally have a little worthwhile assistance, I am all at sixes and sevens, impatient for sign of Rosamund.

At length, the paste bucket stands empty and, while Standford busies himself in the preparing of a fresh batch, Facey and me settle ourselves upon the trestle for a breather. I take the opportunity to raise a matter which has lately occurred to me. 'I do not pretend to understand the intricacies of the law, but it seems that Galton has some claim to the Belmont estate.'

'You are a quick study, Sammy,' grins Facey. 'The man has scarcely mentioned it…on no more than, say, a hundred occasions.'

'He is most insistent on his rights: these fees, tails and suchlike, and you have seen with your own eyes his cold and ruthless nature.'

'I have and cannot say I like him the better for it. What of it?'

'All that stands in his way is that young and friendless boy. You do not think he means him harm?'

Facey runs a hand through his hair, in cogitation before nodding slowly. 'I would not put it past such a man, but the lad is not entirely without confederates. Your own good wife stands picket for one, and you will not take it amiss when I tell you, I rate her a most formidable obstacle.'

'She is, at that.'

'And never forget the ogress Parkes who has made it her business to frustrate Galton's machinations at every turn. No, there are too many sharp eyes on the fellow and, though a vicious enough brute, I do not take him for a complete fool.'

'I daresay you are in the right of it,' I concur.

Facey grunts with displeasure. I look up to find a grinning Standford bustling towards us with a full pail of fresh paste.

It is early afternoon by the time my wife appears in the anteroom carrying a sheaf of music sheets. With a nod to the three of us she settles herself at the piano, lifts away the dustsheet and arranges her sheets upon the music rack. I mutter a brief apology to Standford and hasten to her side.

'There is a little time whilst William is about his letters,' she whispers, before opening the keylid and settling her fine long fingers across the keys. 'First, come stand at my shoulder to make a show of turning the music sheets should Mrs Parkes or Jenkins appear. Now, what news, my love?'

Rosamund begins to play softly as we conduct a murmured conversation which, for the most part, consists of my recollection of this day's events. When I am done, Rosamund continues the piece, taking her time to consider all that I have recounted.

'Mr Beethoven's pianoforte sonata number Fourteen,' she informs me, 'which I have had by heart since I was a girl. It is has been such an age since I was able to play and it seems these clumsy fingers of mine no longer quite answer.'

'It is the most beautiful thing I have ever heard,' I say.

'Pish, Sammy,' she replies, though she smiles up at me.

'No, no, no,' bellows Standford from the far side of the room. 'It won't do at all. 'Tis all crookeder than a tinker's cudgel and shall have to be reset.'

'I ain't a ape, Mr Standford, to be swinging from the ceiling the entire long day,' retorts Facey.

'True enough,' concedes the foreman, 'and I find I could use a smoke, Mr Facey. Shall we first remove this cock-eyed strip and perhaps come again at the section after we have took a spell?'

'You will hear no argument from me on that account,' announces Facey, as he climbs down from the steps.

The pair set to removing the kinked strip of wallpaper, which Standford carefully lays out on the floor and assesses. 'Spoiled for this here work, Mr Facey. But at a shocking quantity of shillings per foot such costly paper should on no account go to waste. When it dries I shall roll it up again and take it home to apply to my own parlour, which is already half-papered with such a motley collection of cast-offs as to resemble a harlequinade. Mrs Standford don't make no objection though, reckoning it exceeding genteel.'

'A working man must have his perquisites,' agrees Facey more affably, as the pair make ready for their respective harbours.

'We leave you for a time that you might enjoy your music in peace, Miss,' announces Standford, respectfully doffing his paper hat as he passes. For his part, Facey grins cheerfully, doubtless heading for the scullery and the kindly ministrations of the cook.

For a while Rosamund continues to play, still cogitating, until of a sudden her fingers cease in the middle of a phrase and she gazes up at me with a look of great penetration. 'You are certain your Mr Skinner specified "Thursday"?'

'I took the utmost care to recall each and every detail. Mr Skinner was most insistent on the day of the transaction and had it writ down in his ledger.'

'Then you will recall Haverford's words on the matter of Edith Belmont?'

'I own, I do not, my love.'

'"Died on Wednesday, buried on Friday." His very words. You will remark from this that the facsimile was purchased the day following Edith Belmont's demise and not before.'

'Certainly,' I say. I had remarked no such thing but have no wish to appear the dunderhead. 'The day after. Just so.' Even still, I cannot feature the direction of my wife's thoughts here.

'Curious, is it not, that this facsimile was not purchased in advance of the murder?'

'I cannot see how that signifies.'

'It does not strike you as the action of one seeking to profit through opportunity rather than by forethought and design?'

'Now that I think on it.' I nod sagely, not the slightest bit wiser.

'Perhaps then the two events are not so connected as we thought. I had imagined a single prime mover, their scheme planned from the outset, the poisoning carried out solely for possession of the gemstone. Now I wonder if these acts of murder and theft might be separate of motive and so undertaken by two entirely different parties. Each unknowing of the other.'

'And where should such conjecture lead?'

'Let us, for the moment, suppose it is Galton accountable for the death of Edith Belmont.'

'Galton is a cold, bloody-minded cove. Not above blackmail and homicide to achieve his ends.'

Rosamund nods. 'All can see that Galton is eager to lay hands on the wealth that remains attached to the Belmont estate and the removal of Edith Belmont has cleared the path. His route now easier by far, through an unworldly child's good graces. Tomorrow, he takes William riding on the Row in company with him. In time, he expects to achieve full guardianship under the law.'

'That don't preclude him wanting the stone along of all else.'

'It does not,' concedes Rosamund, 'though why, after he had achieved those loftier ends, take such unwarranted risk to possess it?'

'Then who other?'

'Someone for whom the opportunity would have been far greater and the risk a deal less. It is Mr Haverford I speak of.'

'But Haverford is a man of the law.'

Rosamund grimaces. 'And they such paragons of probity? Many and many attorneys would put their own kin to the Marshalsea if there was but a ha'penny profit in it. It was those grasping men of law that destroyed my pa and all that he had built with their writs and affadavits. No, my love, I cannot imagine Haverford to be less inclined to leap at the main chance than any other. Think on it for a moment. Who was it knew of Edith Belmont's wishes to be interred with her finery? Indeed, it was Haverford's duty to attest she be accompanied by Eye of Brahma on her final journey. I do not say he knew of the poisoning, indeed, most likely he did not, believing, as all others, that it was the work of the Blue Death. But is it not conceivable that he sent some fellow to purchase the facsimile on his behalf, the day after he had news of her demise, thinking to make a substitution afore the casket was sealed? You will own that the facsimile was of sufficient quality to convince any who might have been present. This fellow with the wen, who your Mr Skinner described as a personage of sober, respectable appearance, might he not have been a lawyer's clerk?'

'He might at that,' I concede. It appears she has smoked it, and it is a wonder to me how she is able to do this. Somewhat like fashioning a quilt, whereby the smallest, most inconsequential scraps may be stitched together to make a worthy whole. 'We must look to Haverford then. Facey and me shall make entry to his chambers this very night, being sure to leave no stone unturned.'

'I wonder what is become of my mild and temperate schoolmaster. You are a bull at a gate, Sammy. Should you be apprehended it is a capital crime without question.'

'I am mindful that our time is all but expired; tomorrow we must produce the article or answer for it. Those pair are neither patient nor merciful men and so surely such desperate measures are called for?'

My wife places her fingers back at the keys and resumes her soft playing. 'You have such faith in me, Sammy. But, alas, I am no oracle. What I have spoke out loud is, for the moment, all musing and rumination, a way of putting my thoughts in order, and it may be that I defame Haverford. Any gate, I would not see you taken up and hanged for a mere supposition, not when a good many hours yet remain; sufficient time, perhaps, to discover this heron sort of fellow with the wen. He is the link to whomsoever now possesses the true Eye, light upon him and our work is all but done. You shall attend your Pimlott and Chuffington at the appointed time, if not in possession of the article, then at the least with the certain knowledge of how it may be found.'

We have used a deal of our precious time and boot leather traipsing about the taverns of Holborn, and it is early evening when Facey and me commence inquiries at The Harrow of Chancery Lane. The place has long been popular with men of the legal trade, being so conveniently positioned between Lincoln's Inn and the Temples.

Though there are manifold blemishes and enflamed nebs aplenty amongst the assembled, there is nary sign of a wen. Deep in conversation by the window are a couple of likely-looking clerks sharing a mug of something, young with grimy collars and black coats all but out at the elbows. Facey plants a shilling piece on the scarred wooden bench between them. 'Gents, what will you take?'

The bolder of the pair eyes Facey with suspicion. 'We do not know you, sir.'

'I seek information regarding a certain party, nothing more.'

'Sir, you ask the one thing we possess in abundance and we should never be averse to another wet, this here being the most indifferent Old Tom. A quarter pint 'twixt the two on us all we can stretch to, even going snacks.'

Facey nods his approval, removing his hand from the coin whereupon the piece is instantly swept off the table by the young clerk.

'We seek a cove with a great wen on his neb, likely a lawyer's man of the older sort,' I say. 'A stooped fellow, holding himself somewhat like a heron.'

The clerk considers for a moment. 'Well, sirs, us ink-pushers are not perhaps the prettiest of professions and certainly you will find all manner of unsightly boils and pustules amongst men of the Inns, but I cannot bring to mind the fellow you describe.'

'There is Henstock of Red Lion Court with a most prodigious carbuncle on his neck that would make you cat up at the sight of it,' announces his companion, slurring a little.

'He is but three and twenty with naught of the heron about him; more of a goose I should say.' Our clerk shakes his head regretfully. 'Alas, I cannot recall ever seeing such a fellow. We are to be found here most evenings, sir, and should know him had he ever showed his dial. You might try the Cock Tavern of Fleet Street, where there is also oftentimes to be found a sprinkling of clerks from the Temples. Forgive us, sirs, that we cannot serve you better and hope you do not intend to redact your shilling in consequence.'

'I do not,' says Facey.

'Then the two on us shall drink to your happy outcome, gents, in something with a mort less of the turpentine about it.'

It is coming on for night as we head down Fleet Street, though the lamplighters are about, as many of the gas lamps hereabouts have already been lit. 'Shadows,' murmurs Facey out the side of his mouth as we close on the Cock Tavern.

'You are certain?'

'Not a doubt of it. Three on 'em, dogging us since we left Dover Street, awaiting full dark most like.'

Time was I should never have missed a tail in the London streets. Back when we were at the resurrection game, there were any number of reasons to be wary of our backs: bobbies, watchmen, rival crews, dippers, bug-hunters and so forth. Now it seems, I am grown a trifle too complacent for my own welfare. I take out my fogle, appearing to fumble with it and allow it drop to the pavement. As I turn, crouching to retrieve it, I spy a pair of obvious bruisers a dozen or so yards back. A few paces ahead of them is a spindly, beaky cove in a bottle-green coat, grimy neckerchief and battered turf hat; no doubt the principal.

We had set out direct from Dover Street and these fine new coats and neckcloths of ours have, I imagine, given us the appearance of being worthy marks. 'You are in the right of it,' I agree, catching up with Facey, 'though none are known to us. I warrant they take us for a couple of pigeons.'

'No doubt we shall see what they are about soon enough,' grunts Facey, pushing through the tavern doors. 'Since we are here, I could stand a nip of something, Sammy.'

'I should not refuse a bracer myself.'

Facey shoves his way through to the counter and raps a heavy coin on the scarred oak. 'Hoy there, landlord, two of rum if you please,' he bellows. Our drinks are readied and handed across in a trice despite the press of coves at the bench likewise clamouring for a fill.

'Why Mr Facey, I remarked your voice. Though that is no especial feat since 'twas likely heard all the way from Southwark.'

Facey grins and takes the proffered hand. 'Bill Blackwell, how d'ye do now?'

At one time Blackwell was a carter running corpses to St Barts, mainly for our rivals, Mutton and Teeth, though on occasion, did run a few for us. Always a straight arrow and never one to quibble over a price. 'Well enough, Mr Facey. And here is Mr Samuel Samuel an' all,' he says, giving my hand a shake. 'It does a heart good to see old friends prosper.'

'Never be deceived by the clouts, Blackwell, we ain't turned swells, nor nothing like it,' advises Facey.

'Merely topping it the nobs over Mayfair way, on account of a little business,' I explain.

'Say no more,' says Blackwell, tapping his nose. 'Though you will not take it amiss if I remark on the quality of your lid, Mr Facey, which it is a twenty or thirty shillin' beaver, if a penny, notwithstanding the trifling holes fore an' aft.'

'Thankee kindly, Bill.' Facey adjusts the hat in question to a more rakish angle. 'I admit, I ain't 'zactly unpleased with the article.'

'You will have a notion that clouts, the buyin' and sellin' of, is Bill Blackwell's game now, gents. I give up with the hauling of karkers a while back. Since the new act of parlingment there ain't sufficient profit in it. These days the cart is for the carrying of old clo' and, on the whole, I kip a good deal easier for it. Should you ever desire to turn that beaver or them fine coats into readies, you will keep Billy Blackwell in mind I'm sure.'

'We shall, Bill. Though I doubt it will come to that.'

'No,' nods Blackwell sagely, 'You ever was too downy a pair to end on your uppers. Speakin' of which, what is it brings you to these parts? Surely you ain't still at the game?'

'Not exactly, Bill,' I say. 'But tell me, would this be your patch hereabouts?'

'It would, Mr Samuel.' Blackwell waves an arm, indicating the throng: a poorly attired, unappetising lot, to be sure. 'You would not think it to look on 'em but there is profit in these coves.'

'How so?'

'They are in the main what you might call the less wholesome sorts at the edges of the attorneys' profession, by which I mean clerks, writ-servers, dunners, straw men and the like. For ten shillin' you may have one of these gladly bear false witness 'gainst the pope hisself in any court of the land, Mr Samuel. For my part, I have only to stand the price of a wet to be notified of a debtor's writ. Assumin' the party concerned do not choose to skedaddle, they must have ready cash to settle, else it is the Marshalsea or the King's Bench for them. You will scarcely credit what precious articles might be offered in return for a few guineas on the nail, though, to be sure, my own dealings are more modest and seldom go further than the purchase of a few good coats, beavers, top boots, a watch or two and fancy weskits at knock-down prices.' Blackwell pauses only to take a good pull at his tankard. 'In course, you might think me a poor sort of fellow to profit from the misfortune of others, but only consider how many of those debtors have themselves preyed for years upon the goodwill and credit of our honest tradesmen. How many milliners, boot-makers and the like have been put to the poor-house along with their families on account of these men who live high on the hog and keep their own carriages whilst dodging their tailors' bills?'

'Never fear, Billy, it ain't hardly for Sammy and me to judge a man for the manner in which he earns his crust,' says Facey, draining his rum with perfect complaisance.

'From what you tell us you must surely be acquainted with a good number of these clerks?'

'Many and many, Mr Samuel.'

While Blackwell has been jawing I notice that the spindly cove has now entered the tavern and has been circumspectly elbowing his way through the drinkers, all the while edging closer towards us. 'Then perhaps you will know of a cove, tolerably respectable and of middle years with a great wen on his neb. Stooped like a heron and likely connected to the law; attorney perhaps, clerk, or some species of factotum?'

Blackwell considers for a moment, taking another sup of his ale for inspiration before finally shaking his head. 'I cannot feature him, gents, though it grieves me so say so.'

'William Blackwell, what's afoot?' We are interrupted by the spindly cove who takes a pace towards us, tipping his turf hat. 'Thomas Tickner, gents. Though I am known to all from here to Bermondsey as Audacious Tom. At your service.'

'You ain't welcome here, Tickner,' growls Blackwell.

'Now, now, William, that is shockin' unfriendly. Any gate, it ain't for you to say. I have took the liberty of imposing upon your conwerse since I could not help but catch the description what these gents just threw out. And it so happens that I am acquainted with the wery man in question.'

'Is that so now?' Facey narrows his one good eye.

'It is, sir. Shocking great furuncle on the tip of his razzo, carries hisself like a bent nail. What's more, the gent in question keeps chambers not fifty yards from this wery tavern. Should you desire it, I shall lead you to him this instant.'

'And what might you have for that service, Tom?'

'Audacious Tom, if you please. There are a great many Toms hereabouts, to be sure, nor there is but one Audacious Tom, distigwitched as I am by daring and enterprise. I shall take naught for the service, sir, but your good opinion of me.'

'Audacious Tom it is then. I accept your offer and take it most kind in you,' announces Facey, handing me his empty tumbler.

I own I have never been much of an asset in a set-to but, as I steel myself to accompany him, Facey places a restraining hand on my shoulder. 'Never trouble yourself, Sammy. I shall be back afore you finish your wet.' He grins wolfishly as the two of them shove their way back through the press of drinkers towards the tavern doors.

Blackwell frowns. 'That cove ain't to be trusted, Sammy, he is a braggart and a fundament and ain't known to none but himself as Audacious Tom.'

'Never fret, Bill. Him and two other coves have been at our backs since Mayfair, it is only that Mr Facey is curious as to their purpose.'

'Ah,' nods Bill sagely, 'then I should not wish to be in their shoes about now.'

We sup in companionable silence for only a few short minutes before Facey reappears through the tavern doors wiping his hands on Tickner's grubby neckerchief to keep the blood from his fine clouts. He strides towards us, the throng parting easily, rightly sensing an abiding air of menace about him.

'Galton's doing,' he announces, reaching for my remaining rum and draining it. 'This Tom fellow and a couple of bruisers was set to learn me my place, by all accounts.'

'You are not too knocked about, I hope?' asks Blackwell, indicating the bloody streaks on Facey's hands.

Facey shrugs. 'The claret ain't mine, Bill. Once out upon the street them bruisers sidle up with cudgels at the ready and Tickner informs me that what I am about to receive comes courtesy of a gent by name of Titus Galton. I tell you, gents, I cannot abide a cove what sets others to do his dirty work.'

'Surely no man could settle with three such in so short a time?' says Blackwell .

'Nor did I, Bill. A gentle love-tap for your Tom Tickner and him squawkin' worser'n a colicky babe was all it took to send them bruisers skedaddling, cudgels an' all,' chuckles Facey. 'Suffice to say, he knows naught of who we seek. Audacious Tom, my arse. Henceforth I 'spect he will be known by all from here to Bermondsey as Crook-Neb Tom.'

We are sharp set when we quit the Cock Tavern and, though no wiser for all our inquiries, elect to repair to the Bolt-in-Tun for our suppers, for it is but a short walk along Fleet Street to our inn.

As we turn into the coachyard we see by the light of the lamps atop the entrance that a small but noisy gathering has assembled outside. A determined lad of about ten years stands protectively before a curious contraption, fending off the crowd. 'Garn, take your grubby paws from the Draisienne lest you lose a finger to the workings.'

On closer inspection, I perceive that it is a wheeled device fashioned from some heavy wood with a leather seat and a set of bowed handles to the front. It stands upright, leaning against the tavern wall.

'An infernal engine is what it is and must be destroyed with fire entirely. You succour the devil's work, boy,' bawls a psalter-brandishing codger through spittle-flecked lips, no doubt one of the many half-cracked ranters so common to the London streets.

'Clamp your cave, you blue-light misanthrope. That there be a glorious example of man's artifice and ingenuity,' retorts a ruddy-faced porter, clasping a leather tankard.

'Hear him,' agrees another.

'True, sir. Very true,' pipes the lad. ''Tis the wonder of the age and since you are assembled for a ogle might consider it only right and fair to pay me a penny for the spectacle.'

'What do it do, younker?' asks a large woman of middle years in a wilting bonnet.

'Why, it transports my guv'nor on its back like a pony, being as it is also knowed as the Dandy Horse, only it don't shit on the cobbles nor require feedin' regular.'

A few in the crowd chuckle appreciatively and a farthing or two is dropped into the lad's eager hands.

'Ain't progress a fine thing,' announces Facey as we pass.

It seems it is become a night for old acquaintants. No sooner have we entered the ordinary than we clap eyes on our old friend, Lieutenant Trench. He sits alone at a trestle table near the fire, set before him a lighted candle, bottle and three glasses. At the sight of us he rises and makes a leg. 'Mr Facey, Mr Samuel. How d'ye do?'

We remove our hats and make our bows, since Trench is a well-bred sort and, though inclined to be stiff, a good-hearted cove.

'Come, join me, if you will,' he indicates the vacant stools.

'What chance, Lieutenant Trench?' says Facey, settling himself.

'Why, none, Mr Facey,' replies Trench filling the glasses with a deep ruby wine. 'I have been waiting on you gents, which is how come I have a good bottle already set by. But first, your health.' We raise our glasses. Trench sips his wine appreciatively. 'Tolerable, tolerable for a tavern Madeira. No, gents, it is not by chance that I am here but in consequence of my work, since I carry a message for Mr Samuel Samuel.' Trench digs into his coat pocket for a folded note, sealed with a wafer. 'A duty I must discharge afore all else,' he announces, handing it to me. I instantly recognise the hand as being that of my wife.

'How is it you come to know of our whereabouts, Lieutenant?'

'You will have observed on your entrance, I make no doubt, the machine in the courtyard?'

'Certainly, it has made quite the stir.'

'Then you have beheld the future, gents. It is my own conveyance and designed to transport a man at great speed and efficiency across the thoroughfares of the metropolis. I have purchased two more just like for the advancement of my messenger service. Mounted upon a velocipede my lads and me can outrun the wind.'

'Velocipede, is it?' repeats Facey, savouring the word.

'More properly a Draisienne, named for its inventor, but known to most as the Dandy Horse. Each afternoon I climb aboard and take a run of the circuit, convening with my young messengers and ticket porters at their stands to ensure all is in order and no dire mischance has befallen.'

'You were ever solicitous of your charges, Lieutenant,' I say, quickly unsealing my note.

'Thankee, Mr Samuel. Now, the lad assigned the Mayfair beat is newish to the area so it falls to me to ensure that he is mindful of the quickest and safest routes. On consideration of his destinations, what do I find amongst his clutch of messages but a sealed note for a Mr Samuel Samuel to be delivered to the Bolt-in-Tun at Fleet Street? Trench, I say to myself, that ain't so commonplace a name that it cannot but belong to your old friend, who you have not seen in an age and should enjoy a bottle with, alongside Mr Facey, for whom you have the greatest respect and affection.'

Facey raises his glass in acknowledgement.

'So, I resolved to deliver this particular message by my own hand and thus take two birds with the same stone as it were: share a bottle of tolerable Madeira with old friends and provide Mr Samuel Samuel with a fine story to relate to his grandchildren that you was amongst the very first to have a message brung, lickety-split, by means of velocipede.' Trench half raises his glass to us before checking himself. 'Ah, come, what a lackwit I am. Forgive me, Mr Samuel. I have been showing away with my Dandy Horses and so prating and flapping my gums as to deprive you of the merest moment to peruse that very note, which has served to bring us together.'

'No matter, Lieutenant Trench, but shall you excuse me, I will certainly now read its contents.'

I flatten out the paper and, though Rosamund writes in a fine, clear hand, set it closer to the light of the candle.

'And what of that young rascal, Pure John?' Trench inquires of Facey. Before we carried him away to Portsmouth with us, young John was one of Trench's messenger boys and, though he was impudent and a scallawag, Trench was always fond of him. Across the table, Facey shoots me a glance. I return the tiniest shake of the head, not through any lack of trust but because, should he be informed of the lad's predicament, the Lieutenant would surely insist on some courageous but foolhardy attempt at rescue. He is one of the few entirely upright, honest coves of our acquaintance and so inhabits a much different world to the one Facey and me are accustomed to, and I should never wish him to come to the attentions of that vile pair, Pimlott and Chuffington.

'The lad thrives 'mongst the crew of the brig, *Pandora*,' Facey replies simply.

'Undoubtedly it was for the best that you removed him from this city. Without the protection of his brother I shudder to imagine what would have become of him else. Besides, as we both well know, a naval life is hard but often the making of a man,' announces Trench, himself a former sea-officer. The discussion turns to sails, dog-watches, belaying and the like, as it was ever wont to do, and so I settle to my note.

My dearest,

Tomorrow, you must come well prepared. Bring your crowbars and, if you are able, lay hands on a good stout hammer.

It seems you were in the right of it all along, Sammy. The article we seek is, after all, concealed behind your wall.

It transpires that the poorly-laid brickwork at the chimneybreast was installed by Jenkins' hand alone. A most singular occurrence, curious enough for Nellie to have come out with the tale at Mrs Stride's table this afternoon. Whoever heard of a butler laying bricks? Moreover, as he laboured, all others of the household were forbidden entry to the rooms.

Not Haverford in the least then. Blinded by an excessive estimation of my own wits, I have made a sorely tangled web of it all and shall henceforth, have a deal more faith in you, my love.

Should you have come upon our gent with the wen by now, all well and good. You may perhaps find him to be a butler or footman, at any rate, friend and accomplice to Mr Jenkins, but, for the moment, he need not be further pursued.

In the meantime, you will keep safe, take no desperate measures nor put yourself in harm's way.

With all my love,
your Rosamund

I fold the paper with care and stow it in my coat pocket, intending it for a keepsake. Trench is in the right of it: here is an article to be preserved for our future issue.

Trench calls out to the can for a couple more bottles.

'News, Sammy?' queries Facey.

'We must prepare ourselves to take down that wall tomorrow, though it breaks poor Standford's heart.'

Facey nods, while Trench fills our glasses. 'The note comes from my wife, Lieutenant Trench,' I explain.

'I had not heard you had tied the knot, Mr Samuel. Felicitations, sir.' He raises his glass.

'I have no doubt that my Rosamund will be proud, sir, and truly amazed when she hears the manner of its delivery.'

'Speed, Mr Samuel, that is the crux of it. You will never believe the competition amongst ticket-porters and messenger services within the metropolis. Why, even now the General Post Office boasts a mighty new depository at St. Martin's Le Grand and should put us all to the poorhouse lest we find a way to provide a superior service. Your fourpenny post is all very well should you have the leisure of a day or two, but in the main, an expeditious delivery, sir, that is what your metropolitan customer truly desires.' Trench notices that Facey's glass is empty and fills it once again before draining his own. 'The world moves on apace, gents. I have heard that the Lancashire Witch can make fifteen miles per hour or more. And what of the Rocket? At the Rainhill Trials it bore a twenty-person carriage achieving no less than thirty miles per hour on an incline. Thirty miles per hour, forsooth. Even my Dandy Horses should be left for dust,' he chuckles.

'Where does it end, Lieutenant? Forty miles, fifty even?' Facey shakes his head in wonderment. 'What then? At such velocities the very breath is stole from your body, if you are not already shook into insensibility by the extreme motion. I am all for progress, as Sammy will attest, but there ought be limits. Asides, why should any man even desire to travel at such speeds? To what purpose? It is beyond all reason. No, sir, Shanks's Pony has always been good enough for the likes of us, though on occasion, a post chaise serves its purpose well enough.'

Trench drinks off his glass with a grin. 'Then, sir, you ought give my machine a try and, once mastered, might fully grasp the exhilaration of the experience.'

Facey shakes his head. 'We are sharp set, Lieutenant, and must regretfully decline.'

'Ah, no, Mr Facey, you will forgive me but I insist,' announces the now flushed and ebullient Trench, 'and I shall call for a supper whilst we put the machine through its paces.' He beckons across the taverner's wife, a stout woman in a greasy mob cap.

'What vittles, mum?'

'Tonight the cookshop do have sarsinges, sir, all plump and glossy along with horseradish, taters and a little of watercress if you please.'

'Then you will kindly send out for the three on us, with all dispatch.'

Not wishing to disappoint Trench, we amble out into the courtyard. Although the crowd has now dispersed, the young lad remains steadfast, standing sentinel over the Dandy Horse. On seeing Trench he grins, opens his palm and reveals a clutch of coppers. 'Lieutenant Trench, sir. I have collected fourpence ha'penny from the muttonheads in exchange for a good gawp and a poke at your contraption.'

'Advanced transportation machine, Matthew. It ain't a contraption,' tuts Trench. 'Well, you have done sufficient duty and should take your ill-gotten gains and get you home for the night. Look sharp now and never tarry.'

'Thankee, sir.' The lad tugs his forelock, claps on his cap and sprints away into the night.

'A scallawag, gents. Not unlike your Pure John I should say.'

'Very like,' I agree, feeling an intense stab of guilt that Facey and me are free to carouse and caper with Dandy Horses while my wife abides alone beneath a foreign roof and our John languishes in the clutches of those pitiless scoundrels.

'Now, sirs, kindly observe as I mount the mechanical steed,' announces Trench, clasping the curved wooden bar at the front and throwing his leg over the machine so that he sits astride the leather saddle. He pushes off, his feet providing propulsion by means of a kind of running motion. At first he is a trifle wobbly, though that may be down to the wine; within moments the wheels spin to a blur as he picks up considerable speed and exhibits such mastery of the apparatus that he is able to describe intricate serpentine loops about the courtyard, twisting and jinking with an astounding virtuosity. We cannot help but be caught up in the spectacle, hooting and clapping as he weaves and capers.

'What ho, Priam. What odds for the Derby?' bellows a facetious groom.

Finally, Trench heads back in our direction and, just as I begin to fear a shocking collision, sets both feet flat to the cobbles and skids to a perfect halt not six inches from us. He remains astride the machine, even more flushed from his exertions, but with an expression of the greatest satisfaction upon his honest face.

Facey is quick to offer his hand. 'I have no words, sir; such mastery. I never saw the like.'

'And now, Mr Facey. What say you take a turn?'

At that moment the taverner's woman pokes her head out the door. 'Should you be quite done with all your whoopin' and hollerin' and them high jinks of yourn, sarsinges is up, sirs. 'Twould never do to let such a fine supper grow cold neither, not if it was ever so.'

Facey feigns disappointment. 'I should like it above all things, Lieutenant, but my belly, growling and groaning as it does, must be allowed the final say on the matter.'

All for progress he may be, but it seems Facey's oft-bruited principle does not apply when it comes to the uncertain motions of a Dandy Horse.

CHAPTER XX

Facey has ever been able to consume great oceans of spiritous liquor without apparent ill effect and, true to form, is, this morning, sprightly and in tolerable good humour. I, on the other hand, am slow and crapulous, enduring a thick head. We are, in consequence, a good deal later than our accustomed hour by the time Nellie offers us entry by the side door. Mindful as I am that we must face Pimlott and Chuffington later today, I am tolerably sanguine about the prospect. Though it has been a vexing and circuitous enterprise, I trust to my wife's perspicacity, and a little to my own instincts, to imagine that we are at the end of it.

'A good morning to you, gents.' Standford rises from his makeshift seat on the toolbox. He waves me closer and, though there is no possibility of being overheard in these great empty rooms, speaks in a low, urgent whisper. 'Mr Samuel, I have a communication for you from the young lady governess.' He gives me a meaningful look, well knowing that we have some connection. 'She wishes you to know that the gent, what is to say, Mr Galton, made his appearance early this morning and has taken the lad riding on the Row. The young lady has been charged to accompany them and begs you might wait upon her return whereupon she finds opportunity to converse with you.'

'Thankee kindly, Mr Standford. You will forgive our lateness, we shall set to with a will by way of amends,' I reply, rating myself the most shocking hypocrite, well-knowing that all this poor fellow's painstaking work must soon be undone entirely. For the moment though, I am content to leave all be till Rosamund's return.

'There remains some yardage yet for the doing,' says Standford, indicating the swathe of bare, plastered wall still to be papered, 'and to be sure, paper hanging is no task for one man alone, else it can never be made to lie straight.'

Facey and me divest ourselves of our old coats, inner pockets heavy with the weight of our crowbars. I have not concerned myself with the obtaining of a hammer since I am aware that there is already a good, heavy article residing in Standford's toolbox.

Standford begins to mix up the paste, Facey adding water from the bucket according to the foreman's instruction. Meanwhile, I give the bare wall a burnish with an old dry cloth to ensure the paper affixes to a good, clean surface.

Standford now unrolls a measured length of his precious paper and we set to applying the paste with our brushes. Once Facey has mounted the folding steps Standford and me hand up the prepared strip with great delicacy, the three of us then apply it to the wall, taking care to avoid all kinks and blisters. When the strip is in place, firmly affixed and smoothed to perfection, Standford takes a pace back, and stands, hands on hips, the better to assess its exactness. Facey and me await his judgement with some trepidation, having no desire to repeat the thankless, uncomfortable process.

'A perfect alignment, gents. Fine work, if I do say so myself,' he announces. 'Another half dozen strips and the wall is done. Once dry, there is but the application of a little paint to titivate the cornices and skirting boards and we may call it quits.'

Our attention is diverted by an urgent and continuous rapping at the front door. Doubtless Galton returned, since it is only he who applies the brass knocker in such an insistent, heavy-handed manner. I glance at Facey, who narrows his one good eye, no doubt anticipating a further reckoning with the man.

For a while there are no further sounds from the lower floor. Indeed, the absence of almost all noise is what is most remarkable. In moments though, we hear swift footsteps on the floorboards outside heralding Nellie's approach. She hurries through the double doors, an anguished expression on her wide-eyed face. 'A most shocking awful thing,' she squeaks, 'you is sent for and must come quick,' and, without tarrying, turns and is gone.

My heart skips a beat, assailed as I am by the spectre of my Rosamund injured or harmed in some way. A thrill of dread runs through me with all the force of a physical blow and before I know it, I find myself careering down the main staircase, almost tripping over my own boots. As I reach the lobby, I find Facey but a step or so behind me.

A grave Jenkins stands in the entrance hall at the foot of the stairs in company with an elderly cove in snuff-coloured coat and grey breeches. The front door is wide open; on the street outside a Berline carriage stands before the house. 'Where is Galton?' I bark, certain that he must be at the foundation of whatever misadventure has occurred.

Jenkins frowns. 'That is none of your concern, fellow. You men will kindly take yourselves to the doctor's carriage and assist in fetching out the young master this instant.'

Still in an agony of suspense, I hasten out to the conveyance. Within, I am relieved to find a tearful but unharmed Rosamund, attired in a riding habit, took, I imagine, from Edith Belmont's armoire. She cradles young William, the lad pale and motionless in her arms, his eyes closed. 'Oh, Sammy,' she sobs at the sight of me.

Facey gently shoulders me from his path. 'Let me have him, Mrs Samuel. He is but a little 'un.' With that he reaches in and scoops young William into his arms. As he carries the boy into the house I hand my wife down from the carriage. She grips my hand tight. 'Poor William,' she whispers. 'I cannot bear it, Sammy.'

Once inside we find Jenkins and the cove I presume to be the physician, still in the entrance hall, conversing in muted tones. Jenkins breaks off at the sight of Rosamund. 'I have directed that the master be taken to the morning room, Miss Howlett.'

There is no objection as I follow behind and we make our way down the corridor past the library and into a bright, well-appointed room with sizeable windows giving out onto the garden terrace.

Facey has laid the boy upon the long oak table and stands sombrely at his side in contemplation, the light shining in from the windows only serving to mark the pallor of the boy's complexion. At our entrance, Facey looks up sharply and slowly shakes his head.

Rosamund approaches the table and lifts William's small waxy hand, gently stroking it. I hear a muffled sob escape her lips. It is a pathetic sight. Heir to wealth and status he may be, but I cannot imagine his life has been the better for it, and I shouldn't wonder if this brief, though tender caress is the first he ever received since residing beneath this unhappy roof.

Facey puts a hand to my shoulder, speaking low and close in my ear. 'Gone, Sammy. You and me have seen enough on 'em to know.'

As though in confirmation we hear the voice of the physician as he and Jenkins approach along the corridor. 'I can do naught but confirm my supposition. He is quite expired, sir, I do assure you.'

The two of them enter the room, Jenkins carrying a lighted candle. 'You will place the flame adjacent to the young gentleman's lips if you please,' instructs the doctor.

Rosamund gently releases the child's hand and steps back to give Jenkins room. There is no draught and so the candle burns steadily. As Jenkins brings the flame almost to William's partially open mouth, it remains unwavering. Not a trace of breath escapes the boy's body.

'It is as I supposed, the boy's neck is broke from the fall. I could only wish there was aught to be done, but alas, a sudden, violent fracture of the cervical spine is beyond the powers of any physician.'

'Nevertheless, this house is grateful to you, doctor, and appreciative of the generous use of your carriage.'

'Certainly, though that is little enough, to be sure. Such a tragedy. In life, we are in the midst of death and that is the Lord's honest truth. And so now the young gentleman must be given over to another, more doleful profession than my own.'

'Indeed, sir. I shall make the necessary arrangements.'

'Perhaps I might, at the very least, do you that small service?'

Jenkins nods, 'Most kind in you, sir. It is Mr Emmanuel Shepherd of Stratton Street who has ever served the family in that mournful capacity.'

'I shall fetch him at once,' announces the doctor, clapping on his hat and giving a brief bow to all. 'My sincere condolences to all of this household. Never trouble yourself, I shall show myself out.'

With the departure of the physician Jenkins sighs, peering blearily about him. 'Where is that confounded child?'

'Coming, Mr Jenkins,' squeaks Nellie as she approaches along the corridor followed swiftly by the purposeful strides of Mrs Parkes. 'I have been at fetching Mrs Parkes, ain't I?'

'What has transpired, Mr Jenkins? I can make no sense at all of Nellie's gabble,' quavers Mrs Parkes, in a tone of considerable trepidation.

Jenkins holds up a restraining hand. 'The very worst news. You must prepare yourself, Madam.'

'No, no, no, no,' she shrieks. Ignoring Jenkins, she dashes into the room. Seeing the tiny body laid out upon the table she howls like a banshee, her legs appear to buckle and she drops slowly to the floor, folding in upon herself in a billow of skirts.

'Out, out,' Jenkins ushers us all from the room and closes the door. We remain in the corridor for the while, a melancholy huddle, Rosamund and Nellie softly weeping; even Facey, who has, for a certain, seen his share of the Reaper's work, is noticeably dejected.

The library door swings open to reveal Galton standing on the threshold clutching a glass of brandy. He spies Rosamund amongst us. 'Well, Miss Howlett. And what is the sawbones' opinion? I cannot imagine it merits all this detestable screeching and wailing.'

'The physician could do naught, Mr Galton. Poor William is killed, sir, of a broken neck.'

Galton reacts with unfeigned dismay, fortifying himself with a great swallow of brandy. 'Good Christ, I had not imagined it near so bad. I myself have taken many a tumble from a horse with little more than a scratch or bruise to show for it. What, and his beast no more than a twelve-hand pony? It ain't hardly to be credited.' He shakes his head in disbelief. 'Well, I am sorry for it. The lad was not such a blackguardly young fellow for all his mumchance ways.' Galton downs the remainder of his liquor, his eye falling upon Nellie. 'You there, girl, you shall inform Mr Jenkins that the decanter here is all but dregs. Be sure and tell him the master of this house requires another without delay.'

We have taken ourselves to the scullery since we all of us have need of a little fortification in the face of this turn of events. A subdued Mrs Stride has laid her hands on a stone bottle of Jenever spirits, which she pours out for the five of us gathered around her table. 'I cannot say I knowed the younker, but the sudden passing of one so young with so little of his life lived is alus a cause for sadness.'

'To the young 'un,' agrees Facey, raising his glass.

'A sweet boy,' adds Rosamund, as we toast the little fellow.

Nellie coughs as she downs the fiery spirit, collecting herself before she turns her great fish-eyed stare on Rosamund. 'You was there, Miss. Was it Galton done away with the boy?'

'Come now, Nellie,' interjects Mrs Stride, 'that is no proper question to be asking the young lady.'

'The Galton gent is now master of this house and ain't that what he has been angling for since the mistress karked it?'

'Nellie, for shame. Besides, that shall not be decided for certain 'til all the lawyer's doings be done.'

Nellie pouts, her face beginning to flush with the unaccustomed spirits. 'We ain't so green as we is cabbage-lookin'. I reckon you might spill what occurred.'

'You will forgive her, Miss. 'Tis but the Jenever gabbing and she do gets some fanciful notions in that head of hers, it being passably empty much else of the time.'

Rosamund nods, fingers playing with the stem of her glass. 'There is naught to forgive, Nellie merely speaks aloud what is in the minds of all and, none here having any great love for Mr Galton, I believe you have a right to hear what passed today.' She takes a deep breath; I see it is not easy for her to recount the tale. 'Mr Galton arrived early this morning to take the boy riding in the Row. You will know in course, he has lately been in the habit of arranging such outings with young William. Perhaps to curry favour with the boy, mayhap from a sense of duty as the child's only extant relation. Such is not for me to say. What I can tell you is that Mrs Parkes was uneasy in her mind over Galton's influence on the boy and, having fetched me a riding habit, begged me accompany them.'

'Afeared of Galton, and so she might have been,' announces Nellie darkly, reaching for the Jenever bottle.

Mrs Stride slaps her hand away. 'Enough now, Nellie.'

Rosamund shakes her head. 'It seemed to me that the boy had little notion of managing a horse; curious in one brought up on a country estate.'

'In recent years they kept no stable at Chilcomb to speak of. Though I do recall there were a dogcart and nag for trips to the village,' interjects Mrs Stride.

'I only wish I had taken notice of my heart, sensing the boy so full of apprehension,' sighs Rosamund. 'At any rate, Galton would brook no objection and William was given the smallest of the livery ponies, long past the mark of mouth, and so I went along, thinking there could be no harm in it.' She pauses, overcome. I pass her my fogle and reach for her hand, no longer concerned with maintaining our subterfuge. 'A runaway dog was the cause of it, scampering across our path, almost trod down by Galton's horse, startling the mounts. When William's pony shied he had not the competence to retain his seat,' she dabs her eye with the edge of my fogle. 'And that is the long and the short of it. There happened to be a physician close to hand who gave what assistance he could but I believe that William was already beyond help.'

Nellie has managed to refill her glass while Mrs Stride has been distracted, drinking it off before the cook can intervene. 'A runaway mutt comes most convenient to Mr Galton's purposes,' she mutters.

'What stuff,' snorts Mrs Stride, 'and you shall leave off the Jenever, my girl, lest you take it into your head to raise the hue and cry and run out for the Lord Chief Justice.'

Rosamund takes a small sip at her own glass. 'Mr Galton may be every bit the black-hearted villain you imagine him to be, but I can assert, and would swear so on the holy bible itself, that he had no hand in poor William's demise.'

'Indeed not,' nods Mrs Stride. 'What's more, he is like to be master of this house soon enough and you shall keep them wild fancies to your own self, young Nellie.'

The table falls silent at the sight of Jenkins slowly ascending the stairs. At the foot he comes to a halt, clearing his throat. 'Forgive me this intrusion, Mrs Stride. It is my sorrowful duty to inform you that Mr Emmanuel Shepherd has come for the young master. I ask that all here assemble in the entrance hall as a mark of our respects.' He turns and slowly commences his ascent.

Once upstairs in the entrance hall we observe Standford already present. He stands morosely, paper hat in hands as we arrange ourselves into a small file by his side. Facey and me have left our own hats in the drawing room, so we content ourselves with bare, lowered heads, hands clasped before us. Mrs Stride and Rosamund dab at their eyes while Nellie's lip begins to tremble. As yet, there is no sign of Mrs Parkes nor Galton.

Jenkins waits by the front door, holding it open in readiness for the undertakers who are not long in emerging from the morning room. William is brought out in a simple pine box fitted with rope handles, carried by a couple of burly men in long black aprons, not a procession precisely but there is yet a certain dignity to it. The slight size of the temporary casket serves to remind us all of how very young he was; it is this, I believe, which provokes a bout of noisy sobbing from Nellie.

A cove in a black frock coat and cravat follows up behind. He pauses, bowing briefly to Jenkins while his men load the casket into a small closed carriage on the street outside. 'Condolences, Mr Jenkins,' he murmurs.

'My thanks, Mr Shepherd.'

'A tragedy indeed. Might I ask how we ought proceed with the arrangements?'

Jenkins shakes his head. 'I could not say, Mr Shepherd. It is for Mr Haverford to decide; he is yet to be informed of this terrible event.'

'Very well, sir. I shall wait on Mr Haverford's instructions, imposing no further upon your grief.' The cove bows once more, puts on his black stovepipe and steps out.

I steal a glance at Rosamund. Though her eyes yet brim with tears, it is evident from her expression that she is not blinded to the most remarkable aspect of this Emmanuel Shepherd: the shocking great wen on his neb.

CHAPTER XXI

The two of us remain standing alone in the entrance hall as the others silently retreat to the basement. Standford accompanies Facey, Mrs Stride and Nellie, while Jenkins, as befits his dignity, follows a little distance behind, likely making for his chamber and the consolation of a bottle.

'You remarked it?' I say quietly.

'Who could not?' affirms Rosamund.

'We none of us featured it, yet all this time it has been plainer than the great carbuncle on his dial. Who better placed to make a substitution within the casket than the undertaker himself?'

''Tis always easier to be wise after the event. It appears that this Emmanuel Shepherd was accomplice to Jenkins and so I am ever more certain that our gemstone is to be found behind the wall.'

I grimace. 'I shall not be sorry to quit this ill-starred house and all its secrets.'

'Nor I.'

I reach out for my wife's hand but she stiffens. I turn to see Mrs Parkes finally emerging from the morning room corridor. Instead of a reprimand there is barely a second glance; the woman descends the stairs to the basement, gazing fixedly ahead as though her eyes are set upon some far distant object.

'Curious how she has took it harder than any,' remarks Rosamund. 'I never heard her utter a civil word to the boy, nor saw a kindly expression and yet she appeared quite unmanned at the news.'

'We all of us grieve for the lad. But now we must see to our own. Come,' I say, squeezing her hand, 'time to rouse Facey and make an end to this business.'

Down in the scullery Facey and Nellie have resumed their places at the table. Facey has finagled a bottle of porter from the cook's store, which stands by him, Nellie has taken for herself a further glass of the Jenever, while Standford sits at the table's head puffing thoughtfully at his old clay pipe. Over at the counter Mrs Stride cuts a loaf into thick slices and the smell of freshly baked bread reminds me that my belly is empty and still somewhat peevish from the excesses of the previous night. At the sight of us she waves with the knife towards the table, indicating that we should sit. 'There is good mutton stew here along of bread and butter should you have a mind. Downcast we may be but life goes on and we must all eat. 'Sides there is naught like a warm braise to bring cheer to a body.'

'You are very good, Mrs Stride, but Mr Facey and me have our labours to attend.' I say, despite my hunger.

'Your work will still be there for you after you have ate, Mr Samuel.'

'Indeed it will,' interjects Standford, tamping the bowl of his pipe with a great blackened thumb afore getting to his feet. 'And there it shall be tomorrow since I do not reckon it right and proper to continue on such a day.' He claps the paper hat to his head, before nodding to Mrs Stride. 'And so, I'm for home and hearth. Thankee kindly for the hospitality, Mrs Stride.'

'Most welcome, Mr Standford.'

'Now then,' announces Mrs Stride once Standford has departed by the backstairs, 'the two on you may sit like Christians and take sustenance with the rest on us.'

'And so we shall,' concedes Rosamund. I do not have the fortitude to resist these tantalizing aromas and Facey will never shift himself while there is yet a single drop of porter in his bottle, so I follow Rosamund to the table.

We have yet to take our seats when the door to the wine cellar opens to reveal Mrs Parkes bringing up a filled decanter. Nellie leaps to her feet like a scalded cat, glancing guiltily at the table where her brimming glass of Jenever sits for all to see.

'Please,' intones Mrs Parkes bleakly, 'never trouble yourselves on my account.'

We sit ourselves in silence, other than for Nellie who remains standing uncertainly. 'Shall I take that for you, Mum?' she inquires.

'No, child. It is the rightful duty of Mr Jenkins. Though lacking both mistress and now master, we shall, I hope, endeavour to maintain the proper regulation of this house.'

'Then ought I fetch Mr Jenkins?'

'Certainly, Nellie.'

Nellie clatters away down the corridor in the direction of Jenkins' chamber.

Mrs Stride bustles over to us with a plate of her buttered bread. 'Should you care for a bite yourself, Mrs Parkes? It has been a sore trial.'

'Obliged to you, Mrs Stride, but I have no appetite.' Despite the obvious presence of the spiritous liquor, she gazes down at us with neither approval nor disapproval and it is somewhat discomfiting to find ourselves within the compass of that flat, blank stare. In the ensuing silence we hear only the muffled sounds of street cries, the clatter of a passing carriage on the cobbles outside and the busy bubbling of the concoction on the stove. No words are passed; even the garrulous Mrs Stride remains mumchance. Only Facey appears untroubled, raising his bottle to take a deep pull at the porter.

At length, the peculiar tension is eased by the return of Nellie followed close behind by the flushed, unsteady Jenkins.

'I understand Mr Galton has called for brandy,' advises Mrs Parkes.

Jenkins smooths his disordered, thinning hair and collects himself. 'Of course, Mrs Parkes, it had quite slipped my mind.'

Mrs Parkes hands over the decanter. 'It would never do to forget Mr Galton nor fail in our duties, Mr Jenkins.'

'Indeed not,' he responds, raising an eyebrow, 'since it seems likely that the gentleman shortly stands to inherit all.'

Mrs Parkes gazes at him for a moment without expression. 'He may, or he may not. We can none of us presume to know the Lord's will. Nor even the workings of the law. No doubt we shall discover how matters stand in due course.'

'At any rate, I have just this minute penned a brief missive to Mr Haverford appraising him of these unfortunate events.' With his free hand, Jenkins produces a small folded paper from his coat pocket.

'Then shall I run out for the ticket-porter, sir?' inquires Nellie.

'I shall see to it,' announces Mrs Parkes, holding out her hand for the note. 'Sit, child. Eat, lest Mrs Stride's good vittles go to waste.'

'As you please,' nods Jenkins. 'I must not keep Mr Galton waiting.'

Though it can scarcely have been described as a joyous gathering, it is as though a pall has been lifted as the pair ascend the stairs and disappear from view.

Mrs Stride ladles out bowls of her vittles for all before joining us at the table. Gratified as I am to be settling my belly, I eat swiftly, shovelling down bread and meat, mindful that Facey and me have pressing business in the drawing rooms. Facey, it seems, has kept pace. He scours his emptied bowl with the last chunk of bread, crams it in his mouth and gives out a great sigh of satisfaction. 'A prodigious fine stew, Mrs Stride. Finest I ever did eat.'

'What stuff, Mr Facey. 'Tis a most ordinary burgoo with some few carrots and taters throwed in. Though I should say there is a trifle more in the pot and you being of such imposing build, might use another ladleful, I shouldn't wonder.'

Nellie shrewdly reaches her hand across for the Jenever bottle, Mrs Stride gives it a light tap with her spoon. 'Now then, my girl, I already said you have had ample sufficiency of these here spirits and it is only a mercy that Mrs Parkes chose to say naught about it.'

Nellie eyes the cook with bleared, red-rimmed fish-eyes before wagging an admonishing finger. 'I shall tell you what it is, Mrs Stride. Mrs Parkes had naught to say to me since she might well have the self-same words with Mr Jenkins, him being such a shocking great lushington as all well knows.'

'Have a care, Nellie, lest you tattle your way to the poor house. Mrs Parkes raised no objection out of decorum on such a day.'

'I don't rightly collect the meaning of that word, but if it do mean Liberty Hall, then I shall have myself another,' she shrugs, pouring herself another glass. ''Sides, if that Galton is to be master here then the high-and-mighty Mrs Parkes shall have naught to say to no one, her being flung out upon the streets quicker 'an you can say "knife", without even a character.'

'Nellie, you must not utter such wicked things, 'specially before strangers. No, nor wish them, neither. Evil be to them who evil thinks.'

Nellie sips at her Jenever and shrugs. 'These ain't proper strangers. Never Miss Howlett, at any rate, who is a rare good soul, and was the only one what gave any 'fection at all to that poor boy. And all with eyes can see you are sweet on Mr Facey.'

Mrs Stride gapes before swiftly rising to her feet. 'I shall fetch the pot, for them what cares for a smidgeon more.' She bustles over to the range, no doubt to spare her blushes. Facey grins and winks at me with his one good eye from over the top of his porter bottle.

'What is it that you must not state before strangers, pray?' Mrs Parkes has returned, descending the stairs unobserved, while we have all been occupied with Nellie's blather.

The housekeeper's hand twitches at the chatelaine, her keys jangle softly in the silence. 'Mrs Stride?'

Over at the range the cook slowly replaces the pot and wipes her hands on an old scrap of flannel. To her credit, she remains quite composed. 'The child was flapping her gums is all, Mrs Parkes. 'Tis but the liquor speaking, which she don't have the head for. If there be fault, it lies in me for permitting her a nip or two.'

'You imagine I am to lose my place here, Nellie?'

Nellie stares down at the table, shame-faced.

'Come now, you may speak what is in your mind, child.'

Nellie swallows, unable to meet the housekeeper's gaze. 'Well, Mum, it is known that you and Mr Galton have had words on occasion. And should the gent stand next in line, as he has so often claimed, then...'

The housekeeper smiles thinly before responding. 'Then I should be put out by that gentleman without a character?'

Nellie makes no reply though Mrs Parkes nods slowly. 'Never fear, child. Mr Galton has no expectations that I am aware of.'

CHAPTER XXII

Mrs Stride shakes her head, perplexed. 'It were understood, Mrs Parkes, that with the passing of young William, God rest him, that Mr Galton should become master here.'

'You know naught, Mrs Stride.' Mrs Parkes who has been standing in her customary upright manner seems to sag. She steps into the scullery, settles heavily upon a nearby stool and there she remains with her head in hands.

Rosamund rises and fills an empty glass from the stone bottle. 'Come, Mrs Parkes,' she says, 'you are indisposed and who can blame you after such calamity?' She steps across to the woman and proffers the spirits. 'Here now, sup this. It may help compose you.'

Mrs Parkes gazes up at her and nods. 'Nellie is in the right of it, Miss Howlett, I am grateful for your kindness to my son.'

'I do not know your son, Mrs Parkes.'

'Indeed you do. The child in your care was my own boy, Ned.'

'His name was William, issue of your late mistress Edith,' corrects Rosamund gently.

'William Belmont has been dead this past fortnight.'

'She has run mad,' announces Nellie, with a certain relish.

'Tush, Nellie,' chides Mrs Stride. 'Mrs Parkes ain't herself right enough, but that don't give you call to make matters worser.'

Mrs Parkes accepts the offered glass. 'These others may think of me as they will, but I believe that you, Miss Howlett, have earned the right to know how matters truly stand.'

'If it should bring some measure of comfort then I should be content to hear what you have to say, Mrs Parkes,' replies Rosamund, fetching another of the stools, which she places close to the housekeeper that they might face one another.

Mrs Parkes sighs heavily. 'A little more than a fortnight past William Belmont was fetched up from the country following the sale of the Chilcomb estate. He was brought here in a hired coach by Walter Price, footman, as was.'

'A fine man what was only doing his duty and didn't he lose his place for it, with not a one in this house to speak up on his account?' interjects Nellie. 'Turned out onto the streets for a naught by that black harlot.'

'I will thank you to keep a civil tongue at my table, my girl,' advises Mrs Stride.

Mrs Parkes shrugs. 'You shall have no quarrel from me on that account, child. Our mistress was a jezebel and a fornicator, a worthless vulgar woman, her only care for her own pleasure and gratification. On arrival, it transpired that the boy had some ailment and so must be put to his bed. By the following morning he had a raging fever on him and, certainly, an inflammation of the chest since breathing had become a mortal struggle. Though I urged Edith Belmont to allow me to call for a physician, she would not, nor even deign to see the boy, considering it a trivial matter, a childhood illness and soon over with. Alas, William expired some few short hours later.'

'And none knew of it?'

'I informed Mr Jenkins, which I took to be my duty. Price had been dismissed and it was the very next day that Mrs Belmont herself was taken ill. With the Asiatic Cholera, you understand.'

'Such misfortune in so short a space of time,' muses Rosamund.

'Some might say justice. "Desire when conceived gives birth to sin, and sin when it is fully grown brings forth death", she intones. 'The woman was a sinner, an adulteress without a shred of motherly instinct. I could not regret her passing and indeed, perceived the Lord's hand in it.'

'How so?'

Mrs Parkes raises her head now, staring at Rosamund with a strange intensity. 'If William was not to be heir then perhaps another, more deserving boy might live that life in his stead. A quiet, obedient, God-fearing boy.'

'Your own son?'

The housekeeper nods. 'No natural, if that is your meaning. Born in wedlock, I assure you. My husband was under-butler at Saltram afore he was carried off by the typhoid in '26. A widow without means and a child not one year old, I was obliged to return to service and the baby Ned sent to be raised by my sister in Enfield, a poor spinster who relies upon what I can send.' Though she appears unnaturally composed as she delivers her desolate tale, Mrs Parkes breaks off for a moment to fortify herself with a little of the spirit in her glass.

'And so, it occurred to me that the good Lord had provided me an opportunity to change the course of my son's life. Few enough of the household had laid eyes upon William and then only for the briefest time. The boys were of an age, and, with Edith Belmont expired and Price dismissed, who might ever say that my Ned was not the true William Belmont? I sent to my sister and had Ned carried to the house late the following night with the strictest instruction that he must now answer to the name of William. I could in no wise acknowledge him nor offer any sign of affection for he did not know me as his mother. He was, as you have seen, by nature, a taciturn child and I believed that, in time, he would become accustomed to his new life and, forgetting the old, come to believe himself to be William Belmont. What I did, I did entirely for his sake, out of a mother's love. I sought to transmute a dismal, uncertain future for my boy into one of promise and expectation, and who can find offence in that?'

'But you say Mr Jenkins had knowledge of William's death. What of his part?'

'Jenkins is a foolish, weak man and inclined to be bibulous.'

Nellie gasps, shocked that the exacting Mrs Parkes should be so openly scathing.

'His silence was easily purchased on the promise of three hundred a year when my Ned achieved his majority. Though you are not married, Miss Howlett, I tell you all this since I believe your role must provide you with some small inkling of that most blessed bond 'twixt a mother and her child. We enter this life with naught and with naught we must leave it. The measure of us is in our issue and the provision we make for them, the lengths we are prepared to go to and the sacrifices we make to ensure their future. That is what we leave of ourselves. It is all we may leave.'

Rosamund places her hand gently on the woman's. 'What we leave of ourselves, Mrs Parkes, is the example we make in this life. The good we do, the memory of certain small acts of decency, kind words, affection, compassion, forgiveness and...' she flicks a glance at me, '...the love we share. But set against that must surely be measured the misery and harm we may cause.'

Mrs Parkes withdraws her hand. She sniffs before smiling bitterly. 'You do not have a child of your own and so cannot know.'

Rosamund rises, posing the question I have been dreading for some while now. 'If what you have said is true, Mrs Parkes, what is become of William Belmont?'

Mrs Parkes shrugs, indicating Facey and me. 'He is to be found at the site of their labours.'

Mrs Stride claps a hand to her mouth in shock. 'A wretched, Godless act, Mrs Parkes,' she cries.

'None of my doing, Mrs Stride, but the work of Mr Jenkins. I only sought to change my own child's destiny.'

'And so you have, Mrs Parkes,' replies Rosamund sadly.

CHAPTER XXIII

Facey pitches away at the wall with a sledge hammer from Standford's toolbox. At the force of his blows the bricks yield beneath the torn and shredded paper to reveal the dark cavity of the hearth.

He steps back, barely out of breath as I set to enlarging the fissure with my crowbar. Sure enough, Jenkins' brickwork has been poorly laid, the mortar weak and inclined to crumble and so the bricks to come away with ease. Peering into the cavity I catch the faint waft of a familiar odour, the sweetish smell of decomposition. 'A lamp, if you please.'

Instead, Nellie rummages in the pocket of her apron for the lucifers, which she keeps to light the fires of this house. With trembling fingers she manages to ignite one and passes it to me so that I may insert it into the gaping hole. The wavering flame reveals that the hearth is empty other than for a little soot, however, by inclining my head upward, I perceive that the flue has been partially blocked by an obstruction of some sort. I extinguish the lucifer and extend my free arm further up inside the shaft. My questing fingers come upon a tightly wrapped bundle, wool by the feel of it. I run my hand around and, finding an edge to the fabric, clasp it tight before pulling. The bundle shifts a trifle though it is still firmly wedged. I crouch lower and now and haul with both hands. With a sharp tug it comes free and drops down into the hearth along with a cloud of soot.

Facey and me haul out the bundle. Though blackened with chimney detritus it is plainly a rug, tightly wrapped and secured with twine. I take out my clasp knife before gazing up at Nellie and Mrs Stride. 'There is no shame in it, should you choose not to remain.'

Nellie, still trembling, stands closer to Mrs Stride who puts a protective arm around her. Mrs Parkes remains impassive, standing apart from the others, arms folded defiantly.

I cut the twine and, between us, Facey and me unroll the rug to reveal a tiny hunched figure, still dressed in a nightshirt, knees tucked up into the belly, hands clasped about the ankles, like a chrysalis. There is a whiff of corruption, though not excessive, since the corpse has a somewhat desiccated appearance. The flesh, where visible, has become parchmentlike and fragile, likely owing to the constant movement of air in the flue.

'Oh, my Lord, the poor mite,' breathes Mrs Stride, consoling Nellie as she sobs.

'In time we would have removed the remains for a Christian burial,' states Mrs Parkes flatly.

Facey gently shifts the tiny body, searching for the presence of the gemstone. He shakes his head.

'Another lucifer, if you please,' I say. Nellie, fumbling, obliges and I resume my examination of the hearth and flue. It is quite empty. I get to my feet, addressing the housekeeper. 'Mrs Parkes, was aught else concealed here?'

She shakes her head. 'What else could there have been?'

'An article of value, perhaps, placed there by Mr Jenkins?' prompts Rosamund.

'I am no thief, Miss Howlett,' snaps Mrs Parkes, offended by the implication, Evidently the appropriation of a life and all its expectations is not such a very great sin in her estimation.

'Mrs Parkes, what mischief is this?' thunders Jenkins from the open doorway.

The housekeeper barely gives him a second glance. Jenkins strides across the room, face flushed, breathing heavily. He comes to a stand before us, a tolerably convincing mask of horror across his face. He glances down at the corpse before glaring at Facey and me. 'Murder is it? By God, you pair shall answer for this.'

'I reckon it is you, sir, who must answer for it,' replies Facey, unmoved. He crouches, gently covering the body once again within the folds of the rug.

'Nellie, run and fetch a magistrate. Mark me, you shall answer to the law for this foul deed,' blusters the butler.

'Do no such thing, Nellie,' interjects Mrs Parkes, turning to Jenkins. 'You may save your outrage, Mr Jenkins. I must tell you, your part is already known to these.'

The look of horror on Jenkins' rubicund countenance is now very real. 'What have you said, woman?'

'Only the truth, Mr Jenkins. My son is gone, there is no merit in dissembling further.'

Jenkins gapes, staring about him. 'She has run quite mad. The death of our young master has quite unmanned her and now this fresh horror...'

Mrs Parkes sighs heavily. 'My son is dead, Mr Jenkins. Sufficient indeed to unseat a body's wits. You may, any of you, fetch a magistrate, should you have a mind to. I no longer care what becomes of me.'

Jenkins instantly changes his tune, becoming placatory. 'No need for that when there has been no foul play. You will have heard from Mrs Parkes, I trust, that the youngster was already passed of a natural cause, a fever or some such, and there was naught to be done for him. My own part in the matter was a trifling one, a matter of concealment: the laying of a few bricks, the arranging of these renovations, though all at the behest of Mrs Parkes. Indeed, I am not to blame here.'

'It is a shocking, blasphemous act, Mr Jenkins,' insists Mrs Stride.

Jenkins lowers his head. 'I know it, Mrs Stride, and should never have been party to it were it not for the persuasive wiles of Mrs Parkes here. I have always rated you a remarkably good-hearted woman, and surely you would never peach an old confederate for such a minor error of judgement?'

Before Mrs Stride can make reply, Mrs Parkes interjects. 'Content enough you were at the notion of three hundred per annum.'

The butler nervously moistens his lips, gazing round at us, a sly look infusing his toad-like countenance. 'I shall tell you what, since we are all friends here. At present our household lacks for master or mistress and, afore the attorney fellow comes poking and prying, it behoves you all to consider that there remains an ample sufficiency of silverware to be had for the taking. To that end I might be persuaded to unlock the butler's pantry and make myself scarce for a short while. I am acquainted with a fellow on Cork Street who will pay cash on the nail for such articles. Nellie, you shall have your pick of Mrs Belmont's armoire. Should you like that, child?'

'Make no answer, Nellie,' instructs Mrs Stride.

Mrs Parkes laughs, though without mirth. 'Not all present are so lacking in scruples as yourself, Mr Jenkins.'

'And what of the famous ferroniere?' I say.

Jenkins gazes at me in surprise, 'Why, you are a bold villain and no mistake. But you aim too high, fellow. That cursed article, and indeed all Mrs Belmont's most precious adornments are long gone, far beyond the reach of man, entombed as they were alongside of her. Content yourself with a fine silver creamer or jug, which you may take with my blessing.'

Mrs Stride purses her lips in disapproval. 'I shall have naught, Mr Jenkins, but neither will I be the one to bring down the law upon this house.'

Jenkins smiles faintly but with evident relief.

'Not for your sake, Mr Jenkins, but for the sake of Mrs Parkes, who has today reaped a harvest of misery beyond all earthly endurance. What purpose would the law serve here? Has it the power to bring these young 'uns back to life? It has not. There is, however, but one condition to my silence. And it is that you, Mr Jenkins, will see to it that this here boy is properly buried in a decent Christian manner.'

'Certainly, Mrs Stride, but...'

'But me no buts, Mr Jenkins. You will find a way to see it done and done with all despatch. I shall not quibble with you and that is my final word on the matter.' With that she gives Nellie a gentle nudge.

'My lips is likewise sealed, Mrs Stride,' she nods. 'Should the poor lad be given a proper sending off.'

I glance at Rosamund, who looks meaningfully at the broken chimney breast before shaking her head, moreover, from his genuinely perplexed expression, I warrant Jenkins truly has no knowledge the ferroniere. To my mind, it is infuriatingly like the thimble-rig, the common street lay in which a pea is concealed under one of three thimbles. Such is the dexterity and confounding patter of the operator, that the flat is certain lose his stake every time. Like the dullest-witted of those bumpkins, we have once again wagered high and come up empty.

Yet, all is not lost. There is still some little time remaining before we must face Pimlott and Chuffington and with one last turn to make: a final thimble to examine, which is to say, a visit to the person of Mr Emmanuel Shepherd.

Plainly, Rosamund is of a like mind. 'Mrs Stride speaks for us all,' she announces. 'But I have no wish to remain a moment longer beneath this desolate roof, nor do I see further reason for me to do so.'

'Then I hope I can say we part on friendly terms, Miss Howlett,' replies the butler, with an ingratiating smile.

'I bear you no ill will, Mr Jenkins, though I believe you to be a man of little conscience.'

The smile melts from his face as he attempts to collect whatever shreds of dignity remain to him. He gestures at the tiny hump concealed within the rug. 'At any rate, I shall make amends here as I have promised. You have my word on that, Miss Howlett. In the meantime, these rooms shall be locked. You will recall that Mr Galton remains ensconced below. I should not wish him to come upon us all in such equivocal circumstances.'

'You have naught to fear from Mr Galton,' announces Mrs Parkes.

'He is like to be the new master here soon enough, though you may wish it otherwise,' retorts Jenkins, seeking to reassert his tarnished authority.

'He shall never be master of this nor any other house.'

'You cannot know that. 'Twill be a matter of testate.'

Mrs Parkes smiles by way of reply, a tight, bitter rictus. There is a deathly silence while Jenkins gapes with growing comprehension. 'What mischief have you wrought, woman?'

'I have done naught, Mr Jenkins. What is done has been by your own hand.' Her eyes glitter strangely. Whether in malice or triumph, I cannot say.

A panic-stricken Jenkins exerts what tenuous authority remains to him, ordering the remaining servants to accompany him as he sets off to discover what has become of Titus Galton. Facey follows, no doubt out of solicitude for Mrs Stride, leaving Rosamund and me alone in the company of Mrs Parkes, who remains grimly silent.

'The decanter you carried up,' sighs Rosamund.

The housekeeper raises an eyebrow. 'You are a sharper one than I gave you credit for, Miss Howlett. The brandy was adulterated with arsenical powders. A dose which no man could survive.'

'Then you have slain an innocent man.'

Mrs Parkes sneers. 'Innocent? I think not, Miss Howlett. Such a man, a gentleman, would never have answered to the law for his crime. And so he has made answer in a swifter, more condign manner.'

'You forget, I was present at the terrible event, Mrs Parkes. 'Twas dire mischance; a runaway dog startled your son's mount. Not a whit of Galton's doing.'

'You seek to find excuse for him. He engineered my son's death for his own purpose but he shall never gain from it.'

Rosamund sighs, 'I see you will not take my word on it and so shall not persist. At any rate, what is done cannot be undone.'

Mrs Parkes' head drops, her body appears to shrink, casting off its customary rigidity. She staggers a few paces to a shrouded chair and lowers herself into it before staring up at us, with an expression of insupportable pain. 'And undo it all I would, in an instant, if only that were possible. You cannot begin to comprehend the desolation of it. My son is gone, all my hopes destroyed in an instant. I cannot bear it, Miss Howlett.' She shakes her head. 'I had imagined that vengeance might bring a measure of relief, if only for a moment. It does not. There is no relief to be had but to make an end.'

'Do not say so, Mrs Parkes.'

'I do say so and it shall be a blessed relief; I shall face the rope and be glad to, since I do not believe that, at the last, the good Lord will judge me so harshly.'

'We cannot pretend to know His will, Mrs Parkes,' she says softly. 'What I can say is that you must live with your own guilt and, in the time left to you, perhaps make what amends you may.'

'And if I tell you there is more?'

'We neither of us wish to hear of it.'

'In truth, Edith Belmont did not die a natural death.'

'None might profit from that knowledge now.'

Mrs Parkes nods with infinite weariness.

Rosamund reaches down and touches her gently on the shoulder. 'I grieve for you, Mrs Parkes, truly, though I cannot excuse your deeds.'

CHAPTER XXIV

Mrs Stride has appointed to have Rosamund's few possessions sent on to the Bolt-in-Tun and so we tarry only for the time it takes her to exchange the riding habit for her own good frock before heading out for Stratton Street.

'What of Titus Galton?' enquires Rosamund, as we hasten along the Hayhill pavements before turning down into the Bolton Road.

'Not to be found within that house,' shrugs Facey. 'Jenkins reckoned him departed for his club.'

'Alas, that will not save him.'

'I do not take your meaning, Mrs Samuel.'

'It seems the brandy given him was adulterated. Mrs Parkes has done for Galton as she did for Edith Belmont.'

'Arsenic?'

'The same, Mr Facey.'

Facey shakes his head. 'I did not care for the gent, it is true, but I should not wish that end on anyone.' He begins to slow as he considers my wife's words. 'The Parkes woman has run mad. I fear for Mrs Stride and the young slavey still under that roof.'

'Never fret, Mr Facey. Her madness comes from grief and so follows a rationality of sorts. Mrs Parkes has done all that her passion and rage has compelled her to do and now intends to give herself over to the law. Your return will accomplish naught.'

'Haverford has been sent for,' I say, gripping his sleeve, 'and we cannot be detained for a moment more lest, after all our pains, we fail our John.'

Facey considers before nodding his assent. 'Pimlott and Chuffington ain't famous for their patience, that I grant you, Sammy.'

The three of us resume our former pace. 'Nor can we appear before those two empty-handed; we should not treat this undertaker with overmuch delicacy,' I advise grimly.

'Then you have come to the right shop for that, Sammy Boy.'

The Stafford Street premises is not hard to find, boasting as it does the name, Emmanuel Shepherd, Undertaker, in gold lettering on a black background above an entrance gate. We pass under the sign and into a small courtyard where there is an unhitched hearse and some few stalls for the horses as well as a modest workshop. A couple of lackeys work away, polishing sundry items of tack; others saw and plane planks of raw timber. Pale curls of elm wood float gently to the cobbles like snowflakes; the result is a not unpleasing aroma of wood, wax and horse.

A long-faced youngster emerges from a door to the main building, wiping greasy lips on a scandalous napkin. From his appearance, in black morning coat, trousers and neckerchief I take him to be apprentice to the undertaker's craft. He makes a brief bow. 'Lady, gents, how might I assist?'

'We are come to speak with Emmanuel Shepherd, if you please,' announces Rosamund.

The apprentice assays Facey and me with a wary, suspicious eye. Rosamund swiftly reconciles him with some eyewash about a recently departed, wealthy uncle and he ducks back into the building.

In a few moments we are ushered inside and admitted into what I take to be Emmanuel Shepherd's place of business. It takes a moment to accustom ourselves to the dreary room, since the thick curtains are drawn and there is only a single wavering lamp for illumination. Shepherd is seated at his desk engaged in paperwork of some description, whilst behind him, against the far wall is a row of open coffins accented with polished brass, standing upright like sentinels. He peers up and gestures at a hard-backed, wooden bench, indicating that we might sit. Even in this gloom the angry-looking wen is evident, a tiny droplet of perspiration or some other manner of effusion hangs at the very tip, trembling in what little light there is. 'A thousand apologies,' he announces, 'I am not ordinarily accustomed to meet with clientele at my own premises and so my accommodations leave something to be desired. You will understand, I am sure, that my patrons are, in the main, personages of some distinction and should never dream of calling upon me, a humble man of trade. It is, of course, for me to call upon them when my services are regrettably required.'

''Tis of no consequence,' replies Rosamund briskly.

Shepherd waves a long-fingered hand at a stone bottle and some few dainty liquor glasses on the desk before him. 'At the least, might I offer you a little of the Batavian Arrack? It is often the case that in the event of a sudden demise within the family, the passing of a loved one, that a little, a very little of spirits might serve to lighten the heart.'

'I should take porter if you have it,' grunts Facey.

'I do not, sir,' replies Shepherd, attempting to conceal his distaste.

'We have no need of spirits, sir, nor any comforts.'

'No, indeed, forgive me. I am informed that it is your poor dear uncle who has need of our services. I suppose you feel obliged to put your duty before all else and see him laid to rest in a manner commensurate with his dignity and status. Just so, my dear, and most commendable. Was he a man of some wealth?' He raises a skeletal hand. 'Do not answer that, pray. I spoke out of turn. Specie don't come into it. We do not care to count the cost when it comes to honouring those dearest to us. It is a liberty, I know, but since you are here, perhaps you would do me the honour of casting an eye over a selection of our caskets.' He gestures to the array of open coffins behind him. 'If these don't suit, 'tis a simple matter to have one run up to your own particular sizing and preferences. Oak, elm, mahogany, good brass handles, even silver fittings, should the fancy take you.'

'We have but one requirement, sir. Mr Facey here will inform you of it.'

The undertaker grimaces as though pained before resuming his practised air of sympathy. 'Certainly, Mr Facey, sir. I am all ears.'

Facey smiles thinly, 'Now then, Emmanuel, old cock. We are none of your well-heeled flats to be fleeced for the cost of a hearse-and-four along with a parcel of ten-bob mutes to lead the parade. And there ain't no uncle, so you may stow your gab.'

Shepherd is momentarily taken aback, that doleful countenance replaced by a quizzical stare. 'You are a good-sized article and, with that patch'd glim of yourn, not an easy man to overlook nor forget. Now that I think on it, I believe I had sight of you at the Dover Street residence this very morning.'

'So you did,' acknowledges Facey.

'Then I can assure you that the young gentleman we brought away has been afforded all due respect and consideration, if that be your purpose here.'

'It is not, though I am gratified to hear it. I shall come straight to it, Mr Shepherd. We are come for the Eye of Brahma.'

The man remains entirely composed, only shaking his head regretfully. 'All I know is that article went to the tomb along with the late Edith Belmont. The tragedy of the world, sir, since it was beyond price. Alas, the infamous Eye of Brahma will never more be seen by the eye of man.' Though it is not overly warm, beads of perspiration have appeared on his forehead; he produces a black fogle from the pocket of his coat and wipes them away along with the drop on the tip of his razzo. 'That is God's honest truth. I might swear it so since I myself was there along with an attorney fellow, who was present that he might testify all was carried out according to the lady's wishes.'

'What was sealed up with the Belmont woman was a worthless facsimile purchased the day following her demise from a jeweller on Jermyn Street.'

Shepherd grimaces, clutching at his belly before collecting himself. 'Mere conjecture. You cannot know that.'

'No conjecture, sir,' I interject. 'For it is no great task for men of our profession to undo what has been done by yours.'

Shepherd smiles thinly. 'Ah, you are resurrectionists then? A most unsavoury trade you pursue. And tell me this now: what is to prevent me calling for my men to detain you all while a magistrate is summoned?'

Facey nods his great head. 'Why, naught, Mr Shepherd, and the fact is, I should enjoy a good mill, though I might warn that you yourself should be first in line for chastisement.'

'An unseemly brawl here should reflect most poorly on the dignity of your business,' notes Rosamund, shrewdly assessing the man. 'Moreover, I should wager that this is not the first time that, in the course of your ministrations, articles of value have found themselves in your hands. No doubt many such may yet be uncovered on this premises, in which case the attentions of a magistrate might be considered most unwise.'

Shepherd dabs at his face once again. 'I concede that the proper decorum of my establishment is of paramount concern. It seems we find ourselves at an impasse and so, what to do, I wonder?'

'Our interest is in the Eye alone. Let us have it and we shall trouble you no further, Mr Shepherd.'

'Let us say, for the sake of conjecture,' he nods at me with a sly look, 'that this Eye is indeed in my possession. What should you give for it?'

'Our word, Mr Shepherd. An oath that none shall ever hear of this matter from our lips.'

Shepherd tuts. 'You are aware of the value of such a piece? I have seen it with these very eyes on the brow of the late Mrs Belmont. It is a flawless black diamond of great size, unlike any other. Were I to have such a stone, you believe I would simply hand it to you for naught?'

'We have not the time nor the wherewithal to bargain with you for its possession, Mr Shepherd. Though there are others who do and on whose behalf we act,' presses Rosamund.

Shepherd leans back in his chair. 'Out of curiosity alone, you understand, I shall hear you out.'

'It is a Mr Pimlott and a Mr Chuffington who are our principals in this matter.'

Shepherd smiles, revealing misaligned brown teeth, aptly for one in his profession, like a row of tumbled tombstones. 'I do not know those men; though, to be sure, I have heard whispers of them. And who has not in this great metropolis?'

'Then you will know they ain't the sort to be trifled with,' asserts Facey.

'The Eye is not a trifle,' retorts Shepherd, evenly. 'But I see that your coming here is something of a blessing and, since we may not readily hold the threat of the law above one another, I shall be direct with you. There are no soirees in the boneyard, sir. The dead have no need of fripperies and baubles. To my mind, those precious items festooning the departed are better left to the living, who may yet find pleasure in them. And should there be a little specie to be had, then what of it? It is the righting of a wrong, is all. Certainly, no worse than the hawking of the flesh itself and, I should say, a deal less of risk to it.'

'True enough,' Facey grunts with a grudging admiration.

'I will tell you that King Cholera has been a great blessing for men of my trade,' he continues, 'not only, as you might imagine, in consequence of its mortal hazard—I have placed two and twenty into the ground this past month alone—but in the manner of their laying out. Such is the terror provoked by the Blue Death that folk are most reluctant to approach an afflicted corpse, no matter how dear. They fear to touch 'em, nor even to look upon 'em oftentimes, and so it falls to me alone to prepare them for eternity and, if they are shorn of a trinket or two afore I screw 'em down into their caskets, why, who now might ever know the difference?' Having been made aware of our connection with Pimlott and Chuffington, Shepherd, it appears, is now most eager to impress us with his own larcenous inclinations.

'Ordinarily, at the passing of an old 'un your relatives will gather round the bed with the greatest asperity, instantly stripping the corpse of its rings, necklaces and sundry valuables before the body is even cold, like a veritable flock of vultures.' He taps his foul, glistening neb and cackles. 'The Blue Death has put paid to that carrion feasting for the nonce.'

'I take it then, you are not yourself afeared of this pestilence, Mr Shepherd?' queries Rosamund.

'By no means. As a young man I was afflicted and hovered close to death for two entire days, quite despaired of until, like Lazarus hisself, rose again upon the fourth day, as hale and hearty as you see me now. I am salted, young lady. You may keep your vinegar, burning sulphur, specifics and what-have-you; miasmas and ground vapours hold no terror for me, nor a corpse with a cobalt countenance.'

'Such as that of Edith Belmont?' I prompt, anxious to conclude our business with this fellow.

'I fear I have given the wrong impression, that all has been easy as kiss-my-hand. Not so, my friend. The procuring of the Eye was not such a simple task as all that.'

'It was necessary to make a substitution. This we know,' states Rosamund.

'Just so, young lady. A little penny-weighting, so to speak.' Shepherd grimaces and clutches at his belly.

'Do you ail, sir?' she asks.

'A gripe, 'tis all. A little cold lamb at luncheon, which I fear was on the turn.'

Rosamund gives him a dubious look. 'What more of the Eye, sir?'

'I see you are eager for the tale and may have it entire, since, no doubt, you carry the information to your principals.' Shepherd settles himself. 'I received a communication from the family attorney, one James Haverford, informing me of Edith Belmont's sudden passing. Since it was the Asiatic Cholera which had carried her off, the arrangements were, as in all such cases, necessarily hurried; no washing, embalming, nor titivating of the corpse. None of the usual ceremony. Though I was directed that the woman was to be briefly laid out, then interred adorned with her most favoured possession, the proceedings to be supervised by the attorney himself.' Shepherd gives his foul neb another tap. 'Now, the existence of a facsimile was well known to all hereabouts and it occurred to me that though I should be watched most closely at the casket, there might be advantage in the purchase of that item. On the off-chance of a little legerdemain, you understand. No great forethought nor stratagem, simply Emmanuel Shepherd trusting to good fortune and nimble fingers.' Shepherd reaches across the desk for the stone bottle. 'You will not take a drop of the Arrak? It is very fine and quite the ticket for a turbulent belly.'

I am on the point of acquiescing when Rosamund interjects, 'My thanks, we will take naught,' she states emphatically.

Shepherd carefully half fills one of the tiny glasses, topping it off with a little water from a nearby jug, turning the mixture milky. 'Quite wasted in a punch,' he announces, before drinking off the concoction with the greatest satisfaction. 'Once at the residence, the body in question was fetched by a couple of my men, likewise salted and immune. They hauled it downstairs to the morning room where it was duly placed in our casket, still in its gown. The household, you understand, was in a mortal terror at the proximity of this dread disease and so only the housekeeper was present, and her for the briefest time. With my men dismissed, there remained but myself and this Haverford fellow in attendance. After a short while, the steward, Jenkins, made his appearance carrying a strongbox. The receptacle was unlocked by the attorney with all due solemnity, whereupon Jenkins, his duty done, and catching sight of the karker's fearful blue phizzog, could not carry himself from the room quick enough.' Shepherd chuckles. 'The box contained a trove of items precious to Edith Belmont, including, in course, the Eye of Brahma. Each and every article painstakingly accounted for and attested to by the attorney afore he would give me leave to adorn the remains.'

Shepherd breaks off to wipe a little perspiration from his brow before continuing. 'I tell you, it all but broke my heart to consign such precious items to the oblivion of the tomb, but do it I must, since the man's gimlet eyes never left me for a second lest I palm a trinket or two. Lastly, I draped that acclaimed ferroniere about the woman's brow and there the matter rested, leaving only the casket to be sealed and thence transported to its mausoleum without delay.

'What a stroke it should have been had I found the opportunity to make my substitution, but it was not to be. Emmanuel, I says to myself, you are but five guineas to the worse; nothing ventured, nothing gained and, in that philosophical frame of mind, I had begun to reach for the casket's lid when there occurred an event of remarkable fortune, miraculous even. A sudden commotion from the hallway, the sound of a voice raised in indignant anger and the door to the morning room flung wide. On the threshold stood a florid gent, sporting bugger's grips, in something of a rare passion, fuelled, I would hazard by immoderation. A family connection, it seems, come to pay respects. Though, to be sure, there was little enough of that, this fellow being in a rare old taking, flinging insult and barbs at the Haverford cove. Aught to do with a matter of fee tail and testate and I know not what. It being scarcely the proper time nor the place for such a set to, the attorney gives him short shrift, bustling him straight from that room, leaving old Emmanuel a brief moment on his lonesome with the karker. Now, I do not need to be told twice to make hay while the sun shines. *Carpe demon*, I says to myself, and, by the time that swivel-eyed attorney had returned, the deed was done. Haverford makes his final inspection and, finding all to be ship-shape and Bristol fashion, gives me leave to seal up.' Shepherd cackles once again, with a sound like a death rattle. 'Then it's away to the boneyard. Edith Belmont off to meet her maker wearing the finest paste and pinchbeck whilst that most valuable of baubles sits happily at the breast of Emmanuel Shepherd. In short, tucked safely away in my coat pocket.'

'Most brazen, Mr Shepherd.'

'You may say so, young lady, but I confess, I find, for once, I have bitten off more than I can easily stomach.' As if to attest to the truth of the statement he grimaces, fleetingly pressing a hand to his belly. 'The Eye of Brahma is a most notorious gemstone, far too well-knowed for it to go to the flash houses or the Jews of Shoreditch. I had thought of breaking it down and selling it piecemeal but its value would be so degraded that it ain't worth the candle. And so, you will apprehend why I should be amenable to a conversation with your patrons: two gentlemen who well know how many beans make five, I have heard it said.'

'We shall take it to those men and they will set a price on it,' announces Facey. 'That price may simply be your life and continued preservation or it may be something more. They will not quibble with you like street hawkers. And you may accept their offer or no. It is all one to us.'

Shepherd looks pained, whether from the griping of his belly or Facey's blunt response, I cannot say. Great oily beads of perspiration erupt from his bone-white forehead, which he quickly dabs away. 'You must take me for the most fearful flat. I have only your word to say you have a connection to those men, and even should that be the gospel truth you cannot expect me to simply offer up such an article into your hands without any form of surety. No, you have been informed of the means by which I came by it and so your principals must come to me with a fair offer; only then might they lay hands on the jewel.' He pauses, struggling to find breath, then hunches before retching dryly into his damp fogle.

Facey rises and takes a step towards the man, looming above him with all his imposing bulk. Before he can articulate his intended threats, Rosamund leaps to her feet, giving Shepherd only the briefest of bobs. 'We shall inform our principals of your stipulation, Mr Shepherd, and you will hear from them in due course.' She glances at Facey and me, 'Leave now and touch naught,' she hisses, before hurrying us from the room.

Once outside, the light and air of the courtyard are an instant and blessed relief to me after the stale fug and oppressive gloom of that office.

'What afflicts you, Mrs Samuel?' objects Facey. 'The Eye is certain to be concealed about that gent's person or within his rooms and I reckon I might easily have persuaded him to cough up the article.'

'We could not have lingered there for a minute more, Mr Facey. It may already have been too long. Shepherd begins to show the early markings of this pestilence and that man's tainted breath has been upon us.'

'But he is salted.'

'There is no such immunity from the Blue Death. For that is what it is, plain as day.'

CHAPTER XXV

'An undertaker, you say?' Chuffington wipes his spectacles with a small silken cloth before affixing them to his neb. Through those twin portals he levels an icy, pitiless gaze upon us once again.

'Indeed, sir. A most audacious substitution carried out under the very eyes of the attorney himself.'

'It appears you have got to the bottom of it at any rate,' he digs into the pocket of his weskit, producing his beautiful silver timepiece, 'though it has took you long enough, to be sure. It is almost one quarter afore the hour of four, Mr Samuel. You are late. If there is one thing Mr Pimlott cannot abide, it is unpunctuality. Is that not so, Mr P?'

'Indisputably, Mr C.'

'A full four days was allowed us, sir.'

'Forgive me, Mr Samuel,' pipes Pimlott, in that fluting tone so at odds with his great bulk, 'whilst it is true that we was sufficiently liberal as to allow you four whole days for your further inquiries, you were instructed to present yourselves along with the gemstone no later than eight and twenty minutes after three this afternoon, precisely. I believe I was perfectly explicit on that point.'

'Precise and to the point. As is his way,' confirms his partner.

Rosamund interjects. 'You set us upon a most perplexing course, sirs, a maze with many and many a blind alley. Not least of which was a murder disguised.'

'That is stale ground, Mrs Samuel, which we have no inclination to revisit.'

The room at the top of this ramshackle New Road house, formerly comfortable and furnished with costly items, is now all but empty. The three of us stand before Pimlott, who lolls in the one remaining armchair, behind him, his partner leans against the mantle over an empty, unlit hearth. There is no sign of Meathook, though behind us, at the door, attends a heavy-set ruffian, fortified by an iron-shod cudgel. The boards are bare, denuded of their ornamental rugs and now sullied by a large, sinister brown stain. The singular Mr Weggums squats over by the far wall, muttering to himself as he holds a morsel of stale cheese to a hole in the skirting.

'We have been waiting on you. Our buyer grows ever more importunate and, as you have no doubt discerned,' Chuffington waves a hand at the surrounding sparseness, 'we ourselves are eager to quit this empty place.'

'There is no comfort to be had,' complains Pimlott, adjusting his great arse in the padded leather seat.

'It has served its purpose. In our line of business it behoves us to relocate ourselves from time to time. Never fear, should the need arise, you shall be informed as to as to where we are next to be found,' announces Chuffington pointedly.

''Tis soiled, this room,' mutters Weggums. 'which accounts for Julius Cheeser will not show hide nor hair.'

Pimlott shakes his great head in exasperation.

'Tush, Weggums. There shall always be plenty more rodents in this city.'

Weggums sighs and slowly rises, eying Facey. 'Was you aware, sir, that your inward parts are composed of blood sausage entirely?'

'I was not,' replies Facey without enthusiasm.

'Enough with your prattle, muttonhead. We conduct business here,' snaps Pimlott.

'Mr Weggums, take yourself to the stairway. Be sure and let us know when our carriage arrives, if you please,' orders Chuffington.

Weggums capers across the floor, stepping light-footed around the stain. 'The very spot where all them links tumbled out after Mr Meathook took his wicked knife to the gent's belly.' He beams at us. 'Great bloody strings of them, I never saw so many in one place, though I should never wish to fry 'em up. Not them, since they raised a mighty stink.'

'Enough, Weggums. Away to your duty, d'ye hear?' warns Chuffington. He waits, tapping his long fingers on the mantle while Weggums scuttles from the room. As the door is closed by the heavy-set cove, Chuffington returns his gaze to us and smiles thinly, indicating the vile stain. 'None of your lad there, I assure you.'

'We are not in the least assured, sir. And you shall have naught further from us until we know our John to be safe.'

Chuffington tuts. 'You forget yourself, Mrs Samuel, we are not street vendors to be haggled with.' He snaps his fingers. 'Mr Pimlott is impatient to be away. The Eye of Brahma, if you please, or it will go ill with you all.'

'We do not possess it, sir,' announces Rosamund.

Pimlott sighs in exasperation, slapping a fleshy palm down upon the arm of his chair; his partner appraises us with dangerously narrowed eyes. 'And yet you claim to have ferreted it out. This is not to be borne, Mrs Samuel. I believe we have been most accommodating and now poor Mr Pimlott is sorely vexed.'

'We have the certain knowledge of its whereabouts. The gent in possession awaits in expectation of your approach,' explains Rosamund calmly.

'That is something at the least, though not precisely in accordance with our instructions.'

'As I said, it has been a sore trial, sir. Release our John and the Eye of Brahma is as good as in your hands.'

Chuffington frowns, mouth twisting at the corners as though he has tasted something foul. 'The identity of this undertaker, if you please.'

'You shall have naught of it, sir, 'til John stands before us.'

'You will recall that the essence of our bargain was the return of the lad in exchange for the gemstone, neither more nor less, Mrs Samuel. You have failed to bring us the article and so can scarcely expect the boy to be instantly restored to you.'

'Then we are at a stand, Mr Chuffington. Our lips are sealed till we have him.'

Chuffington shakes his head in disbelief. 'You think to toy with us? Perhaps you mistake us for soft-hearted men of sentiment, Mrs Samuel?

Your youngster is not to hand, the house has been entirely cleared of our doings. We have washed our hands of him.' He brings forth his timepiece for inspection once again. 'Though there remains time enough to recover him should you comply with our wishes.'

'How can we be certain he is safe?' objects Rosamund, her resolve beginning to crumble.

'How can we be assured that you have, in truth, found our Eye, Mrs Samuel?' counters Chuffington.

Pimlott shakes his head in exasperation, setting his jowls to wobble like a great pink junket. 'Surely, it cannot have escaped your notice that our Mr Burton is present and stands ready with a good stout bludgeon.'

'It has not,' interjects Facey. 'Though you must know that I am well able to give a good account of myself, cudgel or no.'

Pimlott pouts pettishly, before producing a dainty enamelled snuffbox from his coat pocket. It appears a very tiny object couched those fleshy paws. With exquisite care he extracts a pinch, lays it across the deep fold of his thumb and forefinger before applying it to a nostril. 'There is neither comfort nor sustenance to be had here, Mr C. I am eager to see an end to this unseemly wrangling.' He sighs, waving a languid hand at the three of us. 'Should these inform us where the Eye is to be found, we shall undertake to do as much in respect of the youngster.'

'An equitable resolution, Mr P. Knowledge in return for knowledge,' affirms his partner.

Rosamund gazes at the man with evident suspicion, never troubling to conceal her distaste.

'Come now, the young one is unharmed for the nonce, according to our instruction. But be aware, time and tide wait for no man.'

For some reason this commonplace utterance delights Chuffington, who claps his hands, cackling with inexplicable mirth like the glocky Weggums. 'Great heavens, Mr P., if that is not the best thing you have ever brought forth my name ain't Chuffington.'

Pimlott sniffs, somewhat mollified, wiping snuff residue from that bulbous razzo with the corner of a pristine white fogle. 'The fate of the lad is entirely in your hands. No harm has befallen him from our doing, nor Mr Meathook's, I assure you. He may be found at a particular stretch of the river, carried to that place at our instruction but an hour or so past.

Had you arrived at the appointed time in possession of the gemstone, you should have been able to retrieve him at your leisure. Instead, you have chose to fritter your time away with a tardy appearance and this stubborn silence.' He shrugs. 'Now, you must make haste, for he is left at the mercy of Old Father Thames; high tide today is expected to be somewhere close about a half of four. You may continue to carp and cavil, but be mindful that even now the tide is on the turn and the waters rise about your precious youngster.'

'So, now you collect, Mrs Samuel,' leers Chuffington, 'why it is that my colleague's quip was so very apposite. Time and tide wait for no man. Do you see? Ain't it precious?'

'It is Emmanuel Shepherd of Stratton Street who has the Eye and may it bring you your just reward,' she cries, 'now I beg you, tell us where our John is to be found.'

Pimlott levers himself from the low armchair with considerable difficulty, grunting and wheezing with the strain. 'He is of no further value to us and so you may have him. The youngster is at Iron Foundry wharf close by Blackfriars Bridge, hale or drownded. Who can say? We do not command the river and its ways.'

'You had best hope hale, for if a hair of his head is harmed, you shall answer for it,' growls Facey. 'Do not imagine your bruisers will save you. No, nor your Meathook neither. Asides, him and me are past due a reckoning.'

Chuffington eyes him blandly, not in the slightest discomfited. 'You would be well-advised to issue no further threats, Mr Facey, imposing as you are. I remind you that our reach is long, our recollection longer still.'

'Nevertheless, gents. You have my word on the matter.'

CHAPTER XXVI

The clock of St Mary le Bone New Church strikes four as we tumble out onto the New Street pavement. By my reckoning, Blackfriars Bridge is almost three miles from where we stand and, if Pimlott has spoke true, we have a little under a half of one hour to cover that distance. Knowing London every bit as well as I do, my companions need no reminding of this grim fact.

'It may yet be done in a hack,' asserts Rosamund, tugging a fogle through agitated fingers; more, I think, to convince herself than us.

'It might,' I agree. Facey throws me a look, not at all sanguine. Nevertheless, he strides forth, no doubt intending to seize upon the first likely conveyance.

'Should we head east and thence down Tottenham Court Road we might easily avoid the congestion of Regent Street,' calls Rosamund.

Out in the busy road, Facey places himself directly in the path of an oncoming hackney, one of the newer types, a two-seater with the driver up behind. The little carriage comes to an abrupt halt, the cabby making his displeasure known with a stream of foul-mouthed imprecations. Facey grasps at the bridle, determined not to let this vehicle pass us by. It is unoccupied, though with Facey's bulk it is plain to see that there will not be room for three. 'Go now,' I urge, giving my wife's hand a reassuring squeeze. 'and never fret on my account. At this hour, it may be that the distance can be covered quicker on foot. And so I shall employ my own two legs, running like the devil himself is at my heels.'

Rosamund has never been one to shilly-shally nor be told which way the wind is blowing and so, without demur, hitches skirts and dashes for the conveyance.

By the time I have raced the length of Upper Harley Street my imprudent boast has been given the lie. My lungs are burning, boots leaden and, devil or no, I have slackened to a pitiful trot as I pass Cavendish Square and onto Holles Street. Moreover, I can scarcely say I have been assisted by the many loafers, strays and street urchins who have made a game of my frenzied haste and frequently sought to impede or trip me in my headlong flight. Swells and the well-heeled have been content to cast suspicious, disapproving looks, doubtless presuming that I am some felon, galloping to outrun the law.

At Oxford Street I pause a moment, awaiting a break in the passage of carriages and sundry varieties of horse drawn transport dashing to and fro across this bustling city like water through a stand pipe. At the kerbside, I bend and clutch at my thighs, gasping and wheezing like an old bellows.

'That's the ticket there. Suck it up now. Suck it up, sir. For that is finest London air and yourn for the taking,' bellows a hoarse-voiced coster. 'Much of it as you like. And you may have your fill of good fresh mussels to go along of it, which ain't to be had so cheap, but near enough, at only a penny a quart.'

I brusquely wave him away, since I am already so perilous close to catting up. A fortuitous break in the flow sees an enterprising young sweeper scuttling out across the cobbled thoroughfare, clearing a path of sorts through the manure and ordure for his waiting gent. I follow directly behind. Once across I head directly down Harewood for Hanover Square but it is slow progress; too slow. My wind is all but gone and my legs no longer answer as they might.

As the plane trees of the square come into view I am reminded of my wife's fondness for these gardens. On one occasion, picnicking here with Pure John and his brother and, being unable to afford ices from Gunter's, she was able to conjure the flavours by her very words alone, prompting the older boy to declare it better by far than the real thing.

Now, sprung into my noggin is another of her wonderous words. One of the many she has shared in our years together, mindful that as I have not been so well-furnished in the matter of education as she, a mighty new word is a more glittering and precious prize to me than any Eye of Brahma or French Blue.

It is epiphany.

To be sure, I never expected to find much use from it since it seemed an article solely reserved for pious biblical coves on the road to places no man has ever heard of. I am no saintly cove, to be sure, nor should I expect to find myself seated at the right hand of the Lord come judgement day— though should He choose to offer me place in his heavenly scullery and, should I find myself there in company with my friend Facey, quaffing a few of porter, and my dearest Rosamund sipping at a little bohea, why then I should say amen to that—but I am certainly on the road, or George Street at any rate, and that, I imagine, is as good a qualification to be granted an epiphany as any.

What strikes me at this moment, like a ball from a barker, is that while Shanks' Pony will never answer, there is, not a few hundred yards from here, a miraculous form of transport, with which I might outpace the wind. Curiously, the realisation instantly revives my weary sinews, fills my lungs and renders me once again, tolerably fleet of foot.

I cover the short distance down New Bond Street and onto Grafton, and, within a minute or so, find myself before Lieutenant Trench's Albemarle Street offices. According to the polished brass plaque affixed to one of the glossy black double doors of number Forty-Eight, the messenger service is now situated on the ground floor. An indication of the increasing prosperity of his business.

I enter to find a good number of boisterous messenger boys occupying the hallway. Some lounge upon a long wooden bench, while others mill about, prattling and bickering. I am gratified to note a pair of Dandy Horses standing propped against the wall. At my appearance a tall, gangling youth steps forward giving me a brief bow. He is perhaps eleven or twelve years but endeavours to maintain a dignified bearing in the midst of all this youthful exuberance. 'Good day, sir. Might we be of service? A message to be carried at all?'

It takes me a moment to recognise him since he has sprouted so over the past two years. 'Why 'tis young Crabshells, if I am not mistaken.'

The lad colours, clearing his throat, prompting sniggers from a few of the smaller boys. 'I have not been called that in an age. My proper name is Charles, if'n you please, sir.'

'Forgive me, Charles.' To spare his further blushes I do not mention that the last time I had sight of him he was but a very tiny lad, staggering swipey and puking on my boots at the Clapham fair. 'I must see your Lieutenant this instant.'

'Ah, sir. He is casting his accounts and never to be disturbed when at them endeavours.'

''Tis a matter of the utmost urgency,' I say, threading my way through the boys. Without pausing even to knock, I fling wide Trench's office door. Sure enough, the Lieutenant is at his desk, hair awry as though he has been wrenching at it, surrounded by papers and piles of slips and tickets, a penner clutched in his inky fingers. His head snaps up at the sight of me. 'Why, Mr Samuel, what a surprise. I had not expected...'

'Forgive me, Lieutenant, I cannot delay for niceties. I am come on account of Pure John; we have reason to believe him in mortal peril.'

Trench leaps to his feet. 'Very well, Sammy, only tell me how I might assist.'

'A long tale, Lieutenant. Suffice to say he has been seized by villains, left near to Blackfriars Bridge and must be reached afore the tide comes full or suffer to be drowned. Time is woeful short, though I have a notion it may yet be done with a Dandy Horse.'

It is typical of Trench that he pauses not a moment, never even to enquire into the substance of our plight, but stands instantly ready to lend a hand. 'Certainly it might. And the tide? Know you its appointed time?'

'At its height, I am told, some few minutes afore the half hour.'

Trench brings out a pocket watch. His face falls. 'Sixteen minutes perhaps. And that being on the generous side.'

'Now, Sammy, with both hands take a firm hold of the steering bar and throw a leg across the machine like you was mounting a nag.'

'I seldom have cause to ride, Lieutenant.'

'No matter. It ain't the same thing in any case,' Trench settles himself upon the seat, a leg on either side of the contraption like he was born to it.

'Lieutenant,' I say, struggling with this front bar, which persists in twisting and turning the fore wheel as I attempt to mount, 'never wait on me, I beg you. It is at Iron Foundry Dock where Pure John is to be found. I shall follow after quick as ever I can.'

'Very well, Sammy,' nods Trench, determinedly shoving off with both feet. His legs swing back and forth, one after the other, like twin pendulums, thrusting down upon the pavement to impart forward motion. The velocity quickly increases yet he readily manoeuvres the machine around oncoming pedestrians. By the time I have managed to settle myself astride the leather seat of my own device, he has quite disappeared from view.

In emulation of the Lieutenant I push away with both feet and feel the Dandy Horse trundle forwards with uncertain motion. Though Trench makes this form of mobility appear effortless, it is no such thing, demanding as it does a deal of concentration to hold the fore wheel steady, a feat which can only be achieved by the careful management of the steering bar. I have been at pains to clasp my battered but much-loved old beaver firmly to my head throughout the course of my headlong dash from New Road, but now, with both hands fully engaged, it is swiftly whipped away as I begin to pick up speed.

'Give way, give way there,' I call out, as I wobble and weave along Piccadilly like a tipsy sailor. I thread my way through dawdling clumps of shoppers, prosperous-looking families and a sprinkling of military types in their fine regimentals. I have discovered that by the employment of a steady, loping gait, the device will indeed serve to carry its rider along at a precious good clip, though constant small adjustments must be applied to the matter of steering. Overmuch, imprudent velocity can be rectified by the scraping of my boot soles along the ground. If is not the wind I am outrunning, then, I should wager, this steady breeze at the least.

I manage to successfully manoeuvre the mechanism southwards onto Regent Street, through Waterloo Place and onto Cockspur without mishap and, despite the constant jouncing and jarring administered to my arms and nether regions, I appear to have the trick of the thing.

Once onto the Strand the pavements are occupied by a less placid, unrulier throng, much inclined to be facetious since many have come from the coffee shops and taverns, which proliferate hereabouts. 'What's the tearin' hurry, cocky? You forget about them rashers on the stove?' guffaws a portly cove, his thumbs tucked in to a yellow chequered weskit. His companion, a raffish-looking fellow in a brown derby, steps aside and gives me an ironical bow as I fly past. 'That old nag of yourn looks like it could use a feed, sir. For it don't appear quite well.'

It is a momentary distraction but, what with the congestion and my uncertain mastery of the machine, is sufficient to undo me. A hefty, coarse-looking woman of middle years obstructs the path ahead, her trade the hawking of apples and cabbages from out of sacks arrayed about the paving stones. She clutches a couple of apples in her grubby mitts, holding forth upon their merits and, such is her enthusiasm and the stupendous volume of her entreaties, quite fails to hear my shouts of alarm.

I haul sharply at the steering bar, which has the effect of sending me careening into her wares. The Dandy Horse overturns, spilling me across the pavement, where I lie sprawled and gasping. The contraption rests among the exploded sacks, front wheel still rotating. The woman screeches her distress, not in anguish at my condition but for her scattered apples and the odd cabbage, which rolls into the gutter.

The two loafers quickly reappear and haul me to my feet. 'We was only larkin', sir, and had no desire to see you catastrophised.'

'The fault is mine, gents,' I wheeze. 'No real harm done, I believe.'

Alerted by commotion, a trio of painted, berouged Cyprians emerge from one of the narrow alleyways, flashing their glims at the fellows and making lewd, antic gestures. The cove in the brown derby tips his lid to them afore righting the Dandy Horse and returning it to me. With its thick wooden struts, it is built like a plough and I am relieved to find that it is, for the most part, entirely unscathed. As for myself, I have been fortunate that these sacks of produce have preserved me from broken bones or serious injury; likely the apples are a sight more bruised than me.

'Well, I ain't never seen a spill quite so astounding outside of Tattenham Corner, sir.'

'Thankee, gents,' I say, attempting to remount, struggling to manage the disobliging fore wheel, 'but I am away. A life is at stake.'

'Aye,' screeches the woman, 'and it be yourn, since I have a mind to throttle you for the mischief you have caused. And don't mind if I swing for it neither. Not if it was ever so.'

'Now, now, Missus, 'tis only a couple of pippins gone astray.' The brown derby fellow begins to collect the errant apples, giving them a burnish with his sleeve.

'Them ain't pippins but immaculit Golden Nobles fetched up from Kent this wery morn and now all flung about the gutters.'

'Stow it, you old brute. They is all maggoty windfalls and well you know it,' cackles one of the Cyprians. For a moment it seems there is to be a set-to until the portly cove intervenes.

'What say you take a nip at this here flask, Missus?' he suggests, producing the item from his weskit pocket. 'Finest French brandy as ever was and just the tonic for agitation of the spirits.'

'Well, sir, I will,' replies the woman, fanning her face and clutching at her breast before accepting the flask, 'but only to preclude onset of the vapours, which, being of a sensitive disposition, I am a martyr to. Though why a body should wish to perch hisself upon such a scandalous object, placing all and sundry in mortal fear of their lives, I do not know. 'Tis against nature.'

The cove tips me the wink and grins as I set myself firmly to the saddle and push away. ''T'aint natural,' shrieks the harridan at my departing back.

I hasten down the Strand without further mischance, despite the many catcalls and comments. I have learned a hard lesson and so determine never to cast my eyes elsewhere but at the path ahead, the sole exception being a hasty glance at the clock of St Clement Danes as I pass.

The clock is much relied upon hereabouts and so the showing of twenty minutes after four is likely exact. I push on into Fleet Street and, reckoning it under a half mile to my destination, am spurred to ever increased endeavour. The pavement here is more sparsely populated and

I cover the distance at a rate of knots. It cannot be the expiration of more than five minutes by the time I cross Blackfriars Bridge.

I am tolerably familiar with the streets of Southwark since Guy's is close by, but Iron Foundry Wharf is unknown to me. A pair of sawdust-shrouded navvies make their way across Albion Place, no doubt off the timber yards close by. By firm application of boot soles to the road, I bring the machine to an abrupt halt and beg direction from them.

'Why, cocky, no distance at all, and on such prodigious conveyance you is likely to arrive afore you have ever set off. 'Tis a short way along Upper Ground Street and a jink after Marygold Stairs. Though the place lies derelict, for the old foundry has seen nary a cinder this past year or more.'

I offer hurried thanks and press ahead with all the vigour that remains to me and, sure enough, pass Marygold Stairs to my right. Some few yards further along stands a factory building, shuttered and boarded with broken hoardings and rotting planks. A great chimney erupts from the far side, bricks crumbling and infused with ivy, yet unmistakeably the once-proud signature of an iron foundry. I turn down the path and there before me stretches the Thames, giving out its ripe, sodden stink. There is no sign of the hack as yet, but abandoned on a patch of cinders, boards and rubble near the water's edge rests the twin to my own device; Trench's shoes and coat lie discarded nearby. I leap off my machine, letting it fall to the ground and sprint to the brink. This being a wharf, the bank here is built up, supported by a wall of thick upright wooden palings, about which the waters lap and swell. I peer down from the edge, where below, I spy Trench's head bobbing about in the murky brown soup. I see that he has Pure John in his arms, struggling to keep the lad above the water.

Unlike Facey and the Lieutenant, I have a mortal fear of the deep and have never mastered the art of natation, but Trench cannot fight this rising tide forever. I shrug out of my coat and feverishly work at the ties of my boots. 'Lieutenant,' I bellow.

Trench glances upwards, 'Thank God, Sammy, I...' he splutters. The breeze has picked up, causing wavelets to wash about him, filling his mouth, cutting off his words.

Some two years past, the boy's elder brother was hauled lifeless from the Thames and I well recall that pale, waxen face. Though it cost me my own life, I resolve not to let such a fate befall our John. So I jump.

I drop like a stone, foul waters closing over my head as I descend to the very bottom where I feel my feet enveloped in a thick layer of mud. I thrash and kick out in blind panic. Released from the ooze, I find myself bobbing back up like a cork in a pail. I break the surface and snatch a breath, arms flailing as I begin to sink once again. I am close enough to the wall and so claw frantically at the wooden palings, seeking some manner of purchase. My hand catches at an object, something cold and solid embedded in the wood a couple of feet below the waterline. A thick iron ring by the feel of it. Buffeted by the currents, I desperately reach for this projection with the very tips of my fingers. A violent thrashing of the legs provides a modicum of forward motion and so I am able to place my hand around the object entirely. By keeping my arm submerged and holding it quite straight, I am well enough supported to extend my head above the roiling surface. 'Clap on, Lieutenant,' I call, holding out my free hand.

'I may not leave go of the lad, Sammy. Else, he is lost.'

It is far too deep for Trench to be standing and I perceive that he maintains buoyancy by means of his legs alone through a kind of constant threshing motion. He is panting with the effort though, struggling to catch a breath against the motion of the river. He cradles John's head, the boy's neck arching backwards to keep his face above the surface. Every so often, the lad coughs as a splash of errant spume enters his open mouth. His eyes dart towards me, round with fear and yet despite his predicament, he gives me a small, brave smile.

'Give me the lad, I shall try to haul him out.'

'You cannot, Sammy, nor can I raise him; he is manacled and chained to the palings.'

I realise now that I am supported by the submerged iron ring through which that very chain has been passed. I give the thing a vigorous shake and, though there is some movement, it refuses to come detached from the wall. I take a breath, allowing myself to descend 'til I am a foot or so under. I bring my knees up to my chest and, placing my feet against the palings, haul against the ring with all my bodily vigour. Again, it shifts but will not come free. Running my fingers along the connected chain, I can feel that it is entirely rigid, already extended to its fullest limit. John's arms have been shackled behind his back, leashed to this short length of chain, which serves to hold him down, mere inches now from drowning.

I break the surface, panting. I can, at the least, assist Trench in somehow keeping the boy's head raised against this rising tide. I snatch at the collar of his linen shirt, bringing the pair close in to the wall.

Trench clasps my shoulder, giving him leave to collect his breath. I keep my one hand firmly on the ring and, with a free arm apiece, we support the boy's head between us, raising him high as the chain's length will allow, sufficient for the while to keep his mouth and nose above these acquisitive waters.

'Oh, Mr Samuel, I knowed you would come,' he gasps.

'Hush now, John. You must keep entirely still and save your breath.'

Trench gives me a look of anguish, bringing his mouth close, speaks low into my ear. 'Sammy, you will observe the trail of slime across the wall here, the high-water mark. It shows that the tide is yet in spate and set to rise a further inch or two.'

'There is not sufficient length in the chain, Lieutenant,' I say, aghast.

'I know it,' he nods. 'But the chain cannot be broke, nor the manacles, without we have tools.'

I am the great muttonhead of the world, divesting myself of coat and boots like some precious dandy afore launching myself into the river, when all this while in the inner pocket of that very coat sits my own short crowbar. The wall of this wharf, asides being sheer and slimy, is too high to be climbed. 'I possess the very article, Lieutenant. Though since it lies above us I cannot fathom how it might be got.'

'Can you manage the lad alone?' he says.

'I can.'

'Then I shall swim for it, clambering out at the Stairs, 'tis but a short way upriver.' Trench looks down at the boy. 'Not long now, young John. I shall be back afore you know it, and with the means to free you.' With that he pushes away from the wall and strikes out. Long smooth strokes of his arms carry him through the waters in the direction of Blackfriars Bridge.

I remain at the wall, steady enough, my one hand supported by the submerged ring, the other cradling John's head.

The boy coughs and chokes as a stray wave washes over his face and so I endeavour to raise him a little higher against the stubborn resistance of the chain. 'Oh, Mr Samuel,' he gasps, 'it hurts.' I have heard tell of a form of torture by name of Strappado, and what John endures here is much the same. Mindful as I am that his arms are so horribly wrenched behind his back, I have no choice; it breaks my heart to see him in such pain but I must do it to preserve his life. Though his arms be displaced from the joints of his shoulders, I will not suffer him to drown in my care.

'Courage, John. The waters yet rise and so you must endure it.'

'I will try, sir. Hard as ever I can.'

'I am proud of you, John. Proud that one so brave chooses to carry my own name.'

'John Samuel is a fine name, sir, and my good fortune to be the bearer of it.'

I cannot say if it is the spume from these wavelets or if it be tears that I find now dampening my cheeks. I gaze down at him. His teeth are clenched against the pain and he fights to fill his lungs against the relentless waves. He is still but a boy, having, at most, by my reckoning, ten years on him and yet, at this moment, shows more manly fortitude than any of my acquaintance. 'You must know too that Mrs Samuel thinks the very world of you,' I add, hoping to bring distraction. 'Not a word of it, mind, but you would never credit the fuss and doings at the news of your return. The rooms all spick and span, the entire house scrubbed and burnished till it was just so. And a grand feast appointed at the Keppel's Head, sparing naught and a great meat pie to boot. Imagine that. Nothing too good for her John, home from the sea.'

'Am I so, Mr Samuel? "Her John"?'

'I believe so, since there is no other.'

For a time the boy remains silent, only grimacing occasionally from the agonies I am forced to put him through. 'Mr Samuel,' he says quietly.

'What is it, John?'

'I should not like to drown. You will not let me drown?'

'I will not.'

'I have your word, Mr Samuel?'

'You do, John.'

We wait in silence.

The brown waters now begin to lap about the boy's mouth, and it is only by breathing through his nose that he yet survives. I steel myself to pull him just a little higher, most likely at the cost of the frail sinews of his shoulders, when I catch the sound of urgent voices from above. I cannot discern the words but it is sufficient to know that Rosamund and Facey are come.

Of a sudden, the boy jerks, head thrashing wildly as the river closes over his face entirely. I am horribly aware of his further agonies as I wrench at him but, despite my efforts, cannot raise him further. Water fills his mouth and nose. He is beginning to drown.

We are buffeted by a great splash as a body enters the water from above. The boy yet struggles as Facey explodes to the surface. Facey bobs up and down but, like Trench, is capable of remaining afloat through the motions of his legs. In one hand I see that he brandishes my short crowbar. 'The ringbolt,' I roar, 'he is chained to the ringbolt below.' Facey instantly nods his understanding. Upturning himself like a duck, he dives down beneath me.

With my hand still on the ring, I can feel the frantic workings of the crowbar as Facey tears and wrenches at the rotten wood around the retaining bolt. John's struggles are weakening now. His small frame sags just as the bolt parts from the wall. Instantly, I relinquish my grip on the ring and leave hold of John. His body, no longer restrained, bobs upwards. For a brief moment I catch a glimpse of Facey rising to the surface like a merman, gathering the limp boy in his arms.

With no ring to support me now, I scrabble desperately at the wall. There is no purchase to be had, only slime and bare wood and so I thresh my legs and flail my arms in a frenzy. If anything, this panicked floundering only has the effect of driving me under.

I sink. Quite slowly, to be sure. In this murk all is still and quiet and so I cease my struggles. I do so deeply grieve the loss of my Rosamund, yet am strangely calm, content enough with the measure of happiness already granted me. Grateful too, that my very last sight was of John, gasping a great lungful of air, coughing and choking at the water pouring forth from his mouth and nose.

He is safe.

And so, I remain a man of my word.

CHAPTER XXVII

My dear Mr Facey,

You will not consider such correspondence overly forward nor out of place, I hope, since you was good enough to leave with me the Bedford in Chase, Portsmouth, as the means by which you might be reached.

I do not have my letters, and so these few words come, not from my own hand, but by a honest, learned soul of my acquaintance who puts them to paper just as I speak them out loud.

Since you are touched by the momentous events of the Dover Street household, I had thought you might wish to learn how matters did unfold since your precipitate departure.

Such doings, sir.

The attorney, Mr Haverford, had been fetched and, you would never credit it, but that it fell to me alone to explicate for him the curious and distressing circumstances of all that had passed.

Forgive me, I run ahead of myself, and might have mentioned that Mrs Parkes had earlier fled, taking naught, even of her own possessions. Not a whit has been heard nor seen of her since.

As was oft his way, Mr Jenkins betook himself directly to the cellars and there incapacitated himself entirely with ardent spirits.

Following my account, Mr Haverford declared it his first duty to protect the reputation of the family name and so would suffer neither magistrate nor constable to be summoned. William Belmont, that poor mite, was after spirited away under cover of darkness by Haverford's men, though I was assured that he should have a proper, decent burial as I had so desired for him.

As for the house and what Belmont fortune yet remains, none can say, not even the attorney, since Mr Galton, who all supposed would become master, was took mortal sick at the club where he was accustomed to reside, and there expired within a day or so. Likely, the matter shall end in Chancery where it shall be wrangled over from now 'til doomsday.

You may consider me a ignorant, credulous woman, Mr Facey, but I shall tell you what is at the bottom of it: The Eye of Brahma, which is to say the gemstone what was carried here from the Indian continent, I have heard it said that it carries a curse, sprung as it was from the wickedest and most heathen of temples. To be sure, its malign influence has brung naught but misfortune and death to the house and family. Aye, even so far as the military gent, though I am not one for tattle, him as was said to be paramour of our late mistress. According to Mr Haverford, that gentleman is despaired of on account of the terrible wound he had from Mr Galton and not expected to last the week.

It is a mercy then, that the dreadful article has been interred alongside our mistress and is gone from the face of the earth.

The residence now lies shuttered and empty and shall so remain 'til the musings of all them attorneys, advocates and what have you are quite done. In consequence, we few remaining servants are let go. I know not what is become of Mr Jenkins but, for my own self, Mr Haverford has generously secured me a place, not at London as you might suppose, but in the provinces. What with the pestilence and such, I had a mind to be quit of the metropolis and most ardently assert that, since I am one of the few who never had occasion to set eyes upon that accursed stone, my own fortunes have, by no means, been adversely affected.

I am to be cook at the Ellis residence at Southsea. A most respectable establishment, where I shall be accompanied by young Nellie, who has took the position of scullery maid. I believe Southsea is no great distance from Portsmouth and it may so happen that we chance to meet again in passing. Any gate, should such an event transpire, I believe I should like it very well.

There is such a deal to be attended to afore I embark and so I must close, but I trust this finds you in the best of health and you have not forgot to take your porter for its many fortifying properties.

Yours, with great esteem

Mrs Elizabeth Stride (which is to say, Bessie)

Rosamund carefully folds the missive, returning it to Facey. Though my friend is lettered, he is somewhat inclined to stumble and has never been comfortable reading out loud to any but me.

'Southsea, Mr Facey. Well here is serendipity for you,' announces Rosamund.

'I do not know this word, Mrs Samuel.'

'It means a little of good fortune, easily achieved. A dip, as it were, into the waters of serenity, not unlike Jack Horner's pie, whereby, with scant effort, one might pluck forth a precious great plumb.'

Such explication might appear to be for Facey's benefit, though I well know this glittering new word is her gift to me alone. She glances across the table with one of her slantendicular little smiles.

Perhaps this self-same notion may be employed to describe my presence here in the Dolphin tavern, surrounded by those most dear to me. Seated by my treasured wife is our Pure John, no worse for his ordeal than for a slight stiffness about the shoulders; the young have supple sinews and so such afflictions do not trouble them long. Trench perches at the table's head, since he is most particular about the wines to be fetched for us all. Next to me is sat my great friend, to whom I owe my life.

It was, in course, Facey who hauled me from the foul embrace of Old Father Thames. Trench, returning at the run from his emergence at Marygold Stairs had spied the fast approaching hack and was able to explicate our desperate predicament and urgent need of the crowbar. I have no recollection of these matters, but am told that once Facey had made short work of the rusty manacles at John's wrists, my sharp-witted Rosamund flung out a scrap of wooden hoarding for the boy to cling to, thereby freeing Facey to seek me out. He discovered me bobbing close to the bottom and, catching me by my locks, brought me, quite insensible, to the surface.

Facey secured my slack arms about his neck. Trench, having re-entered the river, did likewise for the boy, and the two of them swam upstream like a pair of grampuses, bearing us on their backs to Marygold Stairs. Back on dry land, they hoisted me by my heels as I discharged water like a parish pump and, after a deal of spitting, puking and coughing, found myself fully restored to this wicked world, where I have every intention of remaining.

⁓⁓⁓

'That ain't such a bad way of putting it, Mrs Samuel, that serendiptitty word of yourn,' announces Facey, grinning broadly. 'I confess, I do have some regard for the lady, and, as it happens, should not myself be averse to further acquaintance.'

'Then we must toast to the prospect,' replies Rosamund, raising her glass.

Facey hoists his own fancy bumper, which resembles a glittering thimble in his great fist. We follow suit, all present nodding and beaming at one another for all the world like a parcel of bedlamites, so pleased are we to see our trials behind us.

Facey refills the glasses while Trench sets to carving at the fine plump goose set before us. 'It is often said, Mrs Samuel,' muses my friend, 'that the wicked shall not prosper, though it don't alus seem that way to me.'

'You speak of Mrs Parkes?'

'I do. She has skedaddled, it seems, and likely never to be found since the hue and cry has not been raised.'

'She failed to prosper for all her machinations. Moreover, I do not believe she accounts herself deficient in virtue.'

'A brace of lives was took by means of poison. I am no saint, as all can testify, yet I collect the commandments well enough.'

'It is a curious thing, Mr Facey, that those quickest to find fault in the conduct of others are often apt to make exception of themselves. No doubt, Mrs Parkes was one such. Yet, I cannot think entirely ill of her.'

'That is on account of you seeing the good in everyone,' I say.

'Perhaps,' muses Rosamund. 'But I have often wondered whether vice and virtue are so absolute as we might believe. Mrs Parkes' actions, though in no wise to be condoned, were, at the least, driven by the desire to provide a better life for her poor Ned. Her mistress, Edith Belmont, clung to her fripperies and that ill-starred ferroniere, even in death, whilst utterly neglecting the one object of true value: her own son. I am no philosopher and so, in truth, cannot say which was the worse.'

234

'Well, that Meathook cove is a regular wicked bugger and that is flat,' offers John, 'same for his masters.'

'John, for shame. Such language.'

'It is how we are accustomed to converse aboard, Mrs Samuel.'

'Well, you are home now. And, though you voyage to the ends of the earth, rising to Lord high-and-mighty Admiral of the Fleet, where you find Mr Samuel and Mr Facey along of myself, that shall always be your home, since it is where you are loved best, whether you like it or no.'

The lad blinks, eyes moistening, as he no doubt recalls his brother. 'Then it is a fine thing to be home at last,' he remarks, in an uncommonly small and wavering voice.

'Come,' says Rosamund, gently patting the lad's hand, 'I am a dry stick at the feast, prating away so, and our Lieutenant has just now settled with our fowl most handsomely.'

Great trenchers are passed about the board, high with succulent goose flesh, venison, ham, fruit, asparagus and all manner of delectables.

'Mrs Samuel,' announces Trench, 'might I take the liberty of proposing an addendum to your musings? It is a scrap which I have retained from my schooldays, though coming as it does from a very ancient Greek cove, I should never wish to be thought of as showing away.'

'A most improbable event, Lieutenant, since all here know you for the most modest of gents, despite all you have done for us.'

'Hear hear,' I say, raising my glass, delighted that Trench, who can be a trifle unbending, is so comfortable in our company. It is not only John's salvation we owe him, but likely our future prosperity to boot. Trench, having posted down to us from London a day ago, took it upon himself to look into the regulation of our tap-room and the parlous state of our monies. A brief inspection of those accounts revealed Griffith, our jobbing keeper, to be, as I had suspected, a consummate rogue and not a particular shrewd one at that. In course, the man was dismissed, flung out into the street by Facey, with the added valediction of his arse being kicked from one end of The Hard to the other.

'Thankee, Mrs Samuel,' replies Trench, taking a pull at his wine. ''Tis but some few words of Pericles of the venerable city of Athens. A cove, it is said, with a noggin like a precious great onion, though that don't signify.' The Lieutenant clears his throat before declaiming in a fine, clear voice: 'What we leave behind is not what is engraved in stone monuments, but what is woven into the lives of others.'

Rosamund applauds, smiling with unfeigned delight, making no attempt to conceal her chipped tooth, which she is oft so mindful of in company. 'It is very wise, Lieutenant, and a deal better put than my own poor discourse.' I gaze fondly at her as she sips from her glass. Even as I watch, her demeanour transmutes. I know her so well, yet I cannot catch the substance of the expression. It is one of solemnity and yet there is something more to it. She takes a breath. 'It may also serve as a suitable preface to another matter, one of some consequence, I believe.'

The clatter of dishes quiets.

'This morning I had reason to call at Hawke Street, upon Doctor Clayton.'

A sudden icy shard of terror impales my heart. All but Rosamund were immersed in the Thames and so, since our return from London, I have been ever vigilant for signs of contagion amongst us. Following the expiration of four days without ill effect, I had imagined us all to be safe. 'For more of John's salve?' I entreat, desperate for there to be any other explication than the one I most dread to hear.

'It was not for John's salve.' She smiles now and I cannot fathom why she would do so. Nor can I even take a breath; it is as though I am drowning once again.

'I am with child, Sammy.'

I hear the words but do not, for the moment, fully comprehend them. 'How...?' I gasp.

The utterance precipitates a gale of mirth which becomes a great bellowing, rapping at the table and stamping of feet. Facey pummels me on the back, over and over, like he was dusting a rug and through all this clamour I spy my wife, smiling her small, secret smile at me from across the table. I gaze back at her in wonder, my eyes brimming.

And I know full well what she will leave of herself.

As for me, it is these poor words I leave behind.

Set against my own many faults might, I hope, be discerned some small measure of virtue. For there may come a day when this child of ours shall read them, and in so doing take a moment to consider what manner of persons was their ma and pa.

ACKNOWLEDGEMENTS

I'd like to thank all of those wonderful readers who gave such generous reviews to *Some Rise by Sin*, the first book in this series. You are the reason we do this. I hope you enjoy the sequel as much.

Once again, I'd like to thank Tanya Morel for reading the drafts and for her many insightful comments.

None of this would be possible without the wonderful Angel Belsey and her team at Deixis Press. My heartfelt thanks for your faith, enthusiasm and attention to detail.

ABOUT THE AUTHOR

Siôn Scott-Wilson writes short stories, novels, and plays and has won many industry awards for his television work, including a BAFTA nomination. His debut novel, *The Sleepwalker's Introduction to Flight*, was listed for the CrimeFest Last Laugh Award. He won the Yeovil Literary Prize for Best Novel in 2013 and was a runner-up for the Fish Publishing Prize in 2008. Siôn holds an MSc (Distinction) in Creative Writing from the University of Edinburgh.

www.sionscottwilson.co.uk

ABOUT DEIXIS PRESS

Deixis Press is an independent publisher of fiction, usually with a darker edge. Our aim is to discover, commission, and curate works of literary art. Every book published by Deixis Press is hand-picked and adored from submission to release and beyond.

www.deixis.press